THE RISE OF THE RED QUEEN

**The Red Solaris Mystery Series
by Bourne Morris**

THE RED QUEEN'S RUN (#1)
THE RISE OF THE RED QUEEN (#2)

Praise for the Red Solaris Mystery Series

THE RISE OF THE RED QUEEN (#2)

"With *The Rise of the Red Queen*, Bourne Morris is poised to become the queen of academic mysteries and suspense."

– Gigi Pandian,
USA Today Bestselling Author of *Quicksand*

"Red Solaris is intelligent, tough, and vulnerable, a tricky combination to pull off, yet Bourne Morris does so beautifully and has given us a lead character we care deeply about. *The Rise of the Red Queen*, second in the series, grabs you by the throat and the heart on page one and never lets go."

– Annette Dashofy,
USA Today Bestselling Author of *With a Vengeance*

"Intriguing characters, a complex, inventive plot with nail-biting suspense—I finished it at two in the morning!"

– Jeanne M. Dams,
Author of the Dorothy Martin Mysteries

"Morris has written another delicious pleasure, providing intrigue, plenty of campus drama, and strong female characters. Academic in-fighting, Red's ambition to become the new Dean, and her detective love interest keep the pages turning."

– Karen Penner-Johnson,
Emerita Professor, Kansas State University

"The story involved me quickly, the suspense mounting so high that when my e-reader battery ran low, the warning buzzer made me jump. Morris has created a complete mystery with suspense and emotions burning like a Nevada sunset."

– Mark Bacon,
Author of *Death in Nostalgia City*

THE RED QUEEN'S RUN (#1)

"Touching upon a very real subject, this author offers the perfect formula of suspects, mystery, and a handsome police detective to heat up Red's fire...a great read about what goes on behind those academic doors."

– Suspense Magazine

"Morris has crafted a suspenseful, thoughtful, sexy debut...Her hero, Red Solaris, is vulnerable but tough, complex but straight-shooting, a woman learning how to wield power by remembering what it's like to have little of it. I'll read about her adventures anytime. Long live the Queen!"

– Christopher Coake,
Author of *You Came Back*

"A psychological thriller that reveals the Ivory Tower to be a hothouse full of monstrous egos, where bullying thrives long past playground days and 'academic discipline' requires research skills of the detective kind."

– Kate Manning,
Author of *My Notorious Life*

"Morris proves herself a masterful storyteller in this compelling debut novel. *The Red Queen's Run* is compulsive reading as it takes on the ripped-from-the-headlines topic of campus violence. I can't wait to follow its smart new heroine."

– Alan Deutschman,
Author of *Change or Die*

"A racy and delightful peek into academia's darker corners. Bourne Morris clearly knows this microcosm as well as anyone, and lucky for us, she also knows how to turn a phrase, twist a plot and spin one hell of a yarn."

– Ben Rogers,
Author of *The Flamer*

THE RISE OF THE RED QUEEN

A Red Solaris Mystery

Bourne Morris

HENERY PRESS

THE RISE OF THE RED QUEEN
A Red Solaris Mystery
Part of the Henery Press Mystery Collection

First Edition
Trade paperback edition | December 2015

Henery Press
www.henerypress.com

ISBN-13: 978-1-943390-29-8

Printed in the United States of America

For my best friends,
Miranda and Temple

ACKNOWLEDGMENTS

First and foremost my gratitude and all my affection to the generous readers of my manuscript: Cecelia Pearce, Kristin Felten, Bob Felten, Margo Piscavitch, Wynn Reed and Ryan Kelly. These are the wonderful people who make me possible, keep me straight and let me know when I've become self-indulgent, cliché ridden or confusing.

I am also indebted to Marc Johnson, President of the University of Nevada, Reno, who paved the way for me to the team who handle sexual assault on his university campus. Many thanks to Denise Cordova, Carol Millie and Jo Harvey as well as Ashley Van Broklin and Nichelle Cieri who helped me understand the problems facing both university administrators and students.

A special thanks to Lori Fralick, supervisor of victim services for the Reno Police Department and to Glen Lovedahl of the Reno office of the FBI. All mystery writers should have such good sources in law enforcement.

Everyone should have friends as useful and well informed as Valerie Glenn and Alan Deutschman who gave me insights into social media and the book industry and Chris Coake who remains my best and favorite creative writing professor.

My editors at Henery Press, Anna Davis and Erin George, always help make the book work and I cannot count the many suggestions they gave me that improved the story. I continue to learn from them and am forever in their debt.

My agent, Kimberley Cameron keeps my spirits up and my vision clear, and I am always thankful to Kendel Lynn and Art Molinares at Henery Press and to the staff at Sundance Books and Music and Book Passage.

For my reviewers Joe Crowley, Marc Bacon, Annette Dashofy, Gigi Pandian, Stacy Burton and Karen Penner-Johnson, I cannot sing enough praise for all the time and kind words you gave this book. Your own works keep me ever inspired to try to be as skilled as you are.

My family sustains me. My dear Bob keeps me sane, keeps me going and loves me through all the cranky moments whether I deserve it or not.   My daughters, Miranda and Temple, are remarkable women, wives, mothers and professionals who never cease to astonish me with their energy and accomplishments. My stepson and web master, Scott Buss, helps me more than he will ever know.

Finally, to my friends and former colleagues all over the country and to Priscilla Cunningham who helped me connect with my old Westover classmates, I lift a glass in your honor with humble thanks for your support.

Jamie's Mistake

She was a careful woman. She avoided online requests from people she didn't know. She never stayed long at parties where people drank too much, never let herself get cornered by a man she wasn't sure about. She always walked on well-lit paths, her keys a weapon in her pocket, each key lodged between two fingers with the longest held like a knife between her thumb and forefinger, a sharp, pointed fist if she needed it. Her grandfather had trained her. She knew a few self-defense moves, nothing fancy, just enough to back off some fellow who really didn't want that kind of trouble.

Because she was beautiful, men stared at her body, so it developed a built-in alarm system. Whenever it went off, she would feel a series of pinpricks on the back of her neck, and if she was truly unnerved, a brief cramp in her abdomen. It had happened twice in Boston when she was walking from campus to her apartment.

On one occasion, she'd stopped and hailed a cab that had just come around the corner on her side of the street. The next time, she'd stepped into an all-night convenience store and telephoned a friend.

She hadn't felt that sensation since transferring to the journalism school in northern Nevada. But that Monday night she felt it when the tall man came to the door of the journalism lab just as she was turning the lock, and asked if he could use one of the computers. "Just for a few minutes."

His manner had been pleasant and friendly. She'd tried to seem sympathetic, but she'd refused entry. The professor who ran the lab and gave her the assistant's job had been adamant about the hours. "Closed at ten. No exceptions."

"I understand. Rules are important," the tall man said, then turned and left.

She'd seen him before. Without giving his name, he'd stopped her as she walked to class and invited her to join him for a coffee at the outdoor food wagon on the quad. The man was older, well dressed, well spoken, looked familiar, someone she'd met somewhere. That was why she'd stopped. But there was something about him that made her say, "Perhaps another time."

He'd smiled and moved aside. She'd hastened her steps toward the classroom building across the quad. She was aware of him watching her as she walked away.

A week later she saw him standing by the iron fence that surrounded the library, hands stuffed in his pockets, leaning against the top railing, one long leg crossed in front of another, as if he had nothing else to do but watch her as she climbed the outer stairs to the entrance. He waved. She nodded but didn't wave back.

On the night he'd come to the lab, he'd been polite and friendly. He hadn't insisted, or done anything she regarded as aggressive or threatening, and he walked away from her when she refused his request.

Once she left the building, the campus around the journalism school felt familiar, comfortable. The night air was warm and soft, and reminded her of her grandfather's home in Las Vegas.

To the new transfer student, Mountain West University also seemed smaller and calmer than the urban college she'd left, and safer than the streets where she grew up. Nonetheless, the alarm system in her neck had kicked in, so she stopped at a kiosk to call for a ride from the campus escort service. They would drive her to the garage and up to the third floor where her car was parked.

After five rings she decided to give up and walk to the garage. Relax, she said to herself, they're busy with insecure newcomers. This is a university town, not a big city. You're safe. The tall man was nowhere in sight and, after all, he'd smiled when he left.

The soft evening enticed her. The lights along the path to the parking garage glowed bright and friendly, illuminating the leaves of the tall maples that lined her path. She'd been sitting all day in class and in the lab. Better to walk than ride.

Once in the three-story garage she decided to avoid the elevator. She'd been a high school track star and missed the exercise. She took the concrete stairs two at a time to the third floor, then paused, hands on her knees, breathing heavily before she headed for her car.

The columns of the top floor of the garage rose high above her, and the spaces in the thick walls opened to reveal the lights of the campus below. As she approached her car in the dim light, she turned and saw the tall man standing at the top of the stairs where she'd paused to catch her breath. On the third floor of the empty garage at ten fifteen at night, they were alone together. The pinpricks in the back of her neck returned in force. He walked toward her. Her stomach cramped. He was not smiling.

Chapter 1

The first thing I did every morning was wake up my mind. With my eyes barely open and my hair an unruly mass, I clutched a mug of hot coffee and plunged into the online edition of *The New York Times*. As a trained academic, I knew the importance of priming the cerebral cortex.

My routine also included mindless but essential activities like feeding my dog. If you've ever encountered a hungry Golden Retriever, you know that trying to do anything before feeding the dog is impossible.

On the morning I was scheduled to meet the search committee for the new dean of journalism, I got up early enough to finish the ritual by seven o'clock. I dressed with great care, pinning my hair back into a bun at the nape of my neck in an effort to look like a serious scholar. It took three times before the bun stayed in place. Then I ate as much protein for breakfast as my nervous stomach could stand.

Charlie, my Golden, lay on the floor watching me. I leaned down to stroke the fur between his ears and he gave my fingertips a lick in appreciation. Following me as I went out the kitchen door, he crashed through his dog door and stood on the back step. He watched me turn the key in the lock and walk to my car.

"Wish me luck, Charlie," I said to his solemn face, knowing luck would have nothing to do with what was likely to happen in the days ahead. I was absolutely confident in my own ability to be the next Dean of Journalism, but university search committees have an unnerving habit of preferring to recommend outside candidates for top jobs, even when highly qualified inside faculty members have applied.

I was ready to compete. Last year, when I had been temporarily appointed to lead the school, the journalism faculty had been at each other's throats, impossible to calm down and as difficult to manage as a roomful of trapped feral cats. But I had brought them together and, once united, the faculty accepted my temporary leadership, nicknamed me The Red Queen, and then—surprise, surprise—championed my candidacy for the permanent position.

My final interview with the search committee was scheduled for nine o'clock that morning. And it was a brilliant morning, the northern Nevada sun so bright it made my eyes hurt. I took that as a good sign. Blue sky stretched over my head as I left my car in the journalism parking lot. Japanese cherry trees, the kind that bloom big pink blossoms every spring, lined the lot. Over the trees' thick leaves, I could make out the Sierra Nevada, towering from five thousand to nine thousand feet above sea level, with views of Lake Tahoe shimmering below. God, I was glad to live in this part of the country.

I arrived at the office early, earlier than Nell, my assistant, but not earlier than a tall, good-looking man who was standing in front of the door to my outer office. Cropped gray hair and deep lines etched in skin the color of mahogany, plus a few discernible crow's feet, suggested he might be sixty, maybe older.

He introduced himself as Wynan Congers and followed me from the hall outside my outer office, insisting I make time to see him. I knew I didn't have more than a few minutes before my interview, but the man looked desperate and, as the interim dean of the school, I was responsible for dealing with desperation.

"My granddaughter, Jamie Congers, is one of your students, and she's been missing for two days," said Congers, without sitting down in the chair in front of my desk.

"I'm sorry to hear that, Mr. Congers. Please sit and let's see what we can figure out." This was not my first time dealing with an anxious guardian unwilling to relinquish the protections and requirements of high school. Their babies had grown up to become college students—on their own, free to skip class (or town) anytime they pleased.

The old man sat but his expression remained fierce, his eyes bright with apprehension. "Dean Solaris, my Jamie is a good girl, a serious girl. She transferred here from a good college so she could be in your journalism school. She wouldn't just take off without notifying me or her roommate or someone."

"When did you discover she wasn't where you expected her to be?" A year and a half as interim dean had given me time to learn how to phrase an inquiry so I didn't sound either defensive or indifferent.

Congers moved restlessly in his chair.

His dark blue shirt was neatly pressed and fit close across broad shoulders. His hands were strong with telltale signs of arthritis on the fingers.

"My granddaughter's roommate, Marilyn Ford, called me Tuesday morning. Jamie hadn't come home the night before and Marilyn wondered if she'd come to see me in Las Vegas. We spoke later that day when she learned Jamie hadn't been to any of her classes." His deep voice quivered.

"Sounds like a caring roommate."

"Jamie and Marilyn grew up together. Marilyn's the one who persuaded Jamie to transfer here to the journalism school. One of her selling points was that Landry was a small town and safer than Boston."

"And Jamie's parents are..."

"Gone. My son and his wife were both killed in Afghanistan."

"I'm sorry to hear that. So Jamie lives with you in Las Vegas?"

"When she's not in school." The man leaned forward and his voice rose. "But Jamie isn't careless. She doesn't make stupid choices. Marilyn and I both believe something happened to her. She doesn't have a boyfriend and hasn't had a lot of time to make any friends since she transferred here. She works hard on her studies, and she has a night job here as one of your lab assistants."

Congers got up and strode to the window. I estimated he was about six foot three. His posture was military straight. He must've been as magnetic as a movie star when he was young. Hell, he still was.

"Dean Solaris, you have to help me. Jamie's car is missing. I've talked to Student Services, the campus police, and the Landry police. I filed a missing persons report even though the Landry police say it's too soon for them to act on it. I know it's too soon. I'm a retired cop." His speech was rushed, words tumbling one after the other. "I also know I have to dig deeper and, fortunately, I know how. I was deputy police chief in Las Vegas before I retired. What I want—what I need to do—is to interview your lab professor and some of the students here."

Oh, dear.

"Mr. Congers, did the Landry police offer to investigate?"

He stopped pacing. "Of course not. Their chief claims they don't have the manpower to check up on every college kid who takes a hike." He sat down in the chair again, looking at the floor. Then he lifted his chin, fixing dark eyes on me. "Dr. Solaris, I know I need your permission to talk to your students. That's why I'm here."

Deep breath. "I'm sorry, but I can't give you permission to interrogate my students. However, I can get ahold of the lab professor, and I may be able to find someone else to help. Did you speak to a Detective Joe Morgan at the Landry police station?"

"I don't recall that name."

One of his hands was resting on my desk.

I reached across and touched it with my fingertips. "Mr. Congers, I understand. I care very much about my students and I know sometimes trouble happens. Let me call Detective Morgan. He's a good friend and I may be able to get him to check around."

"I could use all the help I can get, Dr. Solaris."

"Joe's good at getting stuff out of students. Also, many of my students know him and might feel more comfortable—more forthcoming."

I heard Nell in the outer office and called to her. At the sight of her curly gray hair and slender figure, Congers rose. "Good morning, ma'am." There was a softness in his voice I hadn't heard when he spoke to me and a look in Nell's eyes I couldn't remember ever seeing before. No doubt she found him as attractive as I did.

"Nell Bishop, this is Wynan Congers. Mr. Congers' granddaughter, Jamie, is a journalism student, and he needs our help. Please get him a cup of coffee and find out where he is staying."

Nell smiled and extended her hand to Congers. I'd never seen my solemn assistant shake hands so eagerly or release a hand so reluctantly.

I turned to Congers, who was still looking at Nell. "Mr. Congers, I have a meeting I must attend, but Nell will take care of you and get in touch with the lab director."

The man's voice was almost a whisper. "I'm truly grateful to you for trying to help me." He took a breath and reset his shoulders. "Jamie's the center of my life."

I put my hand on his arm and felt it tense beneath my fingers. "We'll figure this out. I promise I'll call this afternoon and we'll get back together again."

After Congers left, I braced myself for the next item on my agenda, the one that had my stomach in knots: meeting the search committee. They'd already interviewed numerous candidates and their questions were probably honed to razor sharpness. I knew my competitors had done brilliantly. Or so the rumor mill said.

Well, not just the rumor mill. I had a spy or two.

My best friend's encouraging words rang in my ears. "Everyone on campus has spoken highly of you, Red. Any committee member checking you out is bound to run into rave reviews for your performance last year." This had come from the former Dean of Liberal Arts, Sadie Hawkins. Sadie was retired, but still a superb source of inside information on the Mountain West campus.

"Sadie, be realistic," I'd said. "I was a journalist for a big city paper, but only for five years before I went to grad school. One of the finalists has a Pulitzer."

"But he has nowhere near your academic experience," Sadie had insisted. "You know how academic battles are won. Arm yourself, my courageous queen. Pin up your gorgeous red hair, take a deep breath, then go into that meeting and earn your nickname."

Remembering Sadie's words, I tried to focus on the importance of my interview, but my mind kept wandering back to the possibility that something unfortunate had happened to Jamie Congers. I prayed for a new boyfriend or an easily explained episode of hooky, but I continued to feel uneasy, infected with the intensity of her grandfather's concern.

Chapter 2

When I'm on campus, I walk everywhere. There are shuttle buses that help you get from one end to another, but I avoid them. The Mountain West campus restores my soul. A vast bed of yellow roses is one of my favorite sights, and it came into sight as I walked to the search committee meeting.

I tried to shake my concern about Jamie as I headed up the steps to the library. My former dean, the late Henry Brooks, used to say whenever I anticipated the worst, "Cheer up, maybe it won't happen." Perhaps Jamie Congers would show up later in the day with a hug for her worried grandfather and reassurances all around.

Meanwhile, I had to stop thinking about her. Mine was the final interview for the permanent dean's position and I should've been rehearsing answers to possible questions from the committee. Sixty-three journalism academics and ten professional journalists had applied for the dean's job, and I was one of only three finalists. But I was an inside candidate and keenly aware of university search committee preferences for hiring outsiders.

"Promoting an insider is not their idea of a task well done," Sadie had warned me. "The university appetite is always for new blood. A dean's position is an opportunity to enrich the cadre of top faculty with a distinguished scholar or a famous professional."

I also knew that my competitors were formidable. The one who worried me most was Manuel Lorenzo, an old friend who'd helped me last year when I was first appointed to lead my school. Manny was a dean at one of the nation's largest journalism schools.

His scholarship was legend and his faculty members adored him. The search committee had probably cheered and opened a bottle of champagne when they got his curriculum vitae—university speak for a complex academic résumé.

My other competitor was Victor Watts, a superhero who held a chair at a prestigious journalism school in the east, was a Pulitzer Prize-winning book author, and a former foreign correspondent for NBC. I wondered what would motivate him to move to a town as small as Landry, Nevada, but he seemed eager for the job.

The search committee for the permanent dean of journalism gathered in a private room on the second floor of the university library. All three finalists met with the committee in the morning, then went to lunch with three of the members, then had dinner with the committee chair.

I was the last on the list of the finalists to be interviewed. I had seen Manny Lorenzo across the quad the week before and waved a cheerful greeting. If I didn't get the job, I reckoned Manny would make a good dean for our school and a good mentor for me.

As for Victor Watts, I had seen him emerging from the library looking much like the photograph on the back of his Pulitzer Prize-winning book. An elegant man, Watts was dressed as if he had just finished a photoshoot for an issue of *Gentlemen's Quarterly*. He nodded a greeting that suggested he knew who I was. I wondered if he really did.

I walked down the wide hall, past portraits of former presidents of Mountain West University. Graceful buildings like the library always comforted me, reminding me of why I'd given up noisy, hectic newsrooms for the carpeted quiet of scholarly surroundings. I loved teaching, but I'd just spent a year learning about academic management and I liked that too. I enjoyed running the journalism school, and I wanted to keep doing it.

"Good morning, Red." A hearty welcome from Bill Verden, Dean of Science—a friend and, I hoped, my supporter.

"Please come in, Dr. Solaris," said Bridget Thomas, Dean of the College of Economics, chair of the search committee and a woman I had never thought of as a friend. Her smile was as thin and as narrow as her lips, not even a suggestion of teeth. Aloofness was her uniform.

"Please call me Red. Everyone does," I said, hoping I could melt her chilliness with a show of cheerful informality.

"Why don't you sit here?" said Mark Froman, guiding me to the head of the table.

I wasn't crazy about Mark, either. His expensive shirts seemed molded to his body, showing off his muscular ropey arms. His eyes were black and beady. He had a bad habit of grasping my shoulders, always trying to steer me one way or another.

Mark was the outside member of the committee, not a university employee.

He had been chosen from the Landry community by Philip Lewis, the university president. A major donor to the university, Froman had inherited a fortune and was independently wealthy. He spent his days serving on non-profit boards in Nevada and California.

The rest of the committee, deans and professors from schools at the university, already sat at the table. I'd met most of them before, and knew a couple of them well enough to be familiar with their families.

Bridget began after unbuttoning and then buttoning a navy jacket that didn't fit her especially well. "Now, Dr. Solaris, since you've just spent the last year as interim dean of journalism, why don't you start by telling us what you think you accomplished. And then, please describe what you failed to accomplish in that post."

Strengths and weaknesses. What a bore. But I had rehearsed for this one.

I cleared my throat. "Well, I led the school through the tragedy of the death of our last dean, Henry Brooks. That loss was particularly hard on many of us and..."

"Brooks was killed by one of your faculty, right?" Mark Froman said, fingering the Rolex on his impressive forearm.

"Yes, but—"

"And he's in jail for it. Right? And for assaulting that student."
Black eyes gleamed.

Bridget interrupted. "Please go on, Dr. Solaris." She glared at
Froman. "I think we're all entirely too familiar with the scandals in
journalism last year and the killing of Henry Brooks."

I swallowed hard. "Yes, well, perhaps my most important
accomplishment was bringing an end to the quarreling among the
faculty and getting the school back on the right path. We improved
our curriculum and prepared for reaccreditation. I was also able to
raise a considerable endowment for a chair in memory of the late
dean."

"Indeed you were," said Bill, "and it was one of the largest
endowments in the history of the university, I recall."

I flashed him a smile.

"And you steered through some cutting edge new courses in
journalism technology, I believe," added the engineering dean.

"Yes," I said, somewhat relieved. Maybe some of these people
might vote for me after all.

"And your failures?" Bridget asked.

"I'm not sure it's a failure so much as a challenge I still have to
face," I said, enunciating every syllable and making sure my
audience had time to take good notes. I was getting to the part that
I considered my unique qualification: my familiarity with the
school's past and my assessment of what needed to happen in the
future. "I still have considerable work to do on restoring the
reputation of the school. I have yet to regain the confidence of some
of our alumni, as well as some of our students. We took a huge hit
last year and my plan is to..."

"You bring up a major problem," said Mark Froman. "Perhaps
too big a problem for someone who was directly involved in the
school at the time of its scandals." So much for the structure of my
argument. Froman had blown it away.

It didn't get easier after that. Bridget Thomas and Mark
Froman seemed determined to dredge up every aspect of last year's
tragic episodes.

On the way back to my office, a group of giggling, pretty girls passed me in the hall and my thoughts rushed back to Jamie. My head rejected it, but my instincts said another one of my students was in trouble—a sense of déjà vu from last year, when I'd witnessed the deep anguish of a student in serious trouble.

I tried to recall if I knew which one of our new black female students might be Jamie. Maybe the tall, beautiful girl I'd seen last week taking the stairs two at a time. Large eyes and incredible skin, she moved with the grace of a dancer and the strength of an athlete. I remembered her grandfather's face and knew I'd help him find her no matter what the cost in time and energy. That was my job.

His words—"Jamie's the center of my life"—echoed in my ears.

Chapter 3

Nell met me outside my office. "Everything go all right?" Her soft eyes were filled with concern. Nell's face is younger than her years, but she looked pale and anxious.

"Hard to say. I think some of the committee members like me but others seem to prefer a candidate from outside the university. One whose hands are clean of last year's mess."

"Oh, Red, we are all sure you did everything you could."

"Not everything, Nell. You know as well as I do that I took much too long to intervene. I'm afraid some of the committee members know it too. If I'd gone to the administration sooner, I might have prevented the assault of that girl." I could still see my student's battered face when she told me what her former lover had done to her. The worst part was her assailant had once been my good friend and confidant, a man I'd trusted way too much.

"We were all fooled." Nell tugged at one of her steel gray curls. "None of us saw the truth until it was too late. You can't blame yourself."

But I could blame myself. And I did.

As I sank into the chair behind my desk and put my hands over my eyes, I remembered the day I finally confronted the killer. Maybe Froman was right.

I was too involved in all the violent events of last year to lead the school as its permanent dean.

My cell phone rang and I glanced at the screen. It was Joe—the man who'd shown up that day at the last minute and saved my life. "How did the search committee go?" His slight note of concern pleased me. Whenever he thought I might be down, he transformed from detective to counselor.

"About as well as could be expected."

"I'm betting it was better than that. You have no idea how persuasive you can be when you put your mind to it."

"I hope you're right."

"We'll see. You're always pessimistic, and you're especially good at expecting the worst to happen. But I have another reason to call you. I got a visit from a Wynan Congers. Says his granddaughter's missing, one of your students. You gave him my name?"

"I did. Congers talked to the police but got nowhere, so I told him to see you."

"You know how much I'd enjoy helping out the next dean of the journalism school, but I'm not sure what I can do for this guy. The girl's over twenty-one and has only been gone a short time. My chief's not likely to put a team on her case for another few days."

"Congers knows that. But he's sure something awful has happened to her. He wants to talk to students and the head of our lab where she worked."

"Okay. Tell me what you know about her."

"Transfer student with good grades, according to her records. Light-skinned African American. Short curly hair. Tall. Great figure and a gorgeous face."

"That's how Congers described her too. Maybe she's gone to Hollywood."

"She'd fit right in, but her grandfather is certain she would have called him before taking a trip anywhere."

"She's an adult, but I'll see what I can find out. Her grandfather gave me her roommate's name and address. He's already talked to the roommate but wants me to see what I can dig up."

"Thanks very much. That will mean a lot to Congers. He's a retired deputy police chief, you know, from Vegas."

"So he said. I plan to do what I can to help the guy."

"Thanks, Joe. You're terrific. I'll help, too. I have Everett Jones, the head of our computer lab, coming in this afternoon so Congers can talk to him."

My thoughts stayed on Congers as I headed out to the parking lot where Bill Verden stood beside his ancient Buick convertible.

"Would it be all right to leave the top down?" he said as he opened the passenger side door for me. "My wife keeps a scarf in the glove compartment if you like."

"Leave the top down, Bill. I can use the fresh air. Where are we going for this lunch?"

"Froman wanted us to meet at Antonio's. You're okay with Italian, right?"

"I'm okay with food. I'm starving. Who else besides you and Froman are going to grill me along with my fish?" I reached for the scarf, remembering I had to look tidy for my official lunch with the search committee.

"Gert Simons. You know Gert."

"Sort of." I didn't know her well, and what I did know was she always seemed timid. I couldn't figure out how Gert Simons had survived the politics of the university, much less achieved the level of director.

The warm wind felt good on my face as we drove out of the south end of campus and took a narrow side street to the main drag of Landry. Shops and bars and three small casinos sat in a row of one-story buildings with the sky and mountains behind. The sky was that absolutely cloudless blue that covers the high desert.

I turned my head to Bill Verden's profile. "Bill, how the hell did I make it into the final three? I felt a lot of negative vibrations in the meeting this morning."

"Oh, c'mon, Red. False modesty doesn't suit you. You've done a terrific job with the school this past year, against incredible odds. Every dean and director on campus knows that."

"But Bridget Thomas seemed..."

"Bridget Thomas has the disposition of a wolverine and is much too occupied trying to second-guess the administration.

Don't worry about her. Her aggressiveness is all show." Bill turned his head and gave me a wink and what he thought was a comforting grin.

But I wasn't comforted. "Okay. But Mark Froman doesn't have to cater to the university brass. He has so much money they cater to him. And he seems dead set against my getting the dean's job."

The grin disappeared. "You're probably right. Froman's overly impressed with Victor Watts. Pulitzer prize winner, ex-*New York Times* writer, and so on. Froman likes fancy company. He may not be inclined to promote an inside candidate, especially a woman, in spite of the great job she's done getting her school through one crisis after another." Bill turned again to me. "Screw Froman. He's one vote."

"I'm sure you shouldn't be telling me things like this until after the search committee sends its recommendation to the provost."

"I know. I shouldn't share the committee discussions or their prejudices. So please don't ever rat me out on this. But I wanted you to know, before we break bread with Froman, that several of us have your back. Remember you were the one who saved the day. You're the right dean for the J-school. Okay?"

I was grateful to Bill. Like Sadie, he was also my friend and my primary spy on the committee. I adored his willingness to be both supportive and indiscreet.

We pulled up to the parking in back of Antonio's and went in the back entrance. Froman and Gert Simons were seated at the table. Gert was a small woman with a round, gentle face, and slim hands with long fingers. She could have modeled rings, but she wore none. She sipped on a ginger ale and studied her menu.

In contrast, Froman looked large and imposing, tilting his chair back, too big and tall for the small table. He had loosened his expensive tie and was halfway through a martini when we came in. He also was talking on his cell phone and ignoring Gert. I am forever amazed at the rudeness of the dedicated narcissist.

Gert looked up and smiled at me as Bill pulled out a chair for me opposite Froman, who continued on his phone call.

Gert whispered, "I'm so glad to see you apply for this position, Dr. Solaris. It's great to have a female top candidate even if she doesn't win. It's so encouraging."

"It will be even more encouraging if I get the job," I said, smiling back as brightly as I could. Gert rubbed her hands together as if she had just put on lotion. We all have our own nervous tells. Mine used to be twisting a strand of my hair, until my father persuaded me it was childish.

It was warm in the restaurant so I removed my jacket and instantly wished I'd worn a high neck blouse instead of a scoop neck silk tee under the jacket.

Froman, still talking on his phone, focused intently on the visible part of my cleavage.

Froman ended his call and finished his martini. After a dab of his napkin, he extended his sizeable hand across the table and shook mine with a heartiness that almost tipped over the salt and pepper. "Well now, Dr. Red Solaris, how are you doing?"

God, I wanted a drink, but didn't dare. "Fine, thank you," I said shifting my attention to the waiter to request sparkling water.

We ordered and when the food came, Froman took over. "Let's get right to it, Dr. Solaris. This morning you told us what you did last year and how difficult it was. Now then, explain to this unenlightened old outsider exactly what a university dean normally does."

I looked at him steadily. "Mr. Froman, I doubt you are all that unenlightened, but for the sake of this conversation, a dean is the leader and key administrator of the college. She normally manages faculty, staff, curriculum, and budget. She must also be a good fundraiser and a good marketer of her school."

Froman attended to a forkful of veal. Bill and Gert ate salads and said nothing. Froman finished chewing. "And what traits or dispositions would you say a dean needs to be successful?"

I swallowed, trying to appear thoughtful. "A successful dean has a clear vision for her school. She is skilled at listening to different points of view and creating effective teams..."

"Ah yes, that's important. Effective teams. And you think you can create teams with those lunatic journalists at your school?" Froman was still having difficulty looking at my face instead of my breasts. I raised my hand up and, with a pointed index finger, drew an invisible line from my breasts up to my face. His eyes obeyed and followed my finger and, for a moment, I was sure the self-important Mark Froman actually blushed at his own lewdness.

Bill came to the rescue with a different tack. Gert listened but had little to say. And, finally, after what seemed the longest lunch of my life, we were done.

On the drive home, Bill said, "I hope you're ready for the downside. A dean's calendar is not her own. You get really tired of the twenty-four hour pace and the lack of control over your own time. And once you've been a dean for a while, you realize that, after you've settled old scores, built teams, counseled faculty and all that, your job can be fairly lonely."

"Any cure for that?"

"Friendship, my friend. Other deans help me all the time. You already have Sadie Hawkins close to you. That's good. She's the wisest of us all. But get to know the rest of us as soon as you can. We can be there for you when you feel blue and isolated."

"So it really is lonely at the top?"

"It can be, my dear."

"After the year I've just been through, I think I know something about that already." But, of course, Bill Verden was right, because the people who pulled me through the chaos of the school last year were Joe and Sadie and good faculty friends who had been loyal throughout.

Verden dropped me off in the parking lot. A group of students had gathered at the front of the lot under the cherry trees, laughing and teasing one another. A few were African-American. None of them was Jamie Congers. Damn.

Chapter 4

Wynan Congers showed up precisely at three that afternoon. Nell followed him into my office with mugs of coffee neither he nor I had requested. Nell was a natural caregiver.

"My father was a chief of police in Tucson," she said, handing Wynan Congers his mug.

"Was he now? And I'll bet he was a good chief," said Congers, still standing close to Nell.

She smiled up at him.

"Did you ever serve?" he asked.

"No. I wanted to join the force, but I wasn't strong enough to pass the physical."

I wondered where this was going. I'd never seen Nell talk about herself to a visitor. And Congers, though obsessed with finding his granddaughter, seemed to have momentarily diverted his attention to my still pretty, if aging, assistant.

Just as I was about to clear my throat and remind them I was in the room, Everett Jones knocked on the frame of my office door.

"Please come in, Ev. Mr. Congers, this is Everett Jones, one of our adjunct professors. He's in charge of the lab where Jamie works. Ev, this is Wynan Congers, Jamie Congers' grandfather. He's worried about Jamie's absence."

"So am I," said Ev. "She's usually very prompt and responsible. It's been a problem for me the last couple of days not to have her. Is she ill?"

"She's missing," said Congers, annoyed but straining for composure. "I'm surprised you haven't reported it."

Ev stuttered. "Uh, I'm sorry, sir. I don't usually report absent students when it's just been a day or so. I mean, I figure they're old enough to know what they're doing...or what they're missing."

The older man made a noise in the back of his throat as close to a growl as I cared to hear.

Ev, who was as tall as Congers but easily intimidated, turned to me. "Actually, when she didn't answer my calls, I thought she might just be cutting class and I was thinking about appointing another student to her job. But I guess if she's missing, I'll wait until she's...uh...found...I mean..."

Nell, sensing the tension between them, interrupted. "I'm sure she'll be found soon, Mr. Congers. And, Dr. Jones, it would be good to hold off on a new assistant and to make sure everyone in the lab knows that the job still belongs to Jamie."

How about that? Nell never interrupted, and this was the first time I'd ever seen her take control of a situation. Perhaps I should give my assistant more responsibility.

Congers looked calmer. "What about the students in the lab on Monday night? Did any of them see anything that would help?"

"I'll be happy to talk to them," Ev began.

"I think I'd prefer to have the dean's detective friend talk to them, if you don't mind."

"Fine," said Ev. "Just let me know." Ev wanted more than anything to be a tenured member of our faculty, and had applied for an assistant professorship.

If he got it, he'd have to prove to me and the other senior faculty that he merited tenure.

The tenure track can be slippery in a university and one major error, or one offended faculty member voting against you, could make all the difference.

My turn. "We will let you know, Ev. You know Detective Joe Morgan of the Landry police?"

"He's the guy who investigated the dean's death last year."

"Right. Joe will want to talk to you, your students, and others. Please make yourself available when he calls."

"Sure will. Nice to meet you, Mr. Congers. Uh...sorry about the circumstances. I hope this works out soon." Ev's feet were already in the hall outside my door by the end of his last sentence.

Congers turned to me. "When do you think I'll hear again from Morgan?"

"I'm sure he'll call you this evening or before. Nell gave him your cell number."

Congers regarded Nell. "Thank you, Mrs. Bishop." He shook my hand and Nell's and left.

When we were alone I gave in to my curiosity. "You like him, don't you?"

"I do. He's very good-looking."

"Never known you to care about how people look." I smiled and sat down in my desk chair.

Nell stepped closer to my desk, her hands folded neatly in front of her. "My grandfather was African-American. Mr. Congers reminds me of him."

"Your grandfather?"

"Yes. A bit darker than Mr. Congers, but every bit as good-looking."

I smiled up at her smooth pale face. "I didn't know."

"Most people don't." She smiled back. "I've never tried to deny it, but I've also never seen much reason to discuss my racial background. I don't mind telling you my tall, handsome grandfather's the one who gave me my big brown eyes."

I swear she turned to leave my office with what looked like a tiny dance step.

Chapter 5

That evening I waited for Joe Morgan to call or show up. I paced my living room, trying not to drink my wine too quickly. This was the kind of evening when I wished I could better predict Joe's movements. A silly thought. No woman can predict the activity or the whereabouts of a man who devotes his life to examining evidence that makes us shudder and hunting down human beings the rest of us call the scum of the earth.

But for all the miserable folk he encountered, Joe understood and shared my soft spot for students. Even though our students were all over the legal age and many very responsible and grown up, I kept tabs on a few who seem to need a bit more *in loco parentis*.

As I once told Joe, "In the olden days, before the liberating 1960s, parents had every expectation that the university would watch over their offspring. Those were the days of deans of students and dormitory housemothers and proctors who monitored students more closely."

He smiled. "Yeah, but then came the student protests, and students' demands for privacy and freedom. And students won. Yet, as a cop, I was still always surprised when parents didn't receive reports of misbehavior."

"They didn't receive grades either."

By the end of the protests, grades were not sent home. Faculty were prohibited from discussing an individual's academic progress. Even the so-called "helicopter parents," who dropped in constantly, were frustrated by university laws on student privacy.

Usually I supported the new rules and respected students' decisions to be on their own. But earlier that day, I'd watched a courageous retired cop rage inside at the thought his granddaughter might be in danger.

I wished we'd kept better track of her. I wished I'd gotten to know her better.

At last I heard the familiar sound of Joe's car in my driveway.

"Hi there," he said with a soft kiss on my mouth. He looked at the wine glass in my hand. "I see you started without me."

"I'm a wreck," I said. "I'm starting to worry about Jamie Congers. I believe her grandfather when he says she would have told someone if she planned to leave."

"I believe him too," said Joe, taking off his jacket and draping it over a chair. "Pour me some of that wine and I'll tell you what little I found out." As was his custom in my house, he sat down in my favorite living room chair, ignoring my books clearly displayed on the side table. "And then I want you to tell me about that search meeting this morning."

"Oh, I can't even think about the search committee right now. It's in the hands of the gods."

"Aren't you supposed to be at dinner tonight with the chair of the committee?"

"Yes, but, just as well, she postponed until later this week. Since she's the chair, I guess she can set the schedule anyway she wants." I sat on the sofa opposite Joe. "Besides, I want to focus on Jamie Congers right now."

Joe's green eyes grew darker and he put his chin in his hands. "Her grandfather's an interesting guy who, from all reports, was a hell of a cop and a hell of a leader in his department. I checked him out. He has a lot of friends on the Vegas force who want me to do whatever I can."

"Did you get a chance to talk to anyone else?"

"Yes, I talked to Ev Jones and the students who were in the lab Monday night, the last people who saw her. I also stopped at Jamie's apartment and talked to her roommate, Marilyn Ford."

"You've been busy. That's great."

"But I haven't gotten much."

"Oh, damn." I poured myself another glass of wine.

"Easy going, sport. You don't want to turn into an alcoholic over a missing student." Joe knew all about my mother's drinking problems.

I put my glass down on the coffee table. "Don't worry. But, please, details."

Joe crossed his long legs. He'd been a basketball player in college and still kept himself lean and in shape. When I first met him, I couldn't take my eyes off him. And even after we began to see each other, I still delighted in the effect his rugged features and surprising humor had on me—and every other woman in the vicinity.

Sadie loved his jokes, even the corniest. "He's my storybook hero. Great body. Strong face. Good mind. You're a lucky woman, Red Solaris." Sadie invariably took Joe's side when we had debates at our dinners together.

Joe took another sip of wine and began. "You know that Jamie was an only child whose parents both died fighting in Afghanistan. And that Wynan raised her in Las Vegas. The guys on the force there told me she's absolutely the light of his life and they really want me to find her because they don't think Wynan can make it without her. I have orders to succeed. They also told me she had a boyfriend there who later joined the force. No lead, though. The rookie is now married and was on duty Monday night."

"What about the students in Ev's lab class?"

"A few were absent, but the ones I interviewed said she was a good lab monitor. Apparently, she really helped some of the freshman with computer programs. They describe her as beautiful and private. They knew her name. That's all. No one saw anyone suspicious that night."

"Could one of the students…"

"Sure. I have to interview those who missed class today and each one, alone, to rule that out. Same for Everett Jones."

"Oh, I hope Ev isn't involved. I won't be able to stand it if another teacher has gotten in trouble with a student."

Joe's face looked grim and he leaned back in the chair, his hands now on top of his head. "Let's not assume Ev Jones had anything to do with it."

Charlie went over to Joe and put his head on Joe's knee. Joe scratched his ears and neck. Charlie loves Joe. In fact, Charlie loves both of us unconditionally, which is more than I can say for most people. Our world might be better if our temperaments were more like dogs and less like dragons.

"Am I cooking tonight or are you?" Joe was a magician in the kitchen, but there was no way he'd found time to shop. And he looked worn out.

"Neither of us. Let's order in some Chinese. I am too tired to light the grill."

Joe stood and walked over to the couch. He put his hands on my shoulders and his fingers reached around the back of my neck and began a slow, delicious massage. He leaned into me, kissed the top of my ear and whispered, "An agnostic professor suffers from insomnia and dyslexia and stays up all night wondering if there really is a dog."

What more could a woman want.

I turned to him and smiled just as he leaned in to kiss me. "Then, of course, there's the dyslexic cop who goes around arresting IUDs."

Chapter 6

After a full day at the office, Joe and I met at the house for dinner. Neither of us had news about Jamie. We worked silently, each a bit restless, although we normally loved being in in the kitchen cooking together.

This was the part of the day we liked best. We each had a task and a glass of wine. Charlie lay curled up under the kitchen table. I chopped carrots on a wooden board and Joe sautéed onions in butter and garlic on the stove. Heaven was the smell of Joe's cooking.

The doorbell rang.

Wynan Congers stood on my small front porch. "I have some news. Maybe a lead," he said.

"Please come in, Mr. Congers."

"Thank you, Dr. Solaris. I was told Joe Morgan might be here."

I indicated a chair in the living room.

Joe emerged from the kitchen. "Hi, Wynan. What's up?"

Congers still stood by the chair. "I may have a lead," he said, clearly exhausted. The flesh under his eyes was swollen. "Marilyn called and said that the tenant in the next door apartment told her she saw a man entering Jamie and Marilyn's apartment when Marilyn was in class."

"Did Marilyn get a description of the man?" said Joe.

"Not really. As soon as she began to quiz the next door tenant, the woman clammed up. Marilyn may have been too eager and too free with information about Jamie being missing. She thinks the woman got spooked and stopped talking."

"Maybe you and I can unspook the lady," said Joe, removing the chef's apron I gave him for his birthday. "Let's go see her now. Just let me turn off the spaghetti sauce."

"I was hoping you'd say that," said Wynan, heading toward the front door.

"If dinner's going to be delayed, may I go too?" I spoke to Joe's back as he turned into the kitchen. "The next door lady might feel more comfortable talking with me than with you two six-footers."

"Three's kind of a crowd," said Wynan.

"But it might help create a sense of urgency in the woman's mind if the dean of the school shows up," said Joe. "Don't worry, Chief. I can assure you that Red knows how to behave herself." I got a wink for that.

"Let's go," said Wynan, opening my front door.

The apartment house where Jamie and Marilyn lived was a three-story brick building on the south end of campus, just across the street from the back entrance to Mountain West University. The elevator looked tiny, so the three of us took the stairs to the second floor.

Marilyn opened her door so quickly I wondered if she'd been braced against it, waiting for us.

She was a pretty girl, darker and not as tall or as elegant looking as her roommate. Dressed in jeans and a Mountain West sweatshirt, she had her hair pulled up in a tight bun on the top of her head. Her large brown eyes filled with tears as soon as she saw Wynan.

"Oh, Mr. Congers, I'm so sorry if I handled this badly. The woman next door has never been friendly, and when she mentioned rather casually that she had seen a man coming in here yesterday, I practically jumped at her."

"It's all right, Marilyn. I brought Detective Morgan with me. You remember him?"

The girl nodded. "Yes. He talked to me last evening."

"And I'm sure you remember me, Marilyn. Meredith Solaris, dean of the journalism school. You were in my media ethics class last year." I held my hand out to the girl, who was trembling and looked as if she could use a strong arm around her shoulders. "Why don't we sit down and you tell us what happened. Would you like me to get you some water?"

"Thank you, Dean Solaris. I'm all right. I'm just glad to see you all here. I've been a mess since I talked to Mrs. Cimaneti next door." Marilyn sank into the couch that took up most of the small living room. "She's old and grumpy and as soon as she knew the man's coming in here upset me, she pulled away. She thought he was a handyman and said she didn't want any trouble and that was all."

"We'll go next door in a minute, Marilyn." Joe spoke in his calm, investigative voice. I'd heard it before and wondered how he always kept it so professional and well-modulated. "Before that, tell us if anything is missing from the apartment."

"I don't think so." She looked at Wynan. "Everything we found of Jamie's and mine is still here just like it was when you first came over and we looked everywhere."

Joe frowned. "Marilyn, could it have been a handyman? Any problems here that needed fixing?"

"None." The girl was emphatic. "I called the landlord while I was waiting for you. He never sent anyone to this apartment for any reason. Not since Jamie and I moved in."

Joe went to the front door and examined the door, the lock, and the frame. "No sign of forced entry here. Does anyone else have a key besides you and Jamie?"

"No," said Marilyn. I could see she was starting to become agitated. "Absolutely no one."

"If it happened Tuesday, after Jamie was gone, maybe the man used Jamie's key," I said. Marilyn's eyes widened. She was shaking all over.

"Maybe," said both policemen simultaneously.

Joe returned to the door. "Let's go see if Mrs. Cimaneti is home and willing to tell us more."

"I think Mrs. Cimaneti's first name is Octavia. That's what I hear the landlord call her sometimes," said Marilyn.

Octavia Cimaneti had an old face, pale gray and wrinkled from forehead to chin. Her hair was white and thinning on top. She stood in the doorway of her apartment regarding us with her arms folded across her chest and her hostility visible and fierce.

"I told that girl next door, I didn't see anything. Just a man going into her apartment. Never saw his face." She raised her folded arms slightly for emphasis and stood with her feet planted squarely in the middle of the doorway.

"May we come in please, Mrs. Cimaneti? This is an important police investigation and your help could be of great value to us." Joe could charm a bird out of a tree.

The old woman eyed the three of us as if trying to decide if we were real police or imposters. Then, without a word, she turned, leaving the door open. Her back was bent and she braced herself with one hand against the wall as she walked over to her chair. The apartment was stuffy, filled with faded upholstered furniture. Yellowed shades and patterned curtains covered the windows. The whole place smelled of fried food. Mrs. Cimaneti indicated the sofa, and I sat down. Wynan stood with his back to the wall. Joe pulled up a dining room chair and sat opposite the still belligerent woman.

"I don't wonder it's a police investigation," she said, her eyes appraising Wynan. "We've had some different kinds of people moving into this building lately and I was just waiting for the first sign of trouble."

Wynan's face remained impassive. No doubt he had encountered similar sentiments from people like Mrs. Cimaneti all his life.

Joe inched closer to the woman until his knees almost touched hers. "You said you thought the man you saw going into the apartment next door was a handyman. Why did you think he was a handyman?"

"He was wearing overalls and heavy work boots. Muddy boots. That's why." Her face grew angrier and her tone more defensive as her hands twisted in her lap. "Unless you're gonna tell me one of those girls has a boyfriend who's a day laborer."

"Neither of them has a boyfriend," said Wynan, still standing and leaning against the wall, making it clear he'd be damned if he was going to sit down in this woman's house.

"You saw him from the back. Right?" Joe had produced a notepad and was writing down her statement. She nodded.

"What color was his hair?"

"He was wearing a cap, so I'm not sure. Gray, or brown maybe."

"What color was his skin?"

"White," she said impatiently. "His hand on the doorframe was white and the back of his neck was white."

"So you saw him quite clearly?" Joe's voice was even—cool, yet still friendly.

"I didn't see his face. That's all I can tell you."

"Just a few more questions, Mrs. Cimaneti. And then we'll let you get back to your evening."

The woman straightened in her chair. She smoothed her skirt and tugged nervously at her sweater.

"How tall would you say he was?" Joe was still writing.

"About as tall as that man leaning against my wall." She avoided looking directly at Wynan. Just as well, I thought. His expression was no more cordial than hers.

"Could you guess at his weight? Heavy, thin?"

"About average...I don't know. He was wearing those loose sort of overalls workmen wear."

"Can you remember anything else that might help find him?"

She closed her eyes. "His arms. The muscles showed through the t-shirt he was wearing. Big muscles."

A popping noise came from the direction of the kitchen. She rose from her chair. "I should tend to my supper," she said, moving toward the sound.

"Thank you for your time, ma'am," said my courteous detective. "We appreciate your help."

Mrs. Cimaneti disappeared into her kitchen. We let ourselves out.

Marilyn opened the door with, "I just found something odd."

"What?"

"I looked again in Jamie's closet, and you know how neat and organized she is. All the skirts in one section, pants in another. She never mixes."

"So?"

"One of her blouses was hanging in the middle of the skirt section. She never does that."

"Do you think the man took some of her clothes?"

"I don't think so. But he might have been looking through her stuff. Something's wrong about where that blouse is hanging."

A girl goes missing and, a day later, a man breaks into her apartment to look through her clothes? Or take some? Strange. Unless it meant Jamie might be in trouble but still alive. I kept the thought to myself.

Jamie

Light crept in from somewhere, but she couldn't make out the contours of the room. Jamie knew she was on a bed, and she could feel she was tied to the head and footboard, both hands and both feet wide apart. Her head pounded and a wave of nausea swept over her. She struggled against the ropes that held her, but they were too thick and too tight. She wiggled her hips. Even with clothes still on her body, the spread eagle position made her feel vulnerable.

Noises came from below. Kitchen noises. A pot scraping against the burner of a stove. A door closing. Her head throbbed again. Terror flooded her mind. She couldn't think straight.

No amount of education or sports training had prepared her for this feeling of helplessness. Strong and smart, she still had no idea what to do next. She felt overwhelmed by the ropes and darkness. None of her grandfather's advice on self-protection applied.

Once, when she was in middle school in Las Vegas, a gang fight had broken out in her classroom. Six boys with knives and two with guns had sent her diving under her desk, hoping the fighters wouldn't see her or involve her. One boy crashed down on top of her desk, his arm gushing blood that spattered her face. Even after the police arrived she had remained in her hiding place, shaking and bloodstained until a teacher persuaded her to come out.

"You did the right thing," her grandfather had said afterward. "You stayed out of the way. You kept yourself safe."

But how was she to keep herself safe in this room?

Chapter 7

Joe called one of his detectives and gave the description of the man seen at Jamie's apartment, then headed for the kitchen to continue cooking his spaghetti sauce. I showed Wynan into the living room.

"Drink?" I asked.

The man's face was a portrait of grief and worry. "Whiskey, please, if you have it."

I poured him a glass and gave myself a refill of red wine. We sat silently, sipping, until Joe came back into the room. "Wynan, I have plenty of spaghetti, if you're hungry."

"Yes, please stay for dinner," I added, embarrassed that I had not thought to ask before.

Wynan shook his head. "Thank you, no. I promised Nell I'd stop by her place to tell her what we learned." He stood up and put his empty glass on the side table. My face must have reflected the question I didn't ask. "She's a nice person, your assistant. We've become friends."

"Good. I think Nell enjoys your company."

"My company isn't too enjoyable these days, Dr. Solaris, but Nell Bishop is a smart woman and a great comfort. Thanks for the drink. I can't tell you how much I appreciate what both of you are doing to help me." The older man's body filled the space of my open front door. "I'll call you first thing in the morning, Joe."

When he'd gone, Joe and I sat down to a solemn dinner.

"Do you think the description you called in will get any leads?"

"Probably not. Not unless a guy with that description has been seen around the neighborhood and reported for suspicious activity.

They'll call me if anything comes up on the computers." Joe twirled his spaghetti absentmindedly. "I feel stymied by this one. We don't even know where to begin to look for Jamie Congers."

"So you think she's definitely been taken by someone."

Jamie

Jamie could see trees and sky through a small window near her bed, but nothing more. She still couldn't figure out where she was. She kept thinking about the parking garage.

Over and over again she remembered standing by her car watching the tall man approach her with a cloth in his hand. At first she'd been baffled. In previous encounters, the tall man's behavior had always been appropriate. He'd always been polite, always walked away.

But in the light of the garage, his expression looked grim, and she could see the muscles in his jaw working. She had panicked, her self-defense responses had locked up. She'd frozen in place as the man had raised his arm and put the cloth over her face.

Why had she frozen when he approached her? Her internal alarm system had gone off, but her instincts had failed to heed it. Perhaps because the tall man had been so manageable in the earlier encounters. Because he seemed so harmless, she couldn't believe she had completely misjudged him. Because, because...

The lock on the door clicked, and the door opened and closed behind a figure. The tall man walked slowly until he stood beside her.

"You're awake."

"Where am I? And who the hell are you?" Her voice sounded hoarse, as if she had been strangled.

His hands reached for the rope that tied her wrists to the bed.

"You must have to use the toilet by now," he said. "I will free you from the bed but you must promise not to try anything foolish or I will have to tie you up again."

She rubbed her wrists as she watched him untie the rope around her ankles. She did have to get up. Her bladder burned.

"Move very slowly," he said. "Any sudden efforts will be punished."

She rose cautiously. The man gripped her elbow and guided her to another door. He opened it, revealing a small bathroom. A toilet, a small sink over a cabinet painted blue. White walls, with blue tiles around the sink and toilet. A small shower took up the corner, partly concealed with an ancient patterned shower curtain.

He stood next to her, taller than she remembered from the garage. He smelled of cologne that seemed at odds with his overalls and heavy boots.

"Are you going to give me some privacy?"

"Sorry." But he didn't move.

Jamie decided she didn't care. Having to urinate in front of him was going to be the least of it.

He stood in the doorway, his eyes focused on the wall just above her head, unsmiling but not threatening. He was over six feet and muscular, with large biceps visible under a long-sleeved knit shirt. His overalls were old and patched and slightly too short over his muddy, thick heeled boots. He was definitely the man who'd approached her on campus, who'd come to the lab last night, and then followed her to the garage. But he looked different in work clothes. On campus, he'd worn a suit and tie. Few people dressed that formally on campus, but he had.

When she finished, he kept his eyes over her head as she stood and pulled up her pants.

"Who are you? Where am I?"

"Put the lid down."

She turned and flushed the toilet. The seat and the lid were old, varnished wood not painted. When the lid met the seat she saw a word carved into the top.

"Obey."

Chapter 8

The hamburger joint was crowded and smoky; most of the customers were students, at the bar or the pool tables drinking themselves into a stupor. Joe and I had seen this scene before, even rescued a young woman who'd almost died from binge drinking.

"It never fails to get to me," said Joe. "Some nights I want to stand on the bar, announce I'm a cop and confiscate their car keys."

"Why don't you?"

"Minor impediment called the Constitution."

Excessive drinking is a huge problem for college students, but, as Joe noted, there's not much a university can do except declare the physical campus "dry." A declaration that just sends the older students to off-campus bars, and the younger ones to off-campus parties.

We made our way to the back through the noise and confusion and sat in a booth. Just as I sat down, I noticed something familiar out of the corner of my eye. Gray curls. I focused on another booth in the opposite corner.

"Well, I'll be damned. Look at that."

In a booth in the opposite corner, Nell Bishop was engaged in serious conversation with Wynan Congers. Her eyes were locked on Congers and neither of them moved.

"No grass growing under that man's feet," said Joe, unfolding his menu.

I was still in a state of disbelief. "But Nell? I've never known her to pay any attention to a man. I don't think she's had a date in years. She's the most appropriate widow I know."

"Well then, it's about time." Joe put his hand over mine. "Decide what you want to eat and mind your own business." He removed his hand. "C'mon, stop staring. You'll embarrass her."

"Yes, sir." I realized I was pleased as well as surprised. Nell had been kind to me from my first day at Mountain West University. And when I took over as interim dean after Henry had been killed, Nell offered me more than loyalty. She became my friend and confidant as well as my assistant. She knew the paths through all the university bureaucracies. She knew all the scandals that had beset the school of journalism. Better yet, she fathomed all the weaknesses of those faculty and administrators who seemed intent on driving me crazy. But most important of all, she kept my secrets and her own counsel.

Nell, my friend, my gentle warrior, my secret weapon. I'd grown to care deeply about her.

She must have sensed my thoughts because she looked over at us. She sent me a little wave of her hand but made no move to get up and come over. She returned to the face of Wynan Congers.

Joe was paying attention. "Congers was a top cop in Las Vegas back in the day, solved several murders, and saved some girls from a prostitution ring. Any number of awards and citations."

"Imagine how frustrated and angry he must be that he can't protect his own granddaughter."

"I'd rather not imagine it. It reminds me of the time when I thought I couldn't protect you."

Now my hand was over his. "You were great. You saved my life, and gave me the strength to deal with the other terrorists on the faculty. You're still my hero, mister."

I felt privileged when I was with Joe. Last winter, he and I had almost broken up for good. I hated to think anything would ever pull him away from me again. In spite of his moods, I wanted us to continue seeing each other.

Joe had told me some of his darker secrets, the worst of which was when he accidentally shot what he took to be an armed robber in a Chicago delicatessen only to discover the man was, in fact, a boy with a ski mask and a defective gun. That's the kind of incident that can haunt a cop for life, and I knew it.

Just as I knew if I didn't find Jamie Congers, it would haunt me. Since our conversation with Marilyn, I had wracked my brain trying to figure out why a kidnapper would go to his victim's apartment *afterward*. What was he looking for, and if he wasn't her abductor but just a common burglar, why wasn't anything taken?

Joe intruded on my thoughts. "You look pensive. What's up?"

"Just trying to exercise my powers of deductive reasoning."

"As I recall from the last case we worked on together, you have some remarkable powers."

"Why would he have gone to her apartment and looked through her possessions after kidnapping her? She didn't have enough money or jewelry worth the risk of being caught."

"Agreed. But there must have been something there that was important to him."

I looked over at Wynan Congers and Nell. "Joe, I think this guy needed to know more about Jamie. It sounds weird, but I think he needed some information because he has some plan for her. A plan that can't be good."

Neither of us spoke, but I could see in his eyes that we both had the same thought. A plan also might mean she was still alive.

Chapter 9

The next evening I found the chair of the search committee for the dean of journalism already seated at the restaurant table. Bridget Thomas had a sheaf of papers in front of her and seemed deeply engrossed by the contents. I wondered if the documents were truly important or just meant to create the impression that my arrival was an unwelcome interruption.

"Good evening, Dr. Thomas," I said, standing behind my chair.

She looked up, her mouth narrow and turned down at the corners. Bridget was what we charitably called a heavy-set woman. Not so much fat as bulky. Her clothes never fit her, usually a size too small for her large frame. Her lipstick was too dark and her eyeliner too thick. She responded with a slight frown. "Please sit down, Dr. Solaris."

I smiled. Just try to irritate me into saying anything that kills my chances, my inner voice said to her frown. "This looks like a nice restaurant. I don't think I've been here before."

Bridget had chosen a restaurant in Reno, where she had a home. No point inconveniencing herself. I was the candidate, no doubt the supplicant in her mind, so it fell to me to drive the hour from Landry.

"Place just opened last month." Her eyes cast down at the papers. "I thought we might give it a try."

"I hope I'm not late." I kept my tone buttery. I knew I was five minutes early.

"You're on time. I always get to appointments a few minutes early," she said with a trace of petulance.

"Well, I know you have an incredible schedule these days, Dr. Thomas. Running a dean search is very time-consuming, and it's good of you to have taken this one on."

C'mon, Bridget, soften up. I'm trying to make friends here.

The corners of her mouth turned up ever so slightly. "Well, I think it's the responsibility of those of us who are established deans to lead the search for new colleagues."

She ordered bourbon, neat. I ordered sparkling water. She ordered steak with fries. I ordered fish and salad.

She asked me about my background as a professional journalist. How long had I worked for a metro newspaper? What did I think of the department head at my old university or the professors who had guided me through my doctoral thesis?

Between her questions I learned she was divorced and the mother of two sons, both in boarding schools back east. "Their father's decree," she said bitterly.

After each inquiry, I tried to segue into my accomplishments as a dean.

"Well now." She tapped her mouth with her napkin and spread her hands on the table. "I know you've been very careful in the search committee interviews to tell us what you have done as interim dean of journalism and why you want the job permanently."

But.

"But I wonder if you have given thought to the lightness of your experience?"

Lightness?

"I'm not sure I know what you mean, Dr. Thomas. Much of what we have been through in journalism this past semester has required a fair amount of heavy lifting on my part."

"Well, yes. It's been very difficult, I'm sure. What with the awful circumstances of the dean's death and the arrest of a faculty colleague. That degree of scandal can be very time-consuming."

"I had more than scandal to deal with. I had to get new courses approved and prepare us to be reaccredited as a school."

"Of course. But what I mean is, you have been an interim dean for less than a year. Your overall university experience is...well...less than what might be expected of a permanent dean."

Take a deep breath. Try again. "Dr. Thomas, I am applying for this position at the urging of the faculty. It would seem I have gained their confidence. I assure you, I know I am not as experienced as you or the other deans on campus, but I learn quickly and I know where to go to ask for advice when I need it."

She clasped her hands and leaned forward. "Dr. Solaris, I understand you did wonders, and I'm sure you're an adept student, but I continue to think you need more. Perhaps I can suggest an activity that would broaden your view of the university, give you a chance to engage in policy discussions, prepare you better for a top job like dean."

Oh, that's what this is about. She has a chore for me.

"I would welcome your suggestions, Dr. Thomas." Much more of this and my nose would start to elongate.

A small, satisfied smile appeared. "I am currently one of only two women on a university committee tasked with developing a policy on sexual assault. You know about that problem, I presume."

I did. Sexual assault on university campuses had been a major news item for over a year. The media had carried story after story about colleges and universities trying to improve the ways in which sexual assault was reported and investigated. The federal government had weighed in with mandates and law professors debated protections for victims versus due process for perpetrators.

"We had a preliminary meeting last week," Bridget continued, "and, frankly, I was appalled that there were a dozen of us around the table and the Director of Student Services and I were the only women."

I opened my mouth to comment, but Bridget was gaining steam and continued before I could say anything.

"I was wondering if you'd like to join us?" she asked. "You could replace one of the male members, one of the athletic coaches. There are three members of the athletic department on the committee and that's too many, in my opinion." She smiled, her first smile of the evening. "Participation in the design of a major university policy would provide useful insight for a new dean. What do you think?"

I returned her smile. "I think if we're going to be fellow committee members, you should call me Red. And I should call you..."

"Bridget, of course." She reached across the table and shook my hand.

Jamie

The man allowed her to remain untied to the bed as long as she made no attempt to escape. He brought her food twice a day, the first early in the morning, the other late at night. Scrambled eggs, toast, and coffee. Then, at night, a slice of warmed ham and some spinach—all nourishing but bland. She had taken one shower, yesterday, while he stood in the doorway watching the shower curtain as she moved. She'd refused at first, terrified of removing all her clothes and making it easy for him. But he'd threatened to undress her himself, and that frightened her even more. As she emerged, he handed her the towel. He scanned her body, then averted his eyes. He made no move to touch her.

What did he want? If not sex, ransom? Why would he think she came from a family that would have enough money to pay a sum worth the crime of kidnapping? And didn't he figure someone in her family would demand to know she was still alive? She was sure her grandfather would insist upon speaking to her on the phone, or seeing her on a computer screen. And none of that had happened.

An hour later, she lay in her bed looking at the night sky outside of the barred window. Marilyn would be frantic by now. Her roommate had probably told her grandfather, who would have jumped on a plane from Las Vegas and come up north to Landry look for her. She reminded herself that Wynan Congers was a good cop. He would know what to do, how to hunt for her. She just had to keep herself safe until he found her.

At daybreak, she stood by the window. She saw nothing but trees and what seemed to be water beyond. No people. No animals. Only the chirp and chatter of birds on the branches nearby.

Where was she?

Why was he keeping her?

The man had refused to answer any of her questions. He'd just said, "Don't try to escape. All the doors are locked and the windows sealed and barred. I'll punish you severely if I discover you have made any effort to leave."

On the second evening, he brought a pile of new clothing with her supper. Jeans, a pale blue denim shirt, two pairs of underpants and two cotton bras, simple with no lace or ornamentation. No shoes or socks. When he had left she examined the clothes. They were her size. Even the bras. How did he know her size just from looking at her? Had he examined her clothes while she showered? No, he'd stayed by the door. Another mystery.

During the day, she had examined every square inch of the bedroom and bathroom, looking for weak spots, looking for ways her physical strength could help her escape. Jamie had been a star athlete in high school: track, basketball, and a state champion Lacrosse player. She had good muscles and strong reflexes. She could outsmart this man. She just wasn't sure she could take him out in a fight. He was bigger and stronger. He might be armed.

She looked for potential weapons: towel racks she could pry away, mirror and window glass she could break into shards, a heavy lamp base she could pull from the wall socket. She examined everything—the wires, the towels, the sheets—as potential weapons or aids to escape.

She worried about time. She still had no clue as to what he wanted of her.

The lock clicked and the door opened.

"You haven't changed into your clean clothes," he said.

"Where did you get them?"

"No questions. Just change now."

He stood and watched. He made no move toward her as she undressed and dressed.

"Pick up the dirty clothes and come with me."

He was going to let her out of the room. She should have created a weapon sooner.

He led her by the hand down a narrow flight of uncarpeted stairs that squeaked under her feet. The stairs led to a long hallway and then into a kitchen. The plaster walls were painted a dull yellow. Two larger but heavily barred windows flanked a double ceramic sink. An electric stove that looked as if it had been purchased in the fifties was matched by an equally outdated refrigerator. Pine cabinets ran the length of the wall. Beyond the kitchen was an alcove with a washer and dryer that seemed slightly newer than the other appliances.

"Put your dirty clothes in the washer."

Above the washer, nailed into the wall, was a large framed document that looked like parchment. Letters similar to those carved into the toilet seat upstairs read: *Ephesians 5:22-6:9. Wives be in subjection unto your own husbands, as unto the Lord. For the husband is the head of the wife.*

She knew Bible verses from her Sunday school days. She knew there was more to the chapter than what was written. Whoever created the document must have wanted a simpler message to be read.

"Pay attention to that," he said. He stood about two feet away, looking at her and then at the parchment.

Husband? Wife? Oh, God, what was he planning? She put her dirty clothes in the washer.

The man moved back into the kitchen, opened a bottom cupboard, and brought out a large saucepan and an iron skillet. "Do you know how to cook?"

"A little."

"There's food in the icebox. Prepare dinner."

Icebox? What century did this man live in? Never mind. She was out of the prison of her upstairs bedroom and now in a kitchen, where the search for escape or weapons might be easier. She opened the refrigerator door. Not much inside. A package of chicken breasts. Two potatoes. A container of green bean salad. A quart of milk. Butter, eggs, half a loaf of bread. The cupboard above the sink revealed basics: salt, pepper, mustard, no spices.

Did he live here or was this just the house where he kept her?

She opened a drawer next to the stove. Two knives. She pulled the larger one out. A good eight-inch blade. He was beside her in an instant. "If anything needs to be cut, I'll do it," he said, taking the knife from her hand.

The kitchen was a larger, newer place for her, and Jamie planned to explore it as thoroughly as she had the upstairs room. A kitchen should offer better opportunity for finding a weapon. The man must've read her mind, because he watched her every move, especially when she touched the knife drawer or maneuvered the heavy skillet.

He stood, arms folded across his chest, his back braced against the wall, watching.

He spoke hardly at all, and then only to give orders. "Scrub out the sink with scouring powder," or "mop the floor starting by the back door."

The back door. It was heavy, solid, no windows. Locked with a dead bolt. And above that, a hasp with a padlock. The padlock had a keyboard with nine numbered buttons. No point looking for a key. She assumed the other downstairs doors were also padlocked.

When she finished mopping, he leaned against the wall by the door. "Now wipe off the table with a damp sponge."

She snapped. "Why the hell should I?"

He pushed off the wall and moved toward her. "Because you are here to do exactly what I want when I want it."

Pinpricks in the back of her neck. She wiped off the table.

*   *   *

Back in her room, Jamie wondered what would happen if she tried to attack him first. Chances were he wouldn't expect it. But then, the few moves her grandfather had taught her in Las Vegas might only work if they were unexpected.

The quick chop to the bridge of his nose, preferably executed with her elbow. "People don't realize how strong the elbow can be," Wynan Congers had said during one of their training sessions. A sharp stomp to the top of his foot. No good when he was wearing boots. Knock the air out of him with a hard jab to his solar plexus. With what weapon? And finally, what if whatever she tried didn't work? How would she break the padlocks while he lay moaning on the floor? What would he do when he recovered from the blow?

She shuddered. She would have to wait for a moment when he was vulnerable, or asleep.

Asleep. God, no. Not that.

Chapter 10

Driving home to Landry through the dark Nevada night along a highway with few houses, under a sky full of stars, my thoughts alternated between my conversation with Bridget Thomas and the puzzle that was the whereabouts of Jamie Congers.

The offer Bridget made to me was not as onerous as she might have thought. The more I thought about the Mountain West committee on sexual assault policy, the better I liked the idea. Serving on a university committee dedicated to dealing with a major campus issue would give me exposure and experience. Besides, I was privately annoyed with Mountain West for taking so long to formulate a firm policy that protected the students, female and male. Maybe I could hurry things up. Other colleges and universities across the country were way ahead of us.

Charlie met me at the door, jumping and running back and forth. He was hungry and I was late with his dinner. I should have asked Joe to come over and feed him while I was with the calculating Dean of the College of Economics.

I gave Charlie his food and telephoned Joe.

"Did Dean Thomas eat you alive?"

"Actually, instead of me she had steak, rare. Almost bloody."

"Hardass, is she?"

"It turned out better than I thought. I suspect she's still not completely on my side for the dean's job, but she needs me to help her on the committee to figure out our sexual assault policy."

"You'll be good at that. You have a good mind for legal problems." Joe had a sixth sense about when I could use a boost to my ego. Another one of the reasons I dated the guy. That, and besides *The New York Times* he read every morning, the man kept books of poetry on the bedside table in his apartment. "Helps me sleep when I have to sleep alone," he'd said without a trace of sarcasm. I loved the idea he led an interior intellectual life. I also loved the idea that when he wasn't with me, he slept alone. Or so I hoped.

"How was your day, Detective Morgan?"

"Long. I spent half of it tracking down the students in Jamie Congers' classes who had been absent the first time I inquired. Then I went through the files my team had come up with on the man with the boots, and finally spent an hour observing two of my detectives testify in court against a local embezzler."

"Oh, I want to hear about the embezzler." Joe's job as chief of detectives in Landry was every bit as interesting as mine.

"You will. I'll tell you all about him."

"You're amazing. Most cops never tell their dates anything about their work. Isn't it against some rule or other?"

"Not really. The press covers most trials so what I might say to you is hardly confidential. And even if some of it were, I don't mind telling you, because I trust you to keep your mouth shut when I ask."

My, how that warmed me up.

Joe continued, "I also don't mind telling you because you really want to hear about my work. Usually the women in a cop's life don't want to hear about police work—or the cop thinks they don't want to hear. Most of what we do all day is either too grisly or too boring to interest women."

"Well, I do want to hear. Any other news on Jamie Congers?"

"Not really. Essentially confirmation that she was nice, very pretty, a good student, and she didn't have a boyfriend anyone knows about."

"Hmm. I kept hoping for a boyfriend."

"You're a romantic, Red. Nice girls don't let their grandfathers and roommates worry this much."

"Speaking of romantic..."

"I'd love to. But I have another hour and a half to put in on a case report and I'm beat. How about I come over tomorrow night and make filet of sole Meuniere followed by awe-inspiring sex for dessert?"

"You do know the way to a woman's heart."

Joe and I discovered our attraction for one another soon after he was appointed case detective on the police investigation of the death of Henry Brooks. Our friendship transformed to romance and was great for a while, but complicated. We broke up when Joe thought he was losing his detective's objectivity trying to solve Henry's death.

Well, that's not quite all the truth. We broke up because he thought I was in love with someone else, but after a month or so of miserable separation, we got back together. Since then, we had been sort of dating and sort of circling each other. Some days I thought Joe would cave into his feelings for me and ask if he could move out of his small apartment into my much larger house. Other days, I wasn't all that sure.

At least Joe was not a cynic. When I needed him, Joe was the kindest and most considerate man I knew. Last summer, when I thought my father might be dying, Joe took an unofficial leave so he could accompany me back to the nursing home in Ohio. Thaddeus Solaris had suffered from Alzheimer's for several years, a disease that had started soon after my mother drove her car into a tree and died. I was sure Dad blamed himself for her death, although he had tried everything possible to get my mother help for her drinking.

Joe accompanied me every day I visited Dad in the nursing home in spite of the fact that my father clearly did not remember me and was unwilling to even acknowledge Joe's existence. Joe held my hand as we watched the man who had raised me and been my mentor, my rock all through childhood. My beloved father had ignored us and sat facing a window, staring at nothing.

We were heading to the airport to return to Nevada when the call came on my cell phone. "I'm so sorry, Dr. Solaris. Your father died about twenty minutes ago."

At the hastily organized funeral held in the church where I had been baptized, Joe's arm circled my shoulders as we listened to eulogies from old friends and colleagues. Thaddeus Solaris had been a great scholar, a more than devoted husband, a husband who had sacrificed much of his life and his peace of mind to a wife he loved beyond all reason. He had been my teacher, my unwavering fan. He had forgotten me, but I would never forget him.

After my father's death, Joe Morgan took over as my champion. Despite the fact that he could be brusque and distant and occasionally disappear into a fog of moodiness, even take off for days of what he called his "alone time," I was sure I could count on him to share my concerns, my holidays, my frustrations, my triumphs, and my occasional bouts of grief.

I also knew he'd never give up searching for Jamie Congers.

Jamie

After dinner, the man said, "That tasted good." It was the first time Jamie had heard him say anything positive. For a moment he was like the man she'd met on campus—the polite one. He watched while she cleared the table and washed the dishes. His elbows were pressed hard against the table, the powerful muscles of his arms visible under the thin fabric of his work shirt. She heard him breathing heavily.

She slowed her washing. *Is this when he grabs me?*

He rose from the table. She tensed and braced herself against the sink.

"Come with me," he said and cupped her elbow in his hand.

Oh, God.

He led her to an interior door, unlocked. Beyond the door was a dark room. He switched on a table lamp revealing a parlor with a sofa against the wall and two upholstered armchairs facing it. A fireplace surrounded by river stones dominated one end of the room. Shelves lined the wall opposite the sofa. A few books, old and without jackets. Three undecorated silver bowls all in need of polishing.

"Beautiful bowls," Jamie said.

"Baptismal bowls for infants," he replied.

Centered between the shelves was another large framed document. He led her to stand in front of it. "Read this out loud."

"Why?"

"Because I said so."

She read slowly.

"Timothy 2:11. Let a woman learn in quietness with all subjection. But I permit not a woman to teach, nor have dominion over a man, but to be in quietness."

He sat on the sofa, indicating she should sit in the chair opposite him. He leaned forward, hands clasped between his knees. He stared at her.

She tried to stare back, to look him straight in the eyes, but after a few moments, he averted his gaze.

"I take it you read the Bible," she said.

"I live it. As did my father before me." He looked up again, directly at her. "And his father before him."

"I know the Bible," she said. "My mother's father was a minister and a biblical scholar. I spent several summers at his house and he taught me the Old and New Testaments."

"My grandfather was a preacher too. He preached in a tent we set up every spring in that meadow." He pointed to the view outside the window. "People came from as far away as Sacramento just to hear him."

"I used to memorize passages from the Bible."

The man opened his mouth, then cleared his throat. "Do you believe? Do you believe the verse you have just read?"

She hesitated. "I believe what the Bible teaches, but most of what I remember was what St. Paul wrote."

His breathing grew heavier. His brow looked damp. "Then perhaps you prefer Corinthians 14: 'Let the women keep silence in the churches: for it is not permitted unto them to speak; but they are commanded to be under obedience as also saith the law.'" His breathing became heavier and beads of sweat appeared on his face.

Where was this going?

"I prefer Corinthians 13," she said, her voice almost a whisper.

"You would. Women always like verses about faith and love more than about obedience."

"Did you create the documents in the frames? They look hand-lettered."

"My grandmother did." He leaned back into the sofa. "They were intended to remind the female reader about the importance of obedience and respect for her husband."

Jamie inhaled deeply. This didn't sound like a prelude to a physical attack. It was the first conversation they'd had that was longer than a one-sentence instruction. Maybe if she kept it going, she could learn more about why he had kidnapped her.

"And did the women in your family agree and obey?"

Again he was silent, this time for several minutes. She sat still as a stone.

"All but one. But never mind that." He rose from the couch, reminding her of his height and strength as well as his demands of her. "This parlor and the kitchen are the rooms you must keep clean at all times. They must be thoroughly scrubbed, dusted, and swept every day."

Jamie stood. "Which woman didn't obey?" She put as much force into her question as she dared.

"My father's second wife. She was like you."

"How was she like me?"

"She was young and beautiful, and she was black. Now, upstairs with you. That's all for tonight."

"What happened to your father's second wife?"

"Silence. Upstairs. NOW."

Chapter 11

The committee to determine Mountain West University policy on sexual assault met two days after my dinner with Bridget Thomas. Twelve of us gathered in a comfortable room upstairs in the administration building that was slightly more elegant than where I'd met with the search committee.

What I noticed first was a large oval mahogany table surrounded by a dozen upholstered swivel chairs, glasses and carafes of water at every place.

Bridget sat next to Karen Milton, Director of Student Affairs. I knew Karen, a considerate woman who had helped my students find counseling services when they needed them. She and Bridget were deep in conversation.

I sat opposite them as we watched the male committee members file in. Three administrators, including the university attorney. Four male faculty members. One I recognized from history and another from biology. Two from athletics, the director and the head football coach.

Nods of recognition and smiles all around.

No one seemed surprised to see that I'd replaced the basketball coach at Bridget's request.

"I'll call us to order in a minute," said one of the administrators, seating himself at the head of the table. "While we wait I'll introduce us to our new member." He turned to me. "I am Bud Chekovski, Vice President of Finance for Mountain West and chair of this committee. And you are Dr. Meredith Solaris, interim dean of journalism. I hope I got that right."

"You did. But you can all call me Red if you prefer. We're not very formal in the school of journalism."

A man across the table from me said, "My students tell me your faculty let all the journalism students call them by their first names. I'm Howard Evans from Biology." I knew exactly who he was. Blond, high cheekbones, incredibly white teeth he maintained at considerable expense. A few years ago, I dated him for about a week. Clearly he did not care to acknowledge our previous relationship in front of the committee.

I couldn't resist. "Nice to see you again, Howard. Still living on Columbus Street?" I reached my hand across the table to shake his. He turned pink. I kept going. "Yes, we do let students call us by our first names. Professional journalists use first names in the industry. And we want our students to get used to feeling professional as soon as possible. Not to mention, it's friendly."

"I wouldn't dream of letting my students call me anything but Doctor Thomas," said Bridget. "Professional titles help keep a respectful distance."

That figures.

The door opened and all the sidebar conversations stopped. Ezra McCready, the new provost, entered the room. Everyone at the table, except the coaches, reported to McCready. We knew he had a significant national reputation, but McCready was still a newcomer and new leader to most of us.

The provost stood with his hand on the back of Bud's chair. "Thank you all for agreeing to serve on this committee. I'll keep your instructions short." Thin smile. He paused, clearing his throat as his eyes circled the faces at the table. "The federal government requires all universities to address the problem of sexual assault on campus. We're seriously behind on this, so we need a written policy before the end of the year. Not much time, but I'm sure you're all up to it."

Karen raised her hand. McCready looked irritated.

"Is this a policy to guide students, or will it cover all university employees as well?'

"Everyone. Students, staff, faculty."

"Should this policy also describe the process for dealing with complaints and with those who...uh...violate the policy?" This came from Howard, who was still pink and fidgeting in his chair.

Howard's question produced a solemn stare. The provost barely looked at him. "I think you should cover process as well as regulations. But be careful. I don't want a document that presumes guilt without supporting evidence. Nor do I expect one designed to protect the privacy of one gender more than that of another."

Silence. No more questions.

The provost lifted his hands off the back of Bud's chair and offered a parting shot: "Be cautious about depending on the so-called statistics bandied about in the press and by advocacy groups. Also be cautious about demanding this university automatically presume that a complaint of assault is valid. Regrettably, sometimes young people...exaggerate."

Karen exhaled audibly. "Statistics suggest most women are telling the truth when..." McCready's cold stare stopped her.

He turned to Bud. "I'll look for a report on your progress next week."

"Thank you, Dr. McCready," said Bud to McCready's back as he left. Then he shuffled some papers and said to the rest of us. "I think this means we'll have to meet almost every day between now and then."

Daily meetings? Karen and Howard both looked shaken. The athletic director frowned. The football coach passed his hand over his face, concealing his expression. Bridget frowned. I slouched in my chair. Fear for a missing student wasn't going to be my only nightmare.

Jamie

Jamie sat on the bed thinking about the father's second wife, her kidnapper's black stepmother who had been "the only one" to disobey the rules. What had happened to her? Had she been banished or run away? Had she been killed for her sins? Was her body buried somewhere behind the house?

Punishment for disobedience was important to this man. Yet he had neither punished her nor made any sexual advances. She mentally ran through the list of what she knew about him. He was tall and physically fit, rarely spoke, dressed at home in jeans or overalls and work shirts. Wore a suit and tie when he left for what she assumed was some sort of office work. She guessed he was in his forties. He was white and she suspected all his family, except the black stepmother, had been white. She couldn't be sure, but no photographs had been in any of the rooms she had been allowed to see, and ordered to clean.

"No family pictures?" she'd asked while dusting one evening.

"None."

He was watchful and wary, yet he left her alone for hours during the day. He locked her in her bedroom after she'd cooked and cleaned up after breakfast. He left at seven and returned at night when she was released to cook dinner and clean. Lunch was fruit and a sandwich in her room.

Her only reading material was a copy of the Bible on her dresser. She assumed the man was Protestant, but not from the liberal Episcopalian faith that had been her maternal grandfather's religion—the one she learned as a child. *John 13:34. A new commandment I give unto you, That ye love one another...*

She suspected her captor would not care to have that verse framed and on the wall of any room in this house.

What else had she learned since waking up with her hands tied to the bed?

The house was old, dark, cold at night. The bathroom fixtures were simple, the tiles blue and white. The closets were small. The bare wooden floors were pale, narrow boards of pine or maple. One rug lay in the parlor. Old yellowed linoleum covered the kitchen floor. The windows upstairs were small and barred with dark curtains he drew at night. The kitchen and parlor windows were larger, also curtained, faced east and looked out on trees and grass, a steel fence and a meadow in the distance. She saw no signs and heard no sounds of other people. She was isolated. No one would hear her cries for help.

She stifled any temptation to weep. She didn't want the man to hear her sobbing and think it a reason to enter her bedroom more than he already did. It was bad enough he'd seen her naked. What might happen if he saw her in tears?

Having failed to discover or craft either a weapon or a tool to attack the bars or the door locks, she spent the day sleeping, reading the Bible, doing pushups and floor exercises, running in place. She knew she must stay strong so that if the chance to escape arose, she would be ready to flee. And, if the man decided he wanted her after all, she would be ready and able to fight.

Chapter 12

"How was the sexual assault committee meeting?" Nell looked up from her desk. Wishful thinking, perhaps, or maybe I was jumping to conclusions, but I would have sworn my assistant looked smoother and prettier than ever before.

"Alarming." I walked past her and into my office next to hers.

"Alarming?" She carried a stack of papers to my desk.

"What's the campus gossip about Ezra McCready?" Universities are like other institutions. Staff always know more than the management. Nell, as a dean's assistant, was a member of the working staff who heard much more about the secrets and foibles of top administrators than I ever would. Moreover, Nell had been around for years before I showed up and had mastered the subtleties of university politics. She was a wizard at maneuvering through the bureaucracy.

She assumed a solemn expression. "Cold fish, according to his office staff. Not one for joking around or bringing flowers to the girls on their birthdays like Stoddard did."

"Is he harder on the women staff than the men?"

"I haven't heard that he is. McCready seems to be an equal opportunity pain in the ass to work for. Of course, he's single and well over forty, so that always gives people something to speculate about."

"Do they speculate?"

"I haven't heard anyone say much about his personal life. Most of them think he's a loner. He's seen as snobbish, reserved, not inclined to make friends with staff. Of course, he may be friendlier with President Lewis and big-time donors. Mind you, this is according to what I get in the employee cafeteria."

"Invariably the best information on campus."

"Was he difficult at your meeting?"

"Authoritarian. His charges to the committee carried a bit of bias, as if he was afraid we were all going to create a policy that only favored females. And he seemed somewhat hostile to Howard Evans and Karen Milton."

"Karen's great. But the provost wouldn't be the first high-ranking male on this campus to get tough with her. Ever since she was put in charge of Title IX on this campus, she's had to deal with men who don't like to receive instruction on how to behave or how to solve their harassment problems."

"Yet our mission is to come up with a special plan to deal with sexual assault. I can't imagine any man on this campus not being supportive of that. Can you?"

Nell busied herself arranging papers on the table opposite my desk. After a moment she said, "I can imagine a few men around here who wouldn't want to see star male athletes, or even star male students, disciplined because they took a young woman's silence for acceptance."

Nell was right. It made me sad. "I know. If the girl didn't beat him with her fists and scream for help, she probably wanted it. Some men just feel entitled, no matter what she says or does."

Nell headed for the door and then turned. "And there's another problem. Sometimes a young woman who's been assaulted is pressured to keep her mouth shut by the other girls. They may know what happened to her but don't want the guy's teammates or fraternity brothers to get angry with them for supporting her and getting the boy in trouble..."

"Is a boy getting into trouble?" The voice came from behind Nell. Sadie moved past Nell and slid her slender body into a chair in front of my desk. Nell was still in the doorway.

"A purely hypothetical boy, Dr. Hawkins," said Nell. "Would you like some tea?"

"Bless you, Nell. I would. Thank you."

Sadie turned to me. Her face was thin and her nose sharp as a raptor's. But her eyes, at least when she met mine, were the gentlest I had ever known. At times, Sadie was more mother to me than my biological mother had ever been. She brushed a strand of white hair back from her face and leaned toward me. "How is the dean search going?"

Unlike Joe and most of my faculty, Sadie had not been pleased when I announced I was applying for the position of permanent dean of journalism. "A dean's job absorbs your life. Too much." Sadie's husband had died two years ago, a few months after she retired. "The hours were long and the work hard, and it kept me from realizing the man I loved needed more from me," she'd said. They had been planning a long-postponed second honeymoon in France when his heart gave out.

"You know, Red, failing to get the dean's job would not be the end of the world. You could go back into teaching."

"I know, and I do love teaching."

"Of course you love it, and you're good at it. As a tenured professor, you are free to do your own work, your own way. University teachers share the satisfaction of famous performers and successful politicians. Few other professions pay us decent money to stand up in front of an audience and feel so confident in our own opinions, so sure that what we believe is true."

"You're right, teaching is fun and I miss it. So not getting the dean's job might not be such a bad thing."

Sadie was on a roll. "Think about it, dear Red. Every year in the fall you get to lead a new group of bright, young, unfinished minds into the thickets, through the jungles, and then out to the open vistas of greater understanding."

"Assuming they've put away their cell phones."

She was undeterred. "Come now, who else but a tenured professor can feel so certain her insights will always be valuable, her views still respected, her mind still sharp even when she's older than dirt?"

"All right. You can dispense with the rhetoric. I promise if I don't get the dean's job I'll be thrilled. Nell and Joe may be a little disappointed in me, but I will view failure as a blessing."

"Which reminds me, how are things with Joe?" Sadie has a way of getting around to her real topic, however circuitous the path. She was worried that if I got the job as dean, it would interfere with my love life.

"Joe's fine. We're fine. And he wants me to be the new dean of journalism."

"I'm sure that's what he says."

"And, Sadie, my love, that's what he means."

Sadie leaned back and smiled. "Very well. Have it your way. I know Joe Morgan is too confident a man to feel threatened by a successful woman. I'm just saying, relationships need nourishment and time together. But I'll shut up about that. So, tell me about your time with the search committee. Is Bridget Thomas behaving herself?"

"Actually, I think Bridget is moving toward liking me. And I know Bill Verden and at least three others seem favorable. The one who worries me most is the outside guy, Mark Froman."

Sadie grunted. "I know Mark Froman. He was a big donor to Liberal Arts before I became dean. Arrogant, self-important son of a bitch, as I recall."

"That's him. He seems to think I am unqualified for this job. Too closely associated with last year's troubles."

"Froman's a misogynist and a predator." Sadie resettled her slim body in her chair. "He thinks pretty women are for sex, not management. Certainly not the management of men, and most of your faculty are men."

"Oh my God. Did Froman hit on you?"

"Heavens, no. I'm a good twenty years older than Froman. But he did harass my associate dean. Brought her to tears one time."

"Do you think it would help my cause if I went to bed with him?"

Teasing Sadie was impossible to resist.

She snorted a laugh. "That would guarantee you Mark Froman would see you simply as a conquest, but never as a leader. Now, what else is on your mind these days?"

I told her about Jamie.

Jamie

Another day gone. No grandfather to the rescue. No weapons. No plan of escape. She was exhausted from housecleaning done late into the night and from worrying. She got little sleep during her daily enforced naps.

And still there were no clues, much less explanations, from the man who had taken her. She had tried for conversation, especially more about his family. He sat mute and tense at the kitchen table.

"I'll tell you more someday," he had finally said after her third attempt. "For now, more work and fewer inquiries would be appreciated." He returned his gaze to his plate.

She had found a paper clip in one of the kitchen drawers and smuggled it into her pocket. For once he hadn't noticed. She thought she could work on the lock to her bedroom. It was deadbolt lock rather than a padlock. She had heard the bolt slide but not heard any clicking of a padlock every night and morning.

After the man had locked her in for the night, she had stayed close to her door listening. A few minutes later, she heard the sound of his footsteps coming back upstairs and going down the hall. Then the opening and closing of a door.

She assumed from the size of the downstairs rooms she had cleaned that there was at least one more bedroom, perhaps two, on the second floor.

She resolved to work on the lock to her door the next morning after he had left for work. One way or another she was going to figure a way out of the house. Or find a telephone. Or find her handbag and her cell phone wherever he had hidden them. Her grandfather would be frantic. She was convinced he would be looking for her by now. But how was Wynan Congers, or any other policeman, supposed to find her?

And the terror inside her went unabated. The tall man hadn't done anything to her, but he could still do whatever he wished. And not knowing what he wanted, what he really wanted, scared the hell out of her.

She wondered what would happen if she set the house on fire when she was cooking. If she did, the man would have to let them both outside. Wouldn't he?

Chapter 13

The story of my life has been punctuated with violence. When I was nine, my mother got blind drunk, took a header down a flight of wooden stairs, and knocked herself out cold. My mother lived hard and died badly.

After college, I got a job as a reporter with a metro newspaper and thought the excitement in my life would be derived less from my own adventures and more from the stories of other people's episodes. About the time I thought my life might calm down and get ordinary, I started dating a man who liked rough sex, and one night, he punched me in the face. I punched back, with a heavy iron lamp base. Broke his nose.

I fled from the abusive man and the busy newsroom and burrowed into the work of the academic. I got my PhD, became a professor and the associate dean of the school of journalism. Peace at last, I thought, until my dean was killed. After that, I worked like hell to make the school function again.

That's why I deeply resented Froman's insinuations about the scandal at my school. It was over. The problems had been resolved. The university had moved on and all the faculty members at the journalism school were getting over it. Why couldn't Froman? Why had he thought it so important to dredge up all those memories of death and betrayal?

As you might imagine, I was not happy when Nell greeted me with: "Good morning. Mark Froman has asked if he can have a meeting with you at eleven this morning. He seemed quite insistent."

"Why? I'm done with all my search meetings. What does he want?"

Nell's brows rose, reminding me of Sadie's opinion of Froman. "He didn't say. Just that he needed time with you at eleven."

I wanted to say no. But Froman was an influential member of the search committee. It wasn't just his vote that worried me. His negative attitude about my involvement in the school's trouble could infect other's votes. And I had heard he had the ear of the new provost. So I said to Nell, "Call him back and say eleven is fine."

I regretted my decision the moment Froman appeared in the doorway of my office. Not too many men in Landry, Nevada wore suits that must have cost a thousand dollars. He took off his jacket and draped it over one of my chairs as if my office was his. His dark silk shirt was tight over his chest and arms. Okay, impressive. He must have spent several hours a day working on those pectorals and deltoids.

Nell brought in coffee. We exchanged guarded pleasantries.

"Thank you for seeing me, Dr. Solaris."

"Happy to oblige, Mr. Froman, but you can call me Red."

"And you can call me Mark." His was an audible inhale and a toothy smile. "Now then, both of us have tight schedules, so I'll get to the point. I understand you have a new problem in the school of journalism."

"And that would be?"

"I'm told a female student is missing, possibly a kidnapping or a homicide."

My turn for an audible inhale. "And where did you hear this?"

"Let's say I have friends in the Landry Police department who share my concern for campus safety."

That wouldn't be Joe, but Wynan Congers had spoken to several in the department. All Joe's colleagues knew that Wynan's granddaughter was missing.

"Well, I don't think we can assume either kidnapping or homicide. The young woman has been away and unaccounted for since Monday, but the police investigating her absence have not yet concluded that any crime has been committed."

Froman was too tall for the slender chair that faced the other side of my desk. His legs sprawled out and he seemed uncomfortable. "I hope for everyone's sake you are right. But perhaps you can tell me what you know so far."

"Excuse me, Mark, but how does this matter concern you? I am not sure why you need to hear what I know so far."

He frowned. "Because you are a candidate for the leadership of this school, a school that has known considerable trouble and tragedy over the past year. I need to know if you are handling this latest matter effectively."

I fought back my rising temper. This was none of his business, and I was damned if I was going to let him interrogate me. I took a deep breath, trying to keep my voice even. "I am handling this. I am working with the Landry Police. The young woman's absence is being thoroughly investigated."

"And what have you and the police learned so far?"

I put my hands on my desk and pressed the wood to keep them steady. "Only that she is somewhere off campus. Her car is gone, and she left no word with anyone."

"Is this kind of absence commonplace among journalism students?"

"Mark, back off. You know from your own college days that students take off on little vacations from their classes. We try to treat them as adults rather than children and, as I am sure you know, they are very particular about their privacy."

"Indeed. But are there no clues to the girl's whereabouts? Was anyone seen with her last Monday?"

"Not that I'm aware."

"And you don't believe she has met with any sort of foul play?"

"For crying out loud, there's no evidence of any play, foul or otherwise. She's not attending her classes, nor is she at her home. But that doesn't mean something sinister has happened. She may've just taken off." I wondered what would happen to my candidacy if I gave in to my rising rage and ordered Mark Froman to leave my office.

Froman frowned and gazed at the wall. He seemed to be thinking about something, but clearly not something he was willing to share. "So she's just gone. Is that it?"

"That's all we know so far." Not a chance in hell I was going to tell Mark Froman about the suspect in muddy boots.

Froman pushed back his chair. "Well, thank you, Red. I'm sorry more isn't known, but as you say, these students are adults and we have to be cautious about meddling in their private lives."

He picked up his jacket carefully, showing me the elaborate lining. We shook hands and he left me wondering why he had insisted on knowing about Jamie Congers, and whether or not I should be more suspicious of his reasons for inquiring. I made a mental note to find out more about Mark Froman and why he cared so much about the absent Jamie Congers.

"Maybe you're the one Mark Froman cares about," said Sadie, thirty minutes later at lunch at Gormley's Grill. "Maybe the girl's absence just provided him an excuse to come to your office and throw his weight around. Impress you. Perhaps he's planning to hit on you after all."

"Damn. Vote against me and then try to lure me into bed, I suppose."

"You forget how attractive you are."

"Thank you, but I don't particularly want Mark Froman to notice my looks. I want him to notice my mind and my experience."

"I told you before. He's rich and arrogant and not especially sensitive or modern in his views of women. He's a throwback."

"Where does his money come from?"

"Froman's father once owned two gold mines and half the ranchland between here and Reno."

"And now?"

"Now, Mark lives in a big house a few miles outside of town, raises thoroughbred horses, and bullies the board members of any number of non-profits."

"And, in his spare time, messes around with university business."

"He likes to be asked to serve on university committees. It makes him feel important."

"Is he married?"

"He was married once, some time ago. Beautiful debutante from Texas. She left Mark after a year of marriage, got a generous alimony settlement, and moved back to Dallas."

"Does he have a problem with women?"

"More likely he has a problem with his zipper."

Jamie

Jamie was sweating. The paper clip was slippery in her hand. The lock was stubborn. She'd been working the clip into it for twenty minutes since the man left. She'd waited until she heard his car pull away and then straightened out the clip and wrapped the end in toilet paper to protect her fingers. She worked intently, praying to succeed.

And then the lower lock clicked open. Cautiously, she grasped the doorknob. She hadn't heard the deadbolt slide this morning. Maybe, if she was very lucky, he'd forgotten the deadbolt. He'd seemed in a hurry at breakfast and he'd practically dragged her upstairs to lock her in. Hoping he'd been careless, she turned the doorknob. The door opened.

The upstairs hall stretched out in front of her.

A door to her left was partially open. She looked inside. An empty crib and a wooden rocking chair were centered on the bare floor. Dark curtains hung at the windows. Against the wall that separated this room from her bathroom was a sink embedded in a counter just large enough to have been a changing table. This must have been a nursery. She explored it quickly, wanting to move on. She found nothing to use as a tool or weapon and no clues about the room's previous occupant.

She went back into the hall. Another door was closed at the end. Only one door suggested it led to a suite or a room much larger than hers. Given the size of the house, she presumed a large room, as wide as the house itself, would be behind the door. His room. She had heard him walk down the hall every night and had heard that door open and close.

She walked tentatively down the hall. Her breathing quickened with excitement. Maybe her handbag would be in that front bedroom. Her heart raced, as if she expected him to return any minute. When she reached the door to what she thought was "his room," she turned the knob. It was locked. She shook the door. Heavy, immovable. The exteriors of two deadbolt locks stared at her. One was above the doorknob, the other near the top of the door, hard to reach and probably impossible to open with the paperclip. This would take a greater effort that would require more skill and more time. Time she was not sure she had.

She decided to stop fussing with his bedroom door and take better advantage of the freedom she had gained so far. The rest of the house might be accessible. The possibility of escape drove her down the stairs and into the kitchen. She headed for the knife drawer. The knives were gone. He had hidden them somewhere. But the heavy skillet was still on the stove. She could break the glass in a window. She grabbed the skillet and headed into the parlor where the windows were barred but larger. She stared at the window. Even if she broke the glass the bars were too thick and too close together for her to squeeze through. Breaking the window would only make sense if she saw someone outside who could see her and hear her screams. Otherwise, all the broken glass would do was tell him she had escaped from her bedroom.

There had to be another way. Skillet still in hand, she tested the exterior door in the kitchen. The large coded padlock held it firm. She turned back to the downstairs hall. It was painted dark yellow like the kitchen and led to two other doors. The one on the left led to the parlor. She assumed the door on the right side must lead to another room opposite but similar in size to the parlor.

At the end of the hall, a massive wooden door looked like it would be the front door of the house. Solid. No windows on either side. She shook it and heard the bang of a heavy lock outside. Another padlock.

She turned back to the door on the right side. It was closed, but not locked. She entered a completely empty room. Not a trace of furniture. The walls showed patches of lighter paint where pictures may have hung. But no pictures, no paintings. She walked around the empty room, testing the barred window. A small bathroom was off to one side. No towels, no shower curtain. Dust on the sink. The same wooden toilet seat as hers carved with the same word, "Obey."

The air was musty and dust was layered on the floor and the windowsills. She had not been asked to clean this room, so perhaps that meant he didn't use it at all. No footprints in the dust on the floor suggested he didn't enter it often.

She explored the walls. The window looked out on the same scene as her bedroom, but the lower view showed what looked like the edge of a lake just barely visible through the trees.

Where would the wall be weakest? Not on the corners. She knew enough about the structure of a building to know the corners would have bearing posts.

She returned to the kitchen for a big spoon and then came back to the empty room and started tapping the wall, waiting for a hollow sound. Between the window and the corner she heard it. She raised the skillet to strike the wall but then noticed a closet at the end of the room.

Inside the closet was empty, except for an old ironing board propped up against what she assumed would be an exterior wall. The wall was about three feet wide.

She moved the ironing board aside and tapped. The edge of the wall sounded dense but the center of the wall sounded light.

Perhaps she would find only plaster and studs between it and the exterior brick. The closet was hidden from the rest of the room by a louvered door. He might not notice.

She swung the skillet as hard as she could against the closet wall. The plaster wall gave. She struck again and, through the gaping hole, she could see wooden studs about twenty-four inches apart between the inner and outer walls. She would be able to slip between them. This could be an escape hole to the outside. As long as he didn't discover it.

She worked slowly and carefully using the skillet to break the edges of the initial hole and widen it. She used the big spoon to scoop up the pieces of plaster and empty them into the space between the interior and exterior wall. She was careful to keep the width of the hole the same as that of the ironing board she planned to use as a cover. It was hot and she felt sweaty and had to leave the closet from time to time to cool off. She checked the sky outside the window so she could figure out the time of day. She had to make sure she would have time to clean up and return to her bedroom before he came home. She missed her watch. He had taken it along with her bag and her cell phone.

Chapter 14

Joe pushed his half-finished dinner away. "No clues on the man in boots yet. Also, no notes or calls to Wynan demanding a ransom. So the longer this goes on, the more I am sure she's been taken prisoner for some reason...or..."

"Or killed." I stared at my food and took another sip of wine.

The phone rang and both of us jumped. But it wasn't for Joe. It was Bridget Thomas for me. No greeting, but a sense of urgency in her voice. "Red, have you looked at your email?"

"No. I just got home."

"Well, you'd better see what our idiot chairman, Bud Chekovski, has to say in addition to tomorrow's meeting time and place."

"Bad?"

"Troubling. I think the provost may have gotten to him after our last meeting. He seems to want us to tread more than cautiously."

"About assault? I've got a missing female student, Bridget. Cautious is not what I'm feeling right now."

I walked over to my computer and brought up my email. There it was, just as Bridget described. "Why is he putting this in an email instead of bringing it up tomorrow at the meeting?"

"I'm not sure, Red. But my hunch is he's been told to frame the discussion the way Ezra wants it, not the way we might want it."

"Damn. I'm not willing to assume that a young woman would arbitrarily accuse a guy of assault. Most of the women students I know are not that vicious. The hell with McCready's caution."

*   *   *

That night sleep did not come easily. Joe had left after dinner to go to the police station to see if any of the checks on the man in the muddy boots had panned out. My mind went back and forth between my worries about Jamie Congers and my concerns that, in the sexual assault policy meetings, I was going to run head on into Ezra McCready's opinions about the reliability of survivor testimony.

And I was personally conflicted. Sooner or later I would have to figure out how to contend with an ugly memory from my own college days. My roommate's boyfriend had come into my room when I was wretchedly ill with flu, pulled off my pajamas and did what he damn pleased. I'd never told anyone.

For years, I'd suppressed the memory because it sickened me. And whom would I have told, even if I had been willing to talk? In those days, the prevailing view of some college administrators was discouraging. And even though the new provost reminded me of that time, was I really willing to do battle with the man who would have the final say on whether or not I would be appointed Dean of Journalism? No matter how the search committee voted, Ezra McCready's view would rule.

So I knew I would be of two minds throughout the discussions of the committee. For one thing, we lacked a clear definition of sexual assault. Did it mean rape, or did it include unwanted kissing and groping? To complicate matters, legal scholars differed as much on definitions as did various college policies.

I tried to brush my concerns away but only found that, when I did, my thoughts switched back to my missing student.

Jamie

She sat on her bed, hands folded in her lap, waiting to hear his footsteps coming up the stairs to release her for her evening chores.

She heard the lock click. He opened the door to her room and stared at the lock for a moment. Did he just realize he had forgotten the deadbolt? He looked up at her. He was carrying a bag and a book in his hand. He measured her with his eyes. "Have a good day?"

"Boring day," she said, looking up at him. She knew she had thoroughly cleaned up the closet downstairs, then washed the skillet and spoon carefully so not a trace of plaster or dust remained. But she couldn't lock the deadbolt on the door to her room without his key, and she feared he would notice.

He didn't seem to notice. He put the book on the bed next to her. "Something new to read," he said. A trace of a smile appeared, almost as if the book was a present he had brought for her.

The bag was labeled "Macy's." Odd, she thought, he didn't look like a Macy's customer. And there was no Macy's in Landry. He would have had to go all the way to Reno.

"Put on these new clothes and then come down to supper." He left and closed the door behind him. This time, he'd decided not to watch her dress.

She pulled at the tissue paper in the bag. A shirt and a pair of khaki pants came out and fell on the blanket, followed by more underwear. Two more bras, two more pair of cotton underpants. Plain cotton pants, not bikini style. At the bottom, a pair of white sneakers and two pairs of thin white socks.

Again, the bra was the right size, as was the shirt. The pants were a bit loose around the hips and waist. The sneakers fit. She wished he'd bought warmer socks.

As she gathered up the bag and tissue, she spotted the book on the blanket. It was a leather journal, small and worn. She opened to find the first page missing.

She was not to know the owner's name.

As she flipped through the first few handwritten pages, she saw the dates had been blacked out with what seemed to be a wide felt-tipped pen. She was not to know *when*, only *what* the writer had written.

The handwriting was clear and delicate, probably feminine. It was also familiar and she knew this was the hand that had created the framed documents downstairs. Her heart sank as she read the first two sentences.

This is a happy day. This is the first day of my marriage.

An hour later, Jamie stood at the sink washing the supper dishes. The man was seated at the table drinking coffee, watching her. She'd resolved to say something, although she'd remained silent all through dinner. She turned from the sink, wiping her hands on a dishtowel.

"What do you want from me?"

"Nothing."

"Nothing?" She twisted the towel in her hands and stepped closer to the table. "Then why are you keeping me a prisoner here?"

He leaned back, his eyes fixed on the coffee cup. "Because I don't want you to run away. And I can't trust you to stay. Not yet."

"Trust me to stay for what?"

"Stay and achieve my objective."

"And what's your objective?" She feared the answer.

"Someday, I hope you will want to be the woman who lives in this house."

"Your wife?" She almost screamed, but kept her voice even. This was more response to her questions than she had ever gotten out of him before.

He looked up at her. His eyes were dark and dead. "I don't believe I said anything about marriage," he said.

"Live in this house as what, then? Your whore?"

He pushed his chair back and stood. He came to her and took the dishtowel and ripped it out of her hands and threw it in the sink. It hit with enough force to rattle a remaining saucer.

He put his hands on her shoulders, his grip so strong she flinched with the pain. "I've no intention of hurting you. Nothing will happen against your will."

She clenched her teeth and looked into his cold eyes. "I'm here in this kitchen against my will," she said. "And you're hurting me now."

He released her. "Give it time. Someday you will be glad I brought you here. Now go to bed, and stop asking questions."

Chapter 15

I might have known that in the midst of my worries about Jamie and my job, my journalism faculty colleagues would come up with a new way to bedevil me. Larry Coleman, recently tenured associate professor of new media writing, was waiting in my office. I'd fought hard for his tenure last year over the objections of three senior professors who had wanted him fired. We'd prevailed, but Larry still seemed tense and unhappy. I wondered what was bothering him this time.

"No rest for the wicked," Larry said as I settled into the chair behind my desk. The morning was bright and sunny, and the leaves of the giant trees that lined the quad outside my window rustled in the constant northern Nevada wind.

"Me wicked or you wicked?"

Nell came in with some files I'd requested and two small bottles of water balanced in her hand. She smiled at me. My, she was looking pretty these days. I knew from her personnel record she was close to sixty, but her face was as smooth as porcelain.

Larry nodded at Nell and took the water. I thanked her for both of us.

"Neither one of us wicked," he said. "Weinstein is wicked and up to his old tricks."

My stomach turned. I'd hoped George Weinstein and Larry would get along this semester and get past their old bitterness toward each other. Dream on. Egotistical hardly described either of them. George and Larry had each come to live in a state of permanent outrage.

"What now?" I dreaded hearing about another fight between the two men. Both of them hit below the belt whenever possible.

"I'm slated to give a paper at an online conference in San Francisco in December. The chair of the panel I'm on knows George, and in a friendly chat yesterday, she asked George what he thought about my paper."

"And?"

"And George gave my paper what she called 'a lukewarm review.'"

"How did George even know what your paper is about?"

Larry chuckled, but there was no amusement in his face. "Oh, George doesn't know a damned thing about my paper. He just ventured an opinion anyway."

"And you found out how?"

"The event chair called me. You know how some people love to spread negative gossip. She thought to give me a heads up about George, as if I needed any warning about that asshole."

"You reassured her, I hope."

"I reassured her about my paper, but I told her what I thought of George, too."

"Great. If she went back to him, George will be in a snit."

Larry stood up and put his water bottle on my desk.

Outside, the sun had gone behind a cloud and the wind had picked up. The rustle of leaves made the trees sound as irritated as I was.

"I'd appreciate it if you would talk to George. I know you want us to have a cordial faculty relationship, but Weinstein makes it impossible for me. He never lets up. The man's behavior is monstrous."

"I'll talk to him. But meanwhile, please don't escalate this matter. The last thing I need right now is another faculty fight."

"I'll be good. I know we all have to behave while you're going through the dean search. And, honestly, we all want you to win this job."

"That's good to know. Thank you."

Larry tugged at his mustache. Then he said, "I am trying to get on with George, I'm trying to be cordial to all the faculty. But George...George's treatment of me constitutes legal harassment. I'm sure I could win a grievance against him because it never stops. It just never stops." He turned abruptly and left.

Please don't file a grievance, I said silently to his back. A grievance garners all the bad publicity of a gang war and would really screw up my chances for the dean's job.

"I don't believe it," said Nell, standing in my doorway. "If those two start up again, I'll put poison in their coffee."

I patted her shoulder as I walked out. "We're not at poison stage yet, Nell. But maybe some antidepressants might help."

If there was one thing I'd learned from last year's faculty quarrel it was that, if the animus gets vicious enough, everyone gets hurt. No matter what the issue, once a quarrel reaches the point where bullying and hateful insults become part of the weaponry, no one escapes the consequences. People who don't want to take sides end up taking sides. Even those who try desperately to remain neutral are drawn into a toxic whirl of accusation and recrimination. I was determined not to let that happen to my school again.

I was also at a complete loss as to what I could do to prevent the next battle. George and Larry were increasingly bitter and trouble seemed inevitable. Wouldn't Mark Froman have a good time watching my failure to prevent another scandal?

The meeting with the policy committee was set for ten a.m. sharp, and Bud Chekovski had scheduled it in a conference room clear across campus from the journalism school. I walked quickly to make up for the time I had been delayed by Larry. I hardly noticed the blue of the bright, cloudless sky or the tall trees that occasionally shaded my path. The Mountain West campus was one of the most beautiful in the country. Defying the high desert that surrounded it, the grounds were green with grass and trees. And all about was a changing array of flowers that bloomed from March until the middle of November. I was so preoccupied I walked past a spectacular stand of purple asters without even seeing it.

I also failed to see Joe and Wynan coming toward me.

"Good morning, Red," said Wynan. Joe grinned, glad we were all finally on a first-name basis.

"Good morning, gentlemen. Any news?"

"Joe's team found a witness who saw the man who matches our guy's description outside of Jamie's apartment house." Wynan's eyes were wide with anticipation.

"And the witness got a partial license plate off the gray Ford van our man drove away in," Joe added. "We're heading to university parking services to see if the plate belongs to anyone on campus. Meanwhile my guys are checking the Nevada DMV for more."

"So we may be making progress." Wynan almost smiled.

"Could the witness add anything more about what the guy looks like?"

"Tall and white, which we knew. Muscular arms. Overalls and muddy boots. Sunglasses and a cap covering the eyes and hair."

"Good hunting," I said, feeling a slight lift in my mood. Maybe we could find Jamie. And maybe we could find her in time.

I continued on toward the other end of campus, wishing I could have stayed with Joe and Wynan and avoided the next hour of discussion.

I spied Bridget and Karen ahead of me as I neared the building.

We walked in together. "A united front," said Bridget, opening the conference room door.

Bud Chekovski was seated at the end of the table. The athletic director and the football coach sat on either side.

Bud looked up. "Morning, ladies." The coach and the athletic director nodded.

Bridget sat down next to the coach and addressed the chairman. "Some of us were wondering why you felt it necessary to send us that quote about dangerous statistics." Bridget didn't start with small talk.

"Just underscoring the point," said Bud, amiable as usual. "We really should focus on this campus and what we know about this campus. Not on some national figures that may or may not be accurate."

"Often what happens to our students doesn't occur on this campus. It occurs off-campus," said Karen.

"What do we know about off-campus assaults?" Howard had come into the room.

Karen paused, waiting for the rest of the committee members to file in and find seats.

"Here's what we know," she said, her voice steady and authoritative. "The Cleary Act requires us to keep records of on-campus incidents. We know that only a few assaults have occurred on the Mountain West campus during the last two years. And only three were reported to my office."

"Only three," repeated the coach.

"Yes, but in the same time period, the Landry police have received dozens of reports from off-campus locations. That's where the parties are, since this campus is officially dry. Most of the incidents the police know about occurred in apartments and houses nearby, but off-campus."

"I know the police chief. I've never heard him say anything about this," said Bud.

"The chief's not the expert," said Karen. "The Victim Services people are. They are the ones who know what's going on. If a student is assaulted and wants to report it, the student goes to them."

"And then when do you hear about it?" This from the university attorney.

"The police are good about keeping me informed," said Karen, sadness in her voice. "When the victim wants to talk to me, or get counseling from us, I see her, or him. When the police tell the survivor that the description given to them isn't enough to identify, or isn't enough to formally charge someone with a crime, then they tell the survivor to come to me."

"When the police don't think they have enough to charge the accused, is that what the provost means when he refers to exaggeration?" Bud was leaning forward.

"No. Not exaggeration," said Karen, her voice rising again. "More like intimidation. All sorts of pressures are put on these young women, many of whom are freshman and new to college. They are shy and uncertain, and it doesn't take much to make them afraid of losing their reputations, or getting all their new friends angry with them."

"I'm told that other girls are often the ones pressuring the victim to keep her mouth shut," I said, remembering Nell's words.

Karen nodded. "Absolutely true. Any of us who deals with sexual assault cases can tell you that happens more often than we would like." Karen sat down heavily in her chair.

The group fell silent. Several pretended to search for something in their briefcases.

"Should we institute the same policy as California? Yes means Yes?" Howard's question surprised me.

Karen nodded but before she could speak, the university attorney cut in.

"Let's remember that a young woman who changes her mind midway, and doesn't get her way, can cause real damage."

"But what kind of young man keeps going when a girl says 'Stop?'" I was beginning to see how this discussion was shaping up.

"A drunk young man," said the coach.

"Or an entitled young man," said Bridget. "Especially a man who doesn't have much respect for women in the first place."

"I think we should keep in mind that sexual activity among our students often starts in high school," said the foreign language professor. "By the time they get to university, the young men expect sex. And sometimes the young women expect it, or assume it's expected." His accent was strong, but his English was exact. And he raised a point that had bothered me too. How much was a history of high school sex mixed with a new freedom to get blind drunk responsible for the degree of assault we were seeing?

"I think we're getting ahead of ourselves," said Bud. "Let's begin with looking at the current law. Karen, perhaps you could lead us through."

When Karen was finished, one of the faculty, whose name I had forgotten, raised his hand. He was a big man seated at the other end of the table. His voice was soft but intense. "Is there anything that ensures the guy who's accused gets a fair shake?"

Karen leaned forward. "Shelby, the law is designed to protect both male and female students."

Now I remembered. Shelby Vane, a tall, large-boned professor from the College of Agriculture. "Yes, I'm sure it protects the victim of either sex. But how does it protect the accused?"

Karen frowned. Bud interrupted. "I think this is a point we should cover in our next meeting."

Shelby Vane sank back into his chair and looked at the ceiling. For a minute, I thought I saw tears in his eyes.

The attorney again, "Dr. Vane, I assure you we will address your concerns, and we will address them thoroughly."

As the meeting broke up, I sidled over to the attorney. We walked out together. In the hallway, I tapped his arm. "You seem to know Shelby Vane. Does he have a particular stake in this issue? He seemed visibly upset."

The attorney looked uncomfortable and drew me aside. "Vane's older brother did some time in prison for rape. Months later, the woman recanted her testimony, but the man's reputation was ruined. I understand the entire Vane family was devastated by the matter. They had a big ranch outside of Landry, and most of them moved away. Shelby and his mother stayed, or I should say, his mother stayed, and Shelby returned after he got his doctorate."

"Do you think he'll be able to be objective about the work we are doing?"

"I don't know. But I do know Shelby Vane asked the Provost to put him on this committee."

"Well, perhaps he'll help represent the interests of the accused."

The attorney cocked his head, "Ever think about taking up the law, Dr. Solaris?"

Nope. Too busy trying to take up the work of a detective.

Jamie

Jamie could still feel the grip of the man's hands on her shoulders and still see the flame in his dark eyes. But he hadn't hurt her. And he said he wouldn't do anything against her will except keep her locked up. She desperately wanted to believe him. But the basic fear sat like a rock in her stomach. He said he wasn't going to hurt her, but he still could. He may not be ready to assault her, but he seemed determined to keep her prisoner. And his reasons struck her as irrational.

Insanity would explain his behavior. But what if he wasn't insane, just cold and calculating, a leopard poised above, waiting for the perfect moment to leap and overwhelm his prey? What if, after he got what he wanted, he planned to kill her? Now more than ever, she had to get away. She had to get back to the closet in the empty room.

She turned on the lamp on her bedside table and picked up the leather journal. He had given her this particular book to read. Perhaps its contents would tell her more about his "objective" and more about who he was and why he had captured her.

The handwriting was elegant and precise.

Penmanship like this was no longer taught in schools, so Jamie deduced that this journal was written by a young woman who had been educated decades ago. The man's mother? Or grandmother? Probably the latter, since the writing was infused with old-fashioned notions of submission and propriety. But certainly the writer was not the stepmother. These were not the words of a woman who had refused to "obey."

Jamie took a deep breath when she came to: *Every day, I shall prepare our home and my appearance before my husband comes home. I will take a few minutes to rest so I will be refreshed from housework. I will apply makeup and curl my hair. I will remember he has spent his day working hard and with others who make him tired and irritated. I promise to be light-hearted and charming when he comes through the door. If he needs a lift in his spirits, I will endeavor to provide it.*

Jamie frowned a few pages later when she read: *Obey! I must not shrink from the word even though it sounds harsh and unreasonable. Instead, I will ask myself if it is truly so difficult to obey him when he commands affection and tenderness. I must find a way to remind myself every day that obedience to my dear husband is Divine Will.*

Jamie closed the journal. She understood the carvings on the wooden toilet seat covers. And she was beginning to understand just what was expected of her. If she'd been afraid he might kill her, the journal convinced her that, at some point, she might have to kill him.

Chapter 16

As I walked back from the committee meeting, the same argument bounced around my tired brain. We needed more time than the provost had given us. No matter what, we couldn't discourage survivors from reporting crimes committed against them. That sort of suppression had gone on for much too long, and in too many cases, had cost good people years of sleepless nights and injured marriages.

Nor could we rush into a policy that denied the accused any chance of self-defense. Even if, most of the time, the survivors were truthful, we couldn't foreclose the possibility that someone could be framed.

We needed more time. But we couldn't wait too long. We had already waited too long.

Three people greeted me in my office.

"Wynan and I have decided to take you two hard-working women to dinner." Joe kissed my cheek and Wynan and Nell stood together off to one side. Wynan nodded, his handsome features softened with a slight smile.

I think that was the first time I had seen him smile. I credited Nell for that. In contrast, Nell looked serious and gave me a wan grin as if to say she was making an effort to enjoy the idea of dinner.

"Great. Where are we going?" I said, still eyeing Nell who seemed miles away.

"We thought we'd try that new restaurant down the street from your house," said Joe.

"Good thought. We'll leave the cars at my house and walk. I could use a stretch."

"So could I," said Nell, still looking dismal.

On the way, Nell and I walked together with Joe and Wynan behind us. I wanted to find out what was bothering her.

"Oh, this afternoon I had a bit of a run-in with George Weinstein," she said. "He may be a senior tenured professor, but he always gives me heartburn."

"Tell me about it. What was today's problem?" I said, hoping it would be minor, but, judging by Nell's demeanor, knowing it was not.

"First, he was angry because you were away at that meeting. And second he wanted me to give him a copy of Larry Coleman's paper. The one Larry told you about. I gather George hadn't read it, but today he wanted it."

"Do you have that paper?"

"Yes. Larry gave me a copy for his personnel file. But I told George he should ask Larry. I don't feel comfortable giving out professor's stuff from their file."

"And George was annoyed?"

"*Annoyed* hardly covers it. I got a ten-minute harangue on how my obligations were to the school and the entire faculty, not just the dean, and how my withholding Coleman's paper was 'way out of line,' as he put it. I'm sure you'll get an earful tomorrow."

I felt my neck get warm. Damn George. Pompous, self-important George.

"I'll deal with that bastard tomorrow. You are the assistant to the dean, Nell, and you don't have to take that kind of crap from George or any of them."

Nell patted my arm. "I know. My first responsibility is to you, and believe me, I like it that way."

The restaurant was cool after the walk and several tables were already filled. Good sign.

We were seated in the back where we could talk, "privately," as Joe had said to the hostess. We ordered drinks. No one spoke.

"Any word on that gray van?" asked Nell finally. I guessed Wynan had told her everything.

"I'm waiting for a report on the DMV search," said Joe. "Maybe later this evening."

We fell silent again until the waitress returned. We ordered food. Not much for any of us—salad and small plates. No strong appetites at the table. We fell silent again after the food arrived.

"It's been too many days," said Wynan, putting down his fork and taking a gulp of wine.

"That's just conventional cop thinking," said Joe. "Jamie could still be okay, even if she's confined and can't reach you."

"You and I both know better. The longer a girl's missing, the more likely she's dead."

"Oh. Surely not." Nell's hand was on his.

"Do you want to bring in the FBI? We can try that. Even without a ransom note or witnesses, we could ask for their help. My team has searched the area pretty thoroughly. At the very least, I can put out the Missing Persons and we all can start putting up posters."

Wynan sighed. "I probably should have asked for all that sooner. But when the FBI comes in, they'll take over and keep me out of the deal. That'll drive me crazy."

Joe's cell phone buzzed and he took the call. "Right. We'll be there in ten." He put the phone back in his pocket. "That was my guy checking the DMV. He thinks he has a match for the partial plate and an old gray Ford van."

"Go," Nell and I said simultaneously.

Later, Nell and I waited in my living room. "I can't go home without knowing," she said.

"Then keep me company. I could use it." I walked into the kitchen to make some coffee.

Nell followed and sat in one of the kitchen chairs. "As long as we don't talk about George and Larry. God, I am sick of the two of them."

"Agreed. How about we talk about you and Wynan Congers?"

Nell blushed. "I haven't had feelings like this for a long time. It's a little dizzying."

"But good?"

"Yes. Very good." Nell glanced out the window. "After my husband died, I thought I would go to my grave without ever meeting another man who interested me." Her gaze returned to me. "Thanks for being my friend as well as my boss. It's good to have someone to talk to."

Charlie left his spot by the kitchen door and went over to Nell. He put his head on her knee and she accepted his invitation to stroke his soft fur. "I used to have a dog like you," Nell said to Charlie, who responded by licking her wrist. "I should get another one."

"When it comes to love, dogs are even more reliable than men."

"I know," she said, scratching Charlie's chest fur. "But being with a good man makes life ever so much richer. Don't you think so?"

My chest tightened. "I do."

Joe and Wynan came in a little after ten o'clock. Joe kept his jacket on and shoved his hands in his pockets. His green eyes were serious and his jaw was set. Wynan looked more tired than ever and barely made it into in a chair.

"The van was registered to an old ranch hand who lives in an apartment a few miles from here," Joe said. "He didn't like the two of us bothering him at night, and at first, didn't respond to questions with more than a monosyllable. But Wynan charmed him and he agreed to show us the shed where he had kept the van."

"Had kept?"

"Yep. He says he sold it for cash last month to some guy he described as white, tall, wearing work boots and jeans."

"Our suspect," said Wynan, breathing heavily. His shoulders came forward, elbows on his knees, hands over his face. Nell got up and went over and put her hands on his shoulders that were visibly shaking.

"Joe, did you get a name for the guy who bought the van?"

"No. The suspect paid cash when he bought the van from the old ranch hand. We checked and the van hasn't shown up again on the DMV records, so that means he never registered it. We figure the man bought the van for some secret purpose and never intended to have it found."

"Do you think the old ranch hand you interviewed is colluding with the man in the boots?"

Wynan shook his head. "We don't think so. Once he realized we were investigating a possible kidnapping, he seemed perfectly willing to tell us as much as he could remember about the suspect and the van. He said the man looked like he might have been a member of a family called Lassiter. The old man said his late aunt had been friends with a Lassiter family years ago. She used to go to revival meetings out in the boonies somewhere, and one of the Lassiters would drive her to and from. The old ranch hand said the man who purchased his van had looked like that driver. So we have just spent an hour checking county computer records for anyone named Lassiter. Nothing."

I didn't like the look on Joe's face.

Jamie

Jamie awoke and heard her bedroom door open earlier than usual. It was still dark out. Her whole body tensed.

"Get up," said the man. "I have to leave early today."

She dressed hurriedly, and just as she was about to leave the room, picked up the leather journal and tucked it under her arm.

She placed the journal next to where she sat for breakfast and went to the refrigerator, pulling out eggs and milk and butter.

"Have you been reading it?" He sat at his place, watching her put the food on the counter.

"It's interesting. Who wrote it?" She cracked eggs into a bowl and tried to sound casual.

"My grandmother. What's interesting?"

"Her handwriting is beautiful, but her thinking seems very old-fashioned. More like something from the nineteenth century than even the early twentieth. And, of course, her sentiments wouldn't work at all today."

He coughed and remained silent for a moment. "That's the problem with women of your generation. You have no respect for the values we used to hold sacred."

"Like slavish obedience to men?"

"I wouldn't call it slavish."

"I would. That's what I am now. Your slave." She turned from the stove and faced him, her hands on her hips. "I'm even the appropriate color, aren't I?"

She could see the redness rising from his shirt up to his chin. He was breathing heavily and his fingers curled into fists. Oh, God. She had gone too far. But she realized some of her fear had been overcome by anger. She had to try, she had to challenge this man, she had to know more about his thinking so she would have a better shot at persuading him to let her out of his awful house. If he turned out to be insane, then she had to know that.

The man seemed to be struggling for self-control. At length he looked up at her. His voice was hoarse and his face gleamed. "I'm not a racist. My stepmother was African-American and I loved her."

She turned back to the stove and poured the egg mixture into a skillet. Neither of them spoke. She served the food and sat quietly across from him. He ate without looking at her.

She tried again. "You may not be a racist, but you are an enslaver. You lock me up every day, you force me to work for you against my will and with no compensation."

"I don't mean to enslave you."

"Then let me go. Unlock the door."

He stood up and walked away from her and stood with his back to her facing the barred kitchen window. The sun was up and the light played against his hair, illuminating the gray strands among the brown. "I can't let you go. You'll...you'll leave me." His voice choked on the last phrase.

Perhaps he was not going to use physical force, but neither was he going to free her. He wanted her. For what? Sex, perhaps. More than that. Submission. He wanted her to want him, to want to be with him, to want to obey him. And as she stared at the back of his bowed head and his broad heaving shoulders, her anger turned to a new kind of fear returning to the pit of her stomach. He wanted her to be his for a long time.

He remained facing the window while she washed the breakfast dishes and scrubbed the sink. She was tempted to continue to force the issue, to demand he realize what he wanted was impossible. She lifted a plate and held it suspended over the tile counter. She was angry and wanted him to know exactly how angry she was. She prepared to smash the plate when she felt him standing behind her, his chest pressed against her back. She could feel the heat from his body. *Oh, God*, she thought, *I've misjudged. He is going for me now.* She started to pull away, but he grabbed both her arms from behind and held her against him. His voice was very soft behind her ear. "I will leave your bedroom door unlocked today so you can go into other rooms."

He stepped away and she turned. His eyes were piercing but his voice stayed soft. "You must stop resisting and learn to accept this house as your home. This is where you belong."

The plate fell from her hand and clattered to the floor, but did not break. He stooped and picked it up and handed it to her. "If you make any effort to escape or tamper with the locks, I will have to confine you to your room again."

That was his plan. If she didn't escape him, or defeat him, she would be in his house for years.

Chapter 17

As I drove to campus the next morning, I worried about Wynan Congers almost as much as I dreaded what we'd learn about the fate of his granddaughter. The retired cop was skilled and realistic but so full of rage and anguish, I suspected that if he ever found the man with the boots, he would turn to savagery. Nell was in early, sorting through papers and slamming the file drawers vigorously to dissipate her nervousness.

"George come by?" I asked without a morning greeting.

"Not yet." She slammed another drawer.

And then, of course, George loomed into sight. I swore he had gained more weight since the last year's faculty quarrels. No doubt consumed with self-pity because he'd lost the battle to deny Larry Coleman's tenure, and because the personnel evaluation I'd given him had been humiliating—George must've been pounding down calories to comfort himself. His light blue cotton sweater strained against his stomach and his collar wrinkled around his neck.

"Good morning, George."

"We need to talk," he said, closing the door to my office and plunking himself down at my small conference table.

I took another chair. "What's on your mind?"

"I don't like the way your secretary treats members of this faculty."

"Nell's not my secretary, she's my assistant. What's your complaint about her?"

"I asked to see that paper Coleman is presenting in December and she refused. She said I had to go to Coleman and ask him for it. Ridiculous. Academic papers should be available to all faculty."

"Well, yes. Once it's ready to be presented, it should become a public document."

"So why won't she give it to me?"

"I think both Nell and I would be more comfortable if you asked Larry directly to see his paper. He may still be editing it. Then again, he may be perfectly willing to give you a copy."

"I have no interest in going begging to Coleman."

"But you do have interest in his work?"

"I just want to be sure that whatever is presented in conferences by members of this school is of high quality and meets our standards for scholarship."

"Keeping our standards high is my responsibility, George. You are not needed, nor required, to police the efforts of others." Damn, the man was infuriating.

George shifted and tugged the front of his sweater, made even tighter across his belly by his seated position. "Coleman's been known to do shoddy work before and I just want to check on this particular paper."

"Hmm. I don't recall shoddy work on Larry's part. And you might do well to tend to your own knitting."

George was on his feet. "Oh, for Christ's sake, Meredith, you defend that second-rater at every turn."

Then I was standing. "George, you promised me civil discourse this semester. No more accusations. No trouble between you guys."

He blew his cheeks. "Yes, I know. Your candidacy for the dean's job is at stake. We must all maintain the pretense of courtesy to each other."

"That's right, George. And, if you want to see someone else's academic paper, that means you must *pretend* good manners. Ask the author politely and *pretend* you are interested in the content. Or else, mind your own damn business."

As I watched George heave out of his chair and head for the door, I remembered a friend in Psychology saying that attitude affects behavior and, conversely, behavior affects attitude. Maybe if George and Larry pretended to respect each other, someday they would actually begin to feel collegial. Or, at the very least, behave themselves. Wishful thinking on my part.

I returned to my desk to find an inter-office envelope containing a confidential memo from Shelby Vane to Karen, Bridget and me. It was politely worded and full of quotes from recent media stories about three young men who had been accused of sexual assault at different American universities. In each case, the young man had been put on suspension and ultimately expelled. And, in each case, the accuser had later recanted the accusations. One young man had been studying to become a doctor and ended up leaving higher education to become a long-distance trucker. Vane's plea was obvious, and I promised myself I would not let our committee lose sight of fairness.

I plunged into the pile of work Nell had left on my desk. The phone rang. It was Joe. A woman's body had been found in a field on the outskirts of Reno.

Jamie

After breakfast, the man had gone to his room. Jamie remained seated in the kitchen, excited at the prospect of having the run of the house and the chance to get back to digging her hole in the closet of the empty front room.

She heard him come down the stairs, but did not see him. He left by the front door, slamming the door and locking the outer padlock noisily and with extra vigor.

She waited, then rose and went to the empty front room. She looked out the window and listened for the sound of his tires on the gravel driveway. She hurried to the closet. The ironing board was just as she left it. She pulled it aside, and there was the hole in the wall. He had not discovered it. She would have all day to enlarge it and break through to the bricks behind it.

But first she wanted to search the house once more. She was still convinced there was a telephone somewhere, although she had not heard ringing. He must have hidden her handbag somewhere in the house. Maybe her cell phone would still be inside it. Maybe, even in this desolate place, it would work.

She raced upstairs back to the one room she had never seen—the front bedroom, his bedroom. She pulled on the door. It did not give. It was locked. She put her face close to the frame, straining to see if the deadbolts had been thrown. Maybe not. He had left in a hurry. She reached into her pocket for the paperclip. Then decided to try a more forceful approach. She ran back to the kitchen, grabbed a butter knife and a pair of old kitchen shears. Then back to the door of his room where she tried the lock, pried at the doorframe, examined the hinges to see if she could use the butter knife as a screwdriver. But the door was large, six feet high, dark wood and heavy. After an hour of exertion, she gave up.

Back downstairs, she took the heavy skillet and the big spoon into the closet in the empty room. She sat on the closet floor and looked at the cuts and scrapes on her hands. She was tired, very tired. She was getting enough to eat, but not enough sleep or exercise. Much as she tried to stay in shape, her confinement in the old house was beginning to take its toll. The stuffy air and barred windows depressed her. Her bed was lumpy and uncomfortable. The food was boring and there was never more than what was exactly needed for a single day. But mostly, there was the man, staring at her, ordering her to do chores, and this morning coming much, much too close.

She went to work on the plaster wall. Because she was tired, work proceeded more slowly. The skillet was heavy in her hand and an awkward substitute for a mallet. She gave up scooping the residual plaster into the space between the interior wall and the exterior brick and let the chunks fall on the floor. Dust covered her clothes and sprinkled her hair. She worked feverishly, planning to clean up later.

Mid-afternoon, hours before she expected it, she heard the front door open.

Chapter 18

I waited for Joe at home, my hands almost too sweaty to open a can of food for Charlie. After I dished it up, the dog ate tentatively, looking up at me more often than usual. When done, he spread his legs and slid down on the floor until his nose rested between his paws. He knew something was wrong, and he knew I was worried about it.

The day had been hard. It was difficult to concentrate on curriculum changes and classroom maintenance problems without feeling uneasy about George and Larry, or without seeing Jamie's lovely face in the back of my mind. Work had ended with a phone call from the provost's office. "Provost McCready would like to see you in his office tomorrow morning. Would ten thirty be convenient?"

"I think so. Can you tell me what it's about?"

"He wants to conduct his own interview of you for the journalism dean position. Can you make it?"

"Yes. I'll be there."

I should have spent the evening trying to prepare myself for the interview with McCready. But I couldn't. I kept going back to Joe's call. Nine o'clock became ten and then the back door opened. I was immediately in Joe's arms, my face buried in his collar.

"It's okay, Red. The body wasn't Jamie's."

"Oh, God. I'm so relieved." I held him tight. "I was so sure the news would be bad. Tell me. Tell me."

He shifted his chin and met my mouth for a kiss. He pulled away. "You and I were both sure it would be bad news. I've been thinking for days that Jamie is dead. But I've tried to keep my thoughts from showing when I'm with Wynan."

"You didn't tell Wynan about the body?" I poured wine and set out some cheese and bread. Neither of us had eaten.

"No. I wanted to be sure, but on the drive to Reno, I kept rehearsing what I would tell him if the body turned out to be his granddaughter's. Wynan's an experienced cop, but he's near delusional about that girl. He keeps wanting to believe we'll find her alive."

Maybe we will find her alive, I prayed silently. "You were gone a long time. I guessed you stayed with the coroner until you were certain. So whose body was it?"

Joe sighed and took a long sip of wine. "The woman was probably in her forties. Hispanic. Much shorter than Jamie Congers. And according to the coroner, dead for more than a month."

"I'm surprised the body wasn't discovered sooner. Your team has been searching every meadow and vacant lot around here for days."

"This body was outside our search area, which I guess we will now have to expand." He looked as morose as I had ever seen him.

Joe rose and put his glass and plate in the sink. I followed him. He pulled me toward him and tugged at my blouse until his hands were on my bare back. "I really need you tonight," he said into my hair.

"I need you too." My mouth was close to his. "Bedtime."

For all our occasional problems with each other, sex has always been our refuge and, in good times, our joy. In bed, Joe and I don't disappoint each other. I sometimes think it's the single aspect of our relationship that guarantees we'll stay together. When his mouth is on mine and his hands move across me, the uncertainty and tensions of the day melt away. At least they melt away for me. I'm never sure about Joe's worries. But at least he sleeps.

After an hour of making love, I watched Joe sleeping next to me. From time to time, his eyelids fluttered and the muscles in his long lean back twitched. He groaned and his legs scissored as if he was running. I leaned over and kissed the back of his neck and rubbed his shoulders. "It's just a dream," I whispered. But I knew it was futile to try and stop his dream. Like Charlie dreaming of chasing a rabbit, legs twitching and mouth open, Joe Morgan was dreaming of chasing a big man in muddy boots.

Jamie

Jamie froze at the sound of footsteps in the hallway. Then the sound of steps in the kitchen followed by steps on the stairs. She had no time to clean up the plaster on the floor, so she lifted the ironing board as quietly as she could and placed it over the now much larger hole in the wall. She slowly crept out of the closet and across the room into the hallway. His steps on the stairs stopped her again.

He looked different. He was wearing a suit and tie instead of his work clothes. He looked the way he had appeared to her on campus.

He stared at her. "What have you been up to? You're covered in dust."

She breathed deeply, brushing the plaster dust off her shirt and pants. "Oh, I've just been doing some cleaning in areas I missed before." Her voice sounded weak and unconvincing.

"Well, then. It's time you cleaned yourself. Here are some things you probably need." He handed her a large plastic bag. "Take these upstairs with you and take a shower. You should wash your hair."

She accepted the bag. He seemed calm to her. "You're home early," she said, her voice stronger.

"Yes. I wanted to get these to you and to see how you had enjoyed your first day of freedom."

Freedom? Hardly. The house was still her prison. But he hadn't caught her in the closet, and maybe he wouldn't look into the empty room.

He turned and started back up the stairs. "I'll see you in an hour for dinner."

Her legs were so shaky she could hardly make it up to her room. She sat on the bed shivering. Then she opened the plastic bag. It contained a hair dryer just like the one she had in her apartment. Next, a bottle of shampoo. Her brand, the one she always bought because it kept her hair soft. She pulled out a box holding a tube of toothpaste. Her brand of toothpaste. And her brand of deodorant and her type of toothbrush and a bar of the brand of soap she had used every day since she was a child.

Oh, Jesus. He must have been in her apartment. That's how he knew what brands she used and the correct size clothes and underwear to buy for her. He'd been examining her things. He knew where she lived.

Chapter 19

Joe left early for work. I heard him start the coffee pot in the kitchen downstairs and then the kitchen door closing behind him. I lay in bed mentally bracing myself for the meeting with the provost. I knew the meeting would be my last chance to convince him that I was the person he should appoint as dean. I also knew I was sitting on a powder keg named George and Larry, and that it could blow up at any time and ruin my chances.

I scolded myself for thinking only of myself. How could I stress out so much over a stupid job when one of my students was in danger, maybe dead?

I got up and brushed my teeth with an energy designed to punish me for my selfishness. I dressed in red, my war color, pulled back my hair and marched to the car, juggling a thermos of Joe's good coffee.

As happens almost three hundred and fifty days a year in Nevada, the sun was shining. In addition, the birds were singing, and the flowerbeds beside my driveway were blooming. Still, I felt like hell. Scared. Angry. Conflicted.

I swung into the journalism school parking lot too fast and stopped just inches from one of the cherry trees. I poured some coffee into the cup that served as the thermos top. My hands shook, my pantyhose itched, and I wished I'd come barelegged to do battle with Ezra McCready.

The path to the administration building was wide and shaded with trees still leafed out in the early fall. I trudged, and I do mean trudged, to my meeting with the provost. The man held my future in his hands, and I didn't like him. I didn't like him at all. He was tall, well built, reasonably good-looking, a bit nerdy when he put on his steel framed glasses. His clothes were conservative and well-tailored. But even if Joe had not been in my life, I would never have been attracted to a man like Ezra McCready. In spite of his academic reputation as a leader, I found nothing to admire. The man struck me as dismissive and interested only in what served his own career, not the welfare of the university. He was a snob, as Nell had said. Perhaps a bigot.

Yet, as I mounted the stairs to the administration building, I vowed to put my private opinions of McCready out of my mind. It was important for me to impress him. I prayed he would think better of me than I did of him. Provost Ezra McCready would have the final say on who would be dean of journalism. Only the president, Philip Lewis, could overrule his decision. The president was my friend but he was ill, infrequently on campus, and not likely to overrule his handpicked executive who was running the university day to day.

McCready's outer office was empty and I felt timid about knocking on the door to his inner office. He might be the sort who preferred to have a secretary announce a visitor.

I waited.

After what felt like an hour but was only ten minutes, the inner office opened. Ezra McCready escorted a man through the door. The man was a bit taller than me, round in face and belly with big dark eyes. My good friend and competitor, Manny Lorenzo.

Manny's smile lit up when he saw me and a big bear hug followed. "Great to see you, Red. More beautiful than ever. My favorite rival."

"Friendly rivals, I hope," I said nervously, glancing back at McCready who stood in the doorway, not a trace of warmth on his face.

Manny turned back to the provost and shook his hand. "Wonderful talking to you, sir," he said in his gentle Texas drawl.

Manny had grown up in El Paso and earned all his degrees in the University of Texas system.

"I enjoyed it thoroughly, Dr. Lorenzo," said McCready. Still no smile but at least some light in his eyes. Manny would be a good catch for Mountain West. A brilliant Hispanic with an impressive record as dean of a journalism school much larger than ours. I figured if the distinguished Dr. Manuel Lorenzo wanted to move from the prestigious university that hired him five years ago to the engaging climate of northern Nevada, Ezra McCready would hand him this job on a platter—with an extra serving of incentives.

Manny moved back to me, gave me another hug and whispered, "Talk soon," in my ear.

McCready watched Manny leave through the outer office without looking at me. "Please give me a moment," he said in my direction, then went back into his office and closed the door. Another five minutes passed. I suspected he enjoyed keeping me on edge and off my game.

The door opened. "Please come in, Dr. Solaris."

The provost's office had been refurnished since my last visit. The former provost, Fred Stoddard, who had helped me through a series of crises last year, had furnished this office with fat leather chairs and a sofa. Not McCready.

A long glass-topped table surrounded by sleek leather swivel chairs dominated the room. A glass-topped desk on chrome legs took over the end of the room in front of the windows.

The carpet was thick and gray, the walls painted a pale gray white. The only color in the room came from the books in shelves lining the walls. A delicate black and white Japanese print hung on the wall to the side of the desk, the only painting in a room that appeared to be as restrained as its occupant.

"Please," he said pulling out one of the black swivel chairs. He unbuttoned his jacket, sat opposite me, and folded his hands on the glass surface.

A file and a carafe of water with two glasses were all that sat on the long empty table.

His face was an unreadable mask. I tried to look cheerful and tugged at my suit jacket. "Thank you, Dr. McCready."

"Now then, Dr. Solaris. Start by telling me why you think you should be the next dean of the journalism school in this university."

I began with the death of Henry Brooks, the former dean, and my appointment to serve as the interim dean. Then I moved on to the horrific faculty quarrel that had preceded and followed Henry's death along with my part in the discovery of the killer.

I must have spoken for ten minutes with no interruption before he said, "Yes, Dr. Solaris. Of course, I know most of this from my conversations with President Lewis and with Dr. Stoddard on the phone a few weeks ago."

I took a deep breath. "Well, I think I have survived something of a baptism by fire over the past several months, and I have learned a great deal from the struggle."

"No doubt you have." His eyes were cold and steady. "I am informed you are popular with several members of the journalism faculty."

"I believe I am respected by most."

"Indeed. Although popularity with faculty members is not necessarily a qualification for leadership." McCready unfolded his hands and placed them flat on the table. "Any more than popularity with students is the mark of a good teacher."

In his chilly, formal office, I felt sweat starting on the back of my neck. "I believe I also have earned the faculty's confidence and that of President Lewis. I believe I have been an effective leader."

"Perhaps so. Perhaps you have even been a brave leader. But I have some questions about your ability and your experience—perhaps I should say, lack of experience. The search committee report is complimentary, but observes you have only been interim dean for not quite a year."

Shades of Mark Froman. Do all tall men in expensive suits plan to put me down as hard as they can?

The provost opened the folder in front of him. "Let's begin with your handling last year of a plagiarist and an admitted sexual predator whom you tolerated for several months even though you knew about his affair with a student."

And that's how it went for the next hour, each of my sins and shortcomings pulled from the folder, one by one. It all felt more like a disciplinary hearing than a job interview.

At length, he stood up and walked to the end of the table. He looked down at me. "Please understand, the university is grateful for your efforts to keep the journalism school together after the tumult that almost destroyed it. And I for one am grateful for your work preparing the school for reaccreditation. But my task is to consider what is best for the future of the school and what leadership skills will be needed for the days ahead."

"I understand," I said, resenting his decision to tower over me at the same time he was expressing his tepid gratitude.

In the end, we shook hands and he walked me to the door. "I plan to make my decision soon. Thank you for your time."

As I descended the stairs from the building, I saw a man heading toward me. Victor Watts, my other competitor. Another tall man in a good suit. This was my day to be treated to displays of Hugo Boss style tailoring. Most of the male faculty on my campus wore sweaters and jeans.

"Interview with the provost?" I asked as he came near. It was almost noon and the sun was high in the sky.

"Oh, hello. Meredith Solaris, right? Actually, I had my interview yesterday. Today, Dr. McCready asked me to join him for lunch." A thin smug smile played across his mouth, as if Watts knew the provost hadn't offered me so much as a cup of bad institutional coffee.

Jamie

Jamie showered, washed the plaster dust out of her hair and dressed in clean clothes. She headed downstairs, determined to find out why he had chosen her specifically from among all the other females on campus. Clearly he'd stalked her at school. Clearly he had entered her apartment and examined her possessions. What was it about her that made him select her among all other women, including women closer to his age, or women who would have been more accepting, more willing to sacrifice some personal freedom in order to get a house and a husband?

He was sitting in the parlor, dressed again in work clothes and heavy boots. His head was bowed as if in prayer. She sat in a chair opposite him and cleared her throat. He raised his head and gave her the usual stare.

"Why me?" She spoke without trembling, hands folded in her lap.

"You're healthy and very good-looking."

"I'm black. You're white."

"I told you. Your race doesn't matter. Never has. My stepmother..." He hesitated.

"Yes. Tell me about your stepmother."

"What do you want to know?"

Jamie wanted to know what had happened to the stepmother, but decided to take a more oblique approach. "How old were you when she married your father?"

He shrugged. "Twelve, thirteen. My mother died when I was eleven."

"Did your stepmother die?"

He busied himself retying the laces of his boots so he could avoid looking directly at her. "She left when I was sixteen. I didn't learn of her death until I was in my twenties."

Jamie leaned forward, addressing the top of his head. "I'm not going to cook dinner until you tell me more about her. Did she look like me?"

He sat back in his chair. "She was beautiful, like you."

"And you loved her?"

"I did."

"Tell me more. Tell me all about her."

"That's enough for now. I'm hungry. You need to start dinner."

Jamie decided to switch tactics. "Why did you break into my apartment and go through my stuff?"

He stood up and turned away from her. His hands became fists that he clenched and unclenched. "Enough questions. Dinner. Now."

She sat still, refusing to move. He turned back to her. His usually unreadable eyes were blazing with anger. She had made him angry, and his expression alarmed her. "Dinner. Now, Jamie."

It was the first time he had called her by name. And her name in his mouth made her skin crawl.

Chapter 20

The red suit I'd worn to the provost's office was too heavy for a warm fall day. I took off the jacket and swung it over my shoulder as I walked. I felt defeated and, at the same time, belligerent. I wanted to go back to McCready and head off what I was certain was going to be his rejection. If he chose another candidate for dean, I would go back to my job as a tenured professor. And much as I agreed with Sadie about the joys of teaching, I really wanted McCready to give me the dean's job. Even if he and I found it difficult to be good friends, I knew I could make him respect me if he just gave me the chance.

I walked, absorbed in my frustration, until I reached the street that bordered the west side of campus. Across the street was Gormley's Grill. Sadie Hawkins was waiting for me inside, along with a generous glass of wine. And, despite my mother's alcoholism and my own conservatism about drinking, I needed a drink more than ever.

Wilson, the owner of Gormley's, gave me a wink as I pushed through into the coolness of the bar.

"Yes, please," I said as I passed him on my way to the corner table Sadie always occupied.

As soon as I sat down, Sadie put her hand over mine. "You look like hell," she said. "How did it go with McCready?"

"Terribly. Just terribly."

Sadie lifted her hand to make room for the wine glass Wilson put on the table between us. "My best Pinot Noir," he said, and patted my shoulder. Wilson had been Sadie's friend for years and she sort of gave him to me as a friend when she and I had become close.

"Thank you." I was as near to tears as I ever got.

"So? Tell me about it," said Sadie. Her sharp features softened by the dim light in the bar. Her white hair glowed in the same dimness. I never could figure out how she read in this light until I saw Wilson place a tiny portable lamp on the table next to her books and papers, a lamp he removed when her companions arrived for lunch. Sadie's hand came back on mine.

"It's the provost, Sadie. And I think he's never going to let me get the dean's job. I'll have to go back into the faculty and work for whomever he chooses."

"But, my dear, as we discussed, you'll still be a tenured associate professor."

"But I'll never be promoted to full professor. McCready will block it somehow." I sipped my wine. "And you know better than anyone, a provost can exert a profoundly negative influence on your career even if he can't outright fire you."

Sadie looked thoughtful. "Who do you think he'll pick for dean?"

"I hope it's Manny Lorenzo. Victor Watts strikes me as an egotist, and I'll bet he's a real prick."

Sadie lifted her hand and pressed my cheek. "Let's change the subject. There's nothing to be done about the provost except to wait for his decision. We should order, and then I want to hear what's happening with the search for the missing girl."

"No good news there, either. Joe's team has been combing the entire city of Landry and much of the outskirts, but no trace of her. Her grandfather has been interrogating just about everyone who's willing to talk to him. The poor man is inconsolable. And Nell and I tag along feeling helpless."

"Will Joe bring in the feds?"

"If he can get some evidence. Right now, we have so little to go on. No one saw the girl with anyone. No one saw her leave campus.

There's been no request for ransom, so we have absolutely no evidence she's been kidnapped. Nonetheless, that's what we all believe."

"That she may have been taken and murdered?"

"Her car is still missing. I keep telling myself that if she'd been murdered, her car would have been dumped somewhere. I mean, who keeps a car after killing the owner?"

Lunch arrived, but I had no appetite. I picked at the salad and ignored the soup. "And there's still the matter of the man who broke into her apartment and went through her closet. I'm so frustrated, Sadie. This girl is my student and she disappeared on my watch. Except that I wasn't watching carefully enough."

"You should eat something. You need to keep up your strength. Tell me, how are things with you and Joe?"

"Joe and I are fine. The other day he put his basketball hoop up on the front of my garage so he could exercise at my house."

"That's a good sign."

"Yes, but he hasn't used it. We're both so involved with the hunt for Jamie and I'm so oppressed by the search for the dean's job that we've hardly had a moment alone with each other."

Sadie gave me her gentlest smile. "And the sexual assault policy committee?"

"That consumes more time than anything else. There's a special meeting called for this afternoon. The third meeting in as many days. We are being pushed hard on this because the provost needs an answer from us quickly."

"And Provost McCready wants things to come out his way on that matter, too."

On the walk back from lunch at Gormley's, I kept reflecting on Sadie's speech about what a good teacher I was and how important my research was and why I should just shuck off the provost's coolness and move on. I had half-convinced myself that I really didn't want the dean's job all that much, when I passed a small building that was occupied by student government offices. It had once been a Bureau of Land Management facility and a small plaque commemorating that use caught my eye. Land Management. Land records. I had an idea and hurried back to my office to call Joe.

It took Joe two hours before he returned my call and I was almost ready to leave for the special committee meeting. "Joe, you said you hadn't found the name Lassiter in any of the county records, right?"

"Right. No DMV, no deeds, no voter registration. No nothing."

"How about old land deeds?"

"Hmm. How old? Recent land ownership is on the county computers. But those only go back twenty years to when the county computerized everything."

"That's what I mean. If they kept them, old land ownership records would still be in the files over at the assessor's office."

"In the state capitol building." Joe's voice rose a bit.

"Want my help? I can ashcan this special committee meeting. I don't want to go anyway."

"Lovely offer. But it's late, and by the time we get there, the state offices will be closed."

"Okay. Tomorrow morning first thing, then. I really want to go with you. I feel very frustrated and I want to help."

"I think it's a long shot, sweetheart, but we'll go. I'm out of strategies for finding this girl."

I was reinvigorated. Maybe I could do something useful for a change and stop feeling sorry for myself.

Jamie

Jamie could not get to sleep. Her mind whirled with speculation about the man and his beautiful black stepmother. She still had no insight into his motives for kidnapping her. She resolved to start more conversations, ask more questions. Each time she did, she learned a bit more about him. In the event she could not escape through the hole in the wall, she might be able to manipulate him if she knew more about how he felt and what he wanted.

When she awoke the next morning, she was tired, but dressed quickly and was downstairs before she heard water running in what she assumed was his bathroom upstairs.

She busied herself with chores that were now routine, setting the table, bringing the eggs out of the refrigerator, putting the bread into the toaster, starting the coffee maker.

He entered the kitchen without saying good morning. He sat at the table and watched her. "What more do you need?" he asked. "I may be able to get to a store later."

She turned from her work at the counter. "What I need is some fresh air and exercise. This house is old and stuffy." She almost added she was an athlete and missed her training but thought better of it. No need for him to know she was strong and agile.

"I'll think about it," he said.

They ate in silence, and she was almost finished with the breakfast dishes when he spoke again. "After you've completed your housework, perhaps I'll take you for a walk outside." She almost dropped the pan she was scrubbing.

"I'd like that very much." Like it. Outside. Oh, God. "But don't you have to get dressed and go to the office?"

"Not today. Today I'm here all day."

Oh no. That meant she would have no opportunity to work on the hole in the closet wall. But at least she would get a walk outside. Maybe, just maybe she could make a run for it. She was a good runner, not stronger than the man, but probably faster. Maybe she would have a chance. But she would have to wait and see. It was essential she do nothing to alarm him. Nothing to give him reason to lock her back up again. She had to use her new bit of freedom cautiously, to stop being scared and start being smart.

Chapter 21

The drive to the assessor's office took us almost an hour, but it was good to be alone with Joe and away from the university. The trees were still full and green and I made a note to return to this road when fall colors began. The maples would turn orange and the aspens and cottonwoods yellow. While not exactly competitive to the New England scenery, the colors of northern Nevada break out after the first stretch of cold nights and are lovely for weeks.

Located in one of the older state buildings, the assessor's office was at the top of a grand staircase leading to the second floor, next door to the new office of the Bureau of Land Management. A slight blond man with a mustache was behind the counter. He looked dubious when Joe told him the computerized state records had not turned up the name we sought. "Even if it was old, we should have it if anyone named Lassiter owned land in this state."

"Could have been purchased a long time ago," said Joe. "May we see the older records that are not on the computer?"

"Sure thing, Detective," said the blond, opening a wooden gate and leading us down a hall to a back room where huge stacks of historical records were kept in large bound books. "Have a good time, folks. Let me know if you need anything copied."

It was a long and boring hunt. The bound books had not been dusted recently. We were almost ready to give up when I spotted a name on an old map. "Morgan-Lassiter."

I showed it to Joe. A hyphenated name might account for why Lassiter alone had not shown up on records. Further searching revealed that an Emily Morgan and Edward Lassiter had owned four separate parcels in the county, all purchased in the early 1900s and inherited by Emily before her marriage to Edward. Two of the smaller parcels were lots in Reno. One was outside of Landry, about a mile from the university campus, and the fourth and largest was east of Landry.

We hurried back to the computerized records up front where, with the help of the disinterested blond man, we learned that Edward Morgan-Lassiter's son Daniel had sold the Reno parcels to homebuilders in the 1970s.

One parcel outside of Landry was still in his name, but appeared to have been for sale. Another was further away.

Little information was filed on either of the remaining parcels. Tax records indicated both parcels were open land with no buildings or development on either.

But the taxes on the larger of the two parcels were paid every year on time, and—here was another surprise—paid by a bank in San Francisco.

No name was associated. And we both knew banks were notoriously protective of their clients.

Another dead end? Maybe, but as Joe and I headed to a local diner for lunch, we felt somehow we had made progress toward finding Jamie Congers.

"Red, it's a long shot. We don't really know if the old man who said our suspect looked like a Lassiter knew what he was talking about. We can't search those properties without a warrant, and we have no evidence to present to a judge to get a warrant."

"I know. But if our man in the muddy boots took her, he'd logically take her to some place no one could see or search. We could at least drive by the property nearest the university and see what it looks like."

"And we will," said Joe. "And I'll have my guys look at those Reno properties Lassiter sold to the builders, too. We'll see if any have structures that might make good hiding places."

"As soon as we get back to Landry."

"Right." Joe took my hand in his. "Thank you for your help this morning. You have very good investigative instincts, and who knows, maybe we are not on a wild goose chase. Maybe you're on to something."

"Anything that makes me feel useful. I have been feeling so stonewalled not knowing what happened to Jamie."

"And by everything else that's going on." He took my other hand and held both. I had told him on the drive over about my meeting with the provost and my concerns about the policy committee. "You're strong, Red. You'll get through all the crap at the university. And we'll find this girl. I don't know where, but we'll find her."

We continued lunch, but an impulse got the better of me. "Joe?"

"Yes?"

"Have you ever given any thought to staying at my house all the time? You already spend so much time there, and you could save the money you pay for rent on your apartment."

Joe touched my arm with his fingers. "I'm not sure this is a good time for me to make that kind of a move. I probably shouldn't have imposed on you by putting up a basketball hoop on your garage." He resumed eating his lunch.

"I don't mind the basketball hoop," I muttered, then pretended to be interested in my salad. *Back off*, my inner voice said. He's not ready and you'll just embarrass him, and yourself.

We drove back to Landry without much conversation. Joe seemed to have a lot on his mind, and I was still thinking about my impulsive request he move in with me. Yet, the more I thought about it, the more I wished he would. The events of the past few days had left me wanting the comfort of knowing I would see him every night.

Maybe Joe wasn't ready. Maybe I was trying to push both of us toward a commitment we were not both ready to make. But, at least I had finally decided what I wanted. And that felt good.

Jamie

The man had gone upstairs after breakfast and left her in the kitchen to wait for the walk he'd promised. She planned to ask him if they could walk toward the water. If it was a lake…People lived near lakes. Maybe she would see someone, or be seen.

"Ready?" The man was standing by the entrance to the hall. He held a length of thick rope in his hand. He approached her. "Don't be frightened. I'm going to tie us together."

"Why? It will be uncomfortable."

"Because you ran the 1600 faster than any high school girl in Nevada."

"You know everything about me and I don't even know your name."

"You will someday." He looped the rope around her waist and then knotted it and looped it around his waist and tied another knot. No chance she could run away. They walked to the back door, tied together, his arm firmly around her shoulders. "Put your head down and close your eyes."

"Why?"

"You still want to go outside? Do as I say."

She obeyed and closed her eyes while he tapped out the code on the padlock. The freshness of the air hit her immediately as they stepped through the back door of the kitchen. It was still warm outside. She calculated it must still be early September. She turned to him, "What's the date?"

"It doesn't matter. Which way do you want to walk?" His grip on her shoulder grew firmer and she could feel the tug of the rope around her waist with every step they took.

"I've seen water through the trees. I'd like to walk that way," she said, hoping he would agree. "It looks pretty."

"It is."

They walked in silence across the lawn toward a narrow path. She noticed the lawn needed mowing. "I like mowing grass. I'd be happy to mow this lawn," she said, trying to sound upbeat.

"I'll bet you would. But being outdoors on your own is a privilege you have yet to earn." Even his speech was stilted and old-fashioned.

The path led through a stand of trees and into a small meadow. She could see water glistening beyond through another stand of trees. His arm around her shoulders grew heavier as he pulled her closer. Past the second stand of trees, they came to the shore of a lake that lay gleaming in the sun, large and wide, more than a mile long.

"It's beautiful. How large is it?" She tried to keep her voice light, although the excitement she felt at being outdoors and the possibility of seeing other people made her heart pound.

"It's actually two lakes," he said quietly as both of them looked out over the water. "The two lakes are connected by a swampy marsh off to the right."

Yes, she could see the marsh.

"The lake's only about twelve feet deep at the deepest part."

Her heart rate increased. She could practically walk across some of this lake, and the rest would be an easy swim.

"This is a eutrophic lake. Do you know what eutrophic means?"

"No. Tell me, please." She wanted to keep him talking and he seemed to want to inform her.

"It means it is a lake that has an abundance of aquatic plants so it's very productive. Biologically speaking, that is." He seemed engaged in informing her about the lake. "And because it's so shallow, the high Nevada winds make it very turbid."

"What's turbid?'

"Clouded, not clear, because the winds stir up the sediment. It's unusually calm and bright today."

But she hardly heard his answer because she was watching an object far across the lake. It appeared to be a rowboat with two people in it. Her breath quickened and her pulse raced. She opened her mouth to shout.

But he saw it too. "Damn trespassers," he said.

He quickly covered her mouth and turned her around so they faced back toward the stand of trees.

"Back to the house." His voice was urgent and unfriendly. He pulled at her as she strained to turn her head and look at the faraway rowboat.

People. Oh God, there were people out on the lake.

This would have to be her escape route if she ever got out of the house. But he hustled her through the trees and over the meadow, back across the lawn and into the kitchen door. He locked the door and untied the rope. Then he moved to the parlor, pulling what appeared to be a large cell phone out of his pocket. He slammed the door but she pressed against it so she could hear.

"There are trespassers in a rowboat on the lake. Two of them. Get down there fast and get them off the property. Call me when they're gone. And make sure they know that lake is on private land, my land, and not to come back."

Who had he called? Private land? His land? Her head was full of questions, but when he came back into the kitchen she remained silent.

"I'm hungry," he said. "Make some lunch."

She worked swiftly. "I need a knife to cut the sandwiches."

He got up and went into the parlor, returning with the eight-inch knife he had taken from her the first time she cooked. That's where he kept it.

Good to know.

"The lake is beautiful," she said when they had finished eating. "Eutrophic, right?"

He looked up from his plate. "Right. You're smart, aren't you? That's good. You learn quickly. And that's good too."

For the first time, she heard the ring of a telephone. The man removed the large phone from his pocket and then she knew what it was: a satellite phone, the kind of phone that uses signals from orbiting satellites, instead of signals from nearby cell towers. The man listened without comment. "Good. Talk later," he said, and with a click of a button, put the sat phone back in his pocket.

So they were as isolated as she suspected. No cell phone reception because there weren't enough nearby towers. Her regular cell would be useless even if she could find it. She decided to continue the conversation, to learn more about him. She briefly considered asking him what he wanted her to learn, but instead said, "Is the lake part of your property?"

His eyes blazed for a moment. "Eavesdropping, eh? Yes, the lake is part of my property, as is all the land surrounding it."

"How much land do you own?"

"Many acres."

"Who did you talk to just now?"

"Not your business. Not yet." He left the kitchen and went upstairs.

Not yet.

Chapter 22

When Joe and I got back to my house, we spread the copies of the land maps out on my dining room table. Two messages from Wynan were on my answering machine.

Wynan showed up about ten minutes later.

"We don't know if there are any leads in this land ownership," said Joe. "But I'm thinking I could check and see if there are any buildings on the parcels near here."

"I can do better than that," Wynan said. "I can get over there now and start looking around."

"Remember, we don't have any search warrants, Wynan."

"I got all kinds of ways to check out a piece of property without a warrant," said the former deputy chief of the Las Vegas PD, with a shrug and a squaring of his jaw. He left and closed the kitchen door behind him.

Two new emails were on my cell phone. The first announced another special meeting of the policy committee meeting at five p.m. "Late dinner again," I said, groaning.

The second was longer and harder to read on a small screen. I went to my computer. "Red, I really need to see you ASAP," wrote Larry Coleman. This was followed by a long paragraph detailing the latest sins of George Weinstein. It seemed George had succeeded at getting Larry's paper eliminated from the presentation schedule of the conference in December.

I called Larry and told him to be in my office in half an hour. But when I arrived at my office, Nell told me Larry had left the school and said he was headed to George Weinstein's house to "settle matters." An alarm bell went off in my mind. I called George's house. After four rings, I got the answering machine with George's rapid-fire diction telling me to leave a message and suggesting I might get a call back if time permitted. Might.

What a day.

The sexual assault policy meeting started promptly at five with chairman Bud Chekovski asking Karen what she would recommend based on her understanding of the federal mandate.

Karen stood. "I think our best course would be to follow the California policy and require," she read from her notes, "'affirmative, conscious and voluntary agreement to engage in sexual activity that is ongoing throughout the sexual activity and can be revoked at any time.'"

"I thought we agreed that's confusing," said the university attorney. "Mr. Chairman, I'd like to make a few observations."

Karen said, "I wasn't really finished."

But Bud Chekovski nodded at the attorney despite Karen's anger.

The university attorney seemed equally belligerent. The fight was on.

"I think we have to avoid any policy that disregards due process. Some of the policies we are seeing from major universities are significantly stacked against the accused."

"Yeah, what about the girl who changes her mind?" said the coach.

Karen interrupted, breathing hard. "Hold on. I was getting to that."

A secretary entered the room and whispered in Bud's ear. He excused himself and called a brief recess.

I sat staring at Karen.

Both of us remembered a student two years ago who had been unwilling to file charges.

The girl's best friend was a fellow student she had known since childhood. She confided in him, but never dated him. One night, after studying for exams together, she had fallen asleep in his room. She awoke to find him on top of her.

I could still remember the girl trembling in my office. "I trusted him. I trusted him," she kept repeating. The next day the girl had left campus for three weeks. When she returned, she refused to speak to either Karen or me about the incident. A year later she committed suicide.

Karen's eyes were glued to me.

A chill ran through me. Jamie was never far from my mind. Stay alive, girl. No matter what happens to you, stay alive.

After five minutes, Bud returned and the attorney resumed his attack on Karen. "As I was saying, I am appalled your recommended procedures offer little guarantee of representation to the accused. When is there a chance to see evidence? Do your recommendations even allow the accused to bring an attorney to any hearing?"

Karen paled. "Yes, they do. But we still have to realize how difficult it is for a young woman, or a young man, to face someone who has hurt them badly, especially someone they may have trusted."

From the other end of the table, Shelby Vane coughed and raised his hand. "And who decides who is telling the truth?"

"We investigate," said Karen. "We interview others who may have been around when the two people were together. We gather the information available."

Shelby again: "And how do you decide the truth?"

Karen took a deep breath. "We consider the preponderance of the evidence, Dr. Vane, and then we make our best call."

"Then what?"

"After a hearing, if we think someone should be expelled or put on probation, we recommend that to the provost's office."

That surprised me. "So the provost decides the punishment?" All the faces turned to me.

"Yes, Red, unless the victim files charges with the police, it's still a civil matter and the provost makes the decision."

"But if a man is accused, it goes on his academic record, right?" Shelby Vane was leaning forward, his face pink with anger. "It ruins his chances for grad school."

"Not necessarily," said Karen. "We view each case on its own merits. There's no rule..."

"I'll bet," said Shelby, pushing back his chair. "Excuse me, folks, I need some air." He grabbed a large denim jacket he had folded over the back of his chair and headed for the door. He hitched his jeans and scuffed one of his boots on the doorsill. "Fairness, folks. That's what our mission has to be." Then he turned and was gone.

Big man. Boots. I made a note to suggest to Joe that he check out Shelby Vane.

"I just want to make one final point," Karen said. "Most of the young men who attack women, especially the freshmen women, do it over and over again. Some of these guys become serial criminals."

Bridget flipped her hand in the air. Karen's soft gray eyes pleaded for support, but I took a different path.

I had been silent too long. "Sorry, folks, but this is bullshit. We're not the right people to figure this out. We're hopelessly divided. We're caught up in rape myths and legal pieties. And we're too old."

Jaws dropped around the table.

"This is not just about law or process, and it sure as hell is not just about us. It's about the students. It's about their culture and their behavior. And they're not even here. They should be."

No one spoke.

A thoroughly befuddled Bud Chekovski ended the meeting.

Jamie

Jamie sat by herself in the kitchen for a long time watching the afternoon sun slowly dip toward the horizon. She could still recall the pressure of his arm around her shoulder and the grip of his hands as he turned her away from the lake. Again too close, much too close.

Before now, no man had ever frightened her this much. True, she had been cautious, especially in Boston. But the men she'd spent time with were decent guys. One had asked for sex a little too soon, but backed off when she denied him. She had never felt so much at risk after the walk to the lake and the hurried return. The man practically dragging her back to the house convinced her of his physical strength and his determination.

The lake was his. All the land around the lake was his. But there was no high fence on the lake side of the house. And lakes attract people just like those two men she had seen in the rowboat. That was the way to go. Even if all the land was his. Even if there were more fences further out. The lake was her best chance. Tomorrow, she would wait until he had left for work and then do her best to break through the brick wall and head for the lake.

She was a good swimmer as well as a good runner. Running in place made too much noise on the wooden floor, so she knelt down knowing she could still do push-ups and sit-ups at night without his hearing her.

Chapter 23

Walking back from the policy committee meeting, my thoughts returned to Jamie and I wondered if Shelby Vane could be involved. He matched the description of the man who'd gone into Jamie's apartment.

He'd asked to be on the committee even though the topic would inevitably be painful for him. But the attorney said his brother had been ruined, devastating the family. Would it be possible for him to kidnap a female student after what happened to his brother? What would've been his motive?

I stopped on the path, realizing I was short of breath. Dr. Shelby Vane might be the least likely suspect. But then I remembered how I had been fooled before. After last year, someone I trusted, a person I would never have suspected of harming another human being, was now in prison.

Perhaps, after all, I should suspect a big man in boots and I should definitely talk to Joe about Shelby.

It was dark by the time I reached the journalism school. I was about to enter the building when I heard a shout from the direction of the parking lot behind the school.

"Damn you, George. Goddamn you."

I rushed around to the back of the building and arrived in time to see two figures illuminated by the parking lot lights. The men were fighting, fists flailing, shouting at the top of their lungs.

"You miserable piece of shit. How dare you come to my house and bother my wife." The larger man landed a punch on the shorter man's face. The short man hit the ground, but bounded back up again and plunged head first into the larger man's stomach. George and Larry. Oh, no.

George pushed Larry hard, and again, the smaller man hit the ground. George stepped back and shouted, "Don't you ever come to my home and talk to my wife again, Coleman. I'll put you in the hospital next time."

Larry got to his feet unsteadily. "You destroyed my chances with the conference, you bastard. You knew how important it was to me and you wrecked it. For no reason except to make my life miserable. You're a sadist, Weinstein, a fucking sadist. That's what I said to your wife, and she didn't seem to be a bit surprised."

I started toward the two men, hoping to intervene. But George came at Larry again, fist raised. I heard the crack of bone against bone.

Larry Coleman lay on the ground, his ear bleeding, his chest heaving.

George glanced in my direction, then wiped spit from his chin. "You had no business saying any such thing to my wife. You're done, Coleman. I don't care what Red says, you're done. I'm going to see you leave this university even if you have to go out feet first." George turned on his heel and headed for his car.

Larry Coleman tried to get up but only made it to his knees. I hurried toward him to help. Larry swayed and struggled to get something from his pocket. A flash of metal and I saw the gun illuminated by the overhead lights. George Weinstein had reached his car a few feet away and opened the car door.

"Weinstein!" Larry came up on one knee and shouted as he raised his hand. George turned toward us. The sound of the gunshot deadened my hearing. We all froze in place. George's eyes grew wide as a small bloodstain slowly formed under his collar. His fingers gripped the top of his car door, then slowly uncurled and let go. His massive body slid to the ground.

I reached Larry and grabbed his arm. He lowered the gun but did not drop it. "Jesus, Larry, what are you doing?"

"He tried to ruin my career too many times. He's threatened me once too often. This time was the last straw." Larry spoke to the asphalt without looking at me.

I hurried to George who was seated on the ground against the driver's seat of his car, his head back, his hand over the hole in his chest. "George. I'm calling an ambulance. Stay still."

But George didn't respond, and as I dialed 911 on my cell phone, I realized he was losing consciousness.

Larry came up behind me. "Is he dead?"

I turned. Larry was white as paper and trembling, blood streaming from the side of his face where George's last blow had landed. He still held the gun in his hand. "I don't know. Why did you do this?"

Larry's breathing was fast and shallow. "I went to his house to make him take back what he did. Get my paper reinstated in the conference. To make him promise to leave me alone. His wife said he wasn't there. I went crazy. I screamed at her about George. She shut the door on me so I came back here to the school." For the first time Larry looked directly at me. "To see you, Red. But you weren't here either."

"What happened?"

"That son of a bitch came to my office. He went behind my desk and grabbed my arms and pulled me over my desk and through the door. I shouted for help but he dragged me down the stairs and out here. He punched me in the stomach, then again in the face. He said he was going to teach me a lesson." Larry started to hyperventilate, then stopped, licked his lips and looked down at George who was now lying on his side. Larry gasped. "Hah! Looks like I'm the one who taught him a lesson."

The sound of sirens caught his attention. "Red, you have to help me out on this. You of all people know what a bad guy Weinstein is. How he bullies and bullies, how he destroys." Larry's face was covered in sweat. He grabbed my arm. "Red. You gotta help me on this. Weinstein deserved it. He was going to beat me to death."

He put the gun back in his jacket pocket and put his face in his hands, sobbing.

An ambulance pulled into the parking lot followed by a police car. The paramedics raced to George, who had toppled over and lay on his side.

"Is he alive?" I asked the medic nearest me.

"Barely," said the man, working quickly over George's body.

Another police car pulled into the lot. I saw Joe running toward me. An officer ahead of him wrenched the gun from Larry's pocket and threw his hands behind his back. Then Joe's hands were on my shoulders, his eyes searching me. "Are you all right? What in Christ's name happened?" Then he released me and stepped back. "Did you get hurt?" His voice was low thunder.

"I'm fine, Joe. I'm not hurt. But I saw it. I got here just before Coleman fired the gun."

"Tell him, Red," Larry screamed as two police officers pulled him away and handcuffed him. "Tell them what a bastard Weinstein was and how he hit me first. Tell them about the threats he made. It was self-defense. You saw it. Tell them."

Joe's hand went into his pocket for his notebook. "Did you see it well enough to know if it was self-defense?"

I shook my head. "I'm not sure. They were fighting. George did hit Larry and knock him down. But..." I had to stop and catch my breath. Joe put one hand on my shoulder to steady me. I watched as Larry was put into the back of the first patrol car. Then the paramedics lifted George, put him on a gurney and wheeled him to the ambulance. "But George was walking away when Larry called out to him and fired the gun."

"So you can't say it was self-defense?"

"More like retaliation."

Joe looked at the ambulance as the paramedics lifted George's body up. We both watched the ambulance pull out of the parking lot, sirens whooping.

Joe moved closer. "You have always worried about those two, haven't you? You said you were afraid something God-awful was going to happen."

"And now it has."

Jamie

Jamie was almost asleep when she heard the door at the other end of the hall close. Then his steps in the hallway and down the stairs. She got up and went to the window. She couldn't see his car but she heard the engine start. For the first time, he'd left the house at night.

She dressed quickly and waited for what felt like an hour. When she didn't hear the sound of his car on the gravel driveway, she crept downstairs and turned on the light in the front hallway. The front door was padlocked but the door to the empty room was still unlocked.

She grabbed the skillet, the spoon and a large flashlight and hurried to the closet. The ironing board was still in place concealing the hole in the wall. She pulled it away and braced it against the opposite wall and went to work on the hole in the plaster. It was almost large enough for her to squeeze through. The flashlight revealed the studs and bricks beyond. The uprights were close together but she thought she could squeeze through. She struck the brick with the skillet. It didn't budge. She hit again and again, the clang of the skillet ringing in her ears with each strike. She stopped to rest her arm and catch her breath. She had been working for a long time. She ducked out of the closet to see if it was still nighttime. It was dark as pitch outside, so back she went to her work.

After what felt like an eternity she kneeled on the floor and scanned the brick wall with her flashlight. She found three bricks that had loosened enough to push out. She inhaled the fresh night air coming in through the hole. She was exhausted but worried if she stopped he would find the bricks on the grass outside and discover her escape plan. She bowed her head. *Please, God, give me the strength to keep going. I have to get out of here.* Her arms ached but she stood and lifted the skillet. It felt as if it weighed a hundred pounds. She struck the wall again. And again. And again. Tears streamed down her face. Two other bricks flew out. She struck again.

Chapter 24

I knew I would have to call the university president, Philip Lewis, even though he was ill and probably in bed. He would call the head of campus security, the provost, the university attorney, and heaven knows who else, and they would all likely converge on the school.

Joe arrived five minutes before the others after taking George's wife to the hospital to be with her husband.

"How is she? Hysterical?" I asked.

"Not at all. In fact, remarkably calm for a woman whose husband has just been shot in the chest."

"I should call her."

"I told her we'd go to the hospital later tonight after you met with the administration." Joe put his arms around me and held me silently for a moment. "Remember, you're strong, Red. You'll get through this mess too."

Noise in the outer hallway sent me to the door and Joe into Nell's office to make phone calls.

We gathered around the table in my office. Philip Lewis looked awful. Pale and shaky, he had gone from thin to skeletal. His disease was wasting him. I felt so sorry to drag him out. He reached out a thin hand and put it over mine. "Well, my dear, I guess our troubles continue after all."

I put my hand over his. "President Lewis, I can't tell you how sorry I am this happened. I have been trying so hard to keep the old quarrel between Coleman and Weinstein tamped down. I'm afraid I have failed you, the school, and the university."

Philip Lewis gave my hand a squeeze. "Red, you can't take responsibility for this. It's not your fault at all. You've made great progress pulling this faculty together. But sometimes the animus between individuals erupts into violence, no matter how hard we try to prevent it. It's not the first time for this campus, and, I regret to say, probably not the last." He withdrew his hand from mine to cover his mouth as a wracking cough shook his frail shoulders.

The university attorney took out a notebook. "We will probably see national media coverage on this. I should prepare a statement."

The provost sat silent, hands folded on the table. I could hardly look at him.

This would be the last straw. There would be no doubt in his mind I was unqualified to lead, to manage the problems of a group of faculty, to prevent scandal and protect my school. After this, there was no way he would give me the chance to be dean of journalism.

The chief of campus security turned to me. "Please tell us what you know from the beginning."

When I finished with the details of what I knew, Ezra McCready spoke. "Dr. Solaris, you say that Coleman went to Weinstein's house and then returned here when Weinstein's wife said her husband was not at home."

"Yes. That's what he told me, and my assistant had told me earlier that Larry had gone to George's."

McCready stretched his arms and massaged his hands. "And then Coleman told you that Weinstein had come to his office, grabbed him by the arms and dragged him downstairs and out to the parking lot?"

"That's what Larry said."

Without looking up from his notes, the attorney said, "And you saw Weinstein strike Coleman and knock him to the ground?"

"Twice."

McCready flashed a look of irritation at the attorney. "Please don't interrupt." Then back to me: "Dr. Solaris, did Coleman tell you how he got hold of the gun before being dragged outside?"

The security chief's chin lifted. "Good question, Dr. McCready. How did Coleman have time to get the gun?"

I shook my head.

McCready looked at me, his eyes dark, steady, and unreadable. "Perhaps Coleman had the gun with him the entire time."

"Took it with him to Weinstein's house and then kept it on him," said the chief.

McCready looked steadily at the chief. "There's really no way for any of us to know that, chief. And we shouldn't speculate." He turned to me. "You've had a rough time with these two, haven't you?" The look in his eyes was borderline sympathetic. "The president's right. You have no reason to apologize, Dean Solaris. This was a deplorable incident, but the fault lies entirely with Weinstein and Coleman."

I felt a twinge of gratitude to finally get McCready's support, quickly followed by a pain in my stomach. If Larry had the gun the whole time, perhaps he'd intended to kill George when he went to the Weinstein's house. If George died, Larry would be charged with premeditated murder.

Philip Lewis had recovered his breath. "The detective we saw in the outer office. Is he on the case?"

I nodded. Joe was always on the case when it came to my university. He was chief of detectives, and Mountain West was the biggest institution in Landry.

As if summoned by the mention of his presence, Joe knocked on the door and came in. "Sorry to interrupt, but I just spoke to the doctor at the hospital. George Weinstein is alive but critical. He's been taken into surgery."

Jamie

She smelled the liquor before she sensed him standing behind her. His hands slammed down on her shoulders. Jamie was frozen in place, still facing the hole in the plaster wall.

"Put the skillet down very carefully," he said, his voice almost a whisper in her ear, the smell of liquor close to her face. "You have been a very disobedient girl, Jamie Congers." His hands still on her shoulders, he turned her around and led her out of the closet. Then he grabbed the back of her neck and pushed her back upstairs. He opened her bedroom door and continued pushing her through the door of her bedroom. His hand was tight and painful around her neck. Jamie was sure he meant to hurt her. He shoved her hard. She fell across the middle of the bed on her stomach, arms outstretched, legs hanging over the edge. She closed her eyes listening to his labored breathing.

Several minutes passed. Then she heard the scuff of his shoes on her floor, the closing of her door, the click of the dead bolt being locked.

Silence.

Then she heard the thud of his steps going down the hall to his room.

Minutes later, she emerged from a daze of relief to the rhythmic banging of a hammer pounding nails into wood, the sound muted but coming from the empty room downstairs.

Chapter 25

The journalism faculty filed slowly into the conference room on the third floor. I stood at the end of the table, waiting for everyone to arrive. Our graphics teacher, Phyllis Baker, walked over and put her arms around me. "Oh, Red. I'm so sorry. I can't believe it."

Outside the conference room windows we could hear the babble of the media that gathered at the entrance. Cameras clicked and reporters thrust microphones into faces, shouting their questions while tugging on sleeves.

Police kept the media outside, but the inevitable noise seeped through.

"How's George?" asked Edwin Cartwell, running his thin hand over his even thinner sandy hair. Edwin had been George's close friend and ally last year, but the two seemed to have drawn apart.

"In recovery," I said, and turned to the faculty and staff members at the table. Some seated. Some standing. Two or three in tears. Not, I thought, because George Weinstein was beloved, or even liked, but because violence begets the nerve-wracking anxiety that brings us to tears.

I started without a greeting. "George Weinstein is in recovery. His condition is critical, bordering on grave, and it's too soon to tell whether or not he'll pull out of this, and if he does, what shape he'll be in." My words seemed rushed and absent of compassion. "I spent a little time with his wife last night while George was in surgery. Dorothy was quiet, probably in shock, but she seemed to be holding up as well as can be expected. I am sure she will welcome cards and letters, but I think phone calls should wait a while until we know more."

Quiet in the room, everyone waiting for the other shoe to drop.

I braced myself against the edge of the conference table. "Larry Coleman is in custody. I believe an arraignment is scheduled for later this morning."

"Do we know what caused it?" from somewhere in the back of the room.

Edwin saw the look on my face and came to the rescue. "George and Larry had been quarreling recently over a paper Larry was due to present in December. It seems that George was instrumental in getting the conference chair to change her mind about Larry's presentation and she cancelled his appearance."

A collective groan.

Another voice. "But is that reason to shoot a guy?"

"No, it's not," I said. "But as some of you know, there was a physical fight in the parking lot. And there were threats. You all are aware these two men had a history of animosity, and I guess this latest just pushed both of them over the edge."

Poor Larry, I thought. Such a smart, fragile, frightened man. How had he let rage take over so completely? And poor George. I would never have wished so awful a punishment as a gunshot wound.

"How would you like us to handle this with our students?" asked Phyllis.

I sighed. "Tell them the truth. They're journalists in training."

After the meeting, I went to my office to prepare for the press conference Philip Lewis and Ezra McCready were planning to give on the lawn in front of the library building.

I would be lucky to get through the crowd downstairs without giving a statement.

Nell followed me after gathering a stack of messages from her desk. On the top was Sadie's. Nell was so wise. She knew Sadie and

Joe would be the only people I'd want to talk to, and Joe was tied up at Larry Coleman's arraignment.

I called Sadie, whose first words were, "Well, chick, at least no one is trying to take a shot at you these days. At least not literally." Sadie had been my firm support and faithful friend all during the last year when I was sure my own life had been threatened.

"Oh, Sadie, I am so sad. I still can't believe what I saw last night and what this is going to mean for the school."

"For the next few weeks it's going to be perfectly dreadful. Every news outlet from here to New York will want a story, an interview, a piece of you. But then the news cycle will change and gradually, this will fade, at least until Coleman's trial. And you, my dear friend, will survive that. And the school will too. Count on it."

I staggered into my chair and put my head down on my desk. Larry Coleman arrested. George Weinstein in critical condition. Jamie Congers still gone. I felt trapped, no way out, no way to get away from tragedy and bitter and inevitable disappointment.

I struggled up from my chair and tried to shake off my gathering gloom. Don't give up. Throw up but don't give up.

I walked down the stairs to Edwin Cartwell's classroom where he taught news writing.

Edwin can be an awful stuffed shirt in faculty meetings, but he's vibrant in front of a group of students. I had learned over the past few months that whenever I felt depressed or defeated, the best cure was to watch Edwin teach.

A small studio room was adjacent to his classroom.

The studio had a window that looked into Edwin's class, and if I kept the studio room dark, I could sit there, unobserved, watching and listening as Edwin reminded me of the joys of great teaching. He moved among the students, pausing to look over a shoulder at what a student was writing on the computer, leaning down to whisper help with a problem, applauding a particular effort. They were writing about the shooting of George Weinstein.

Edwin moved back and forth and then to the head of the room where he raised his voice to remind them about a famous blind editor. Edwin was in full animation as he told how the editor would pound the floor with the tip of his white cane as he commanded his reporters to write vividly. "Make me see. Make me see," the blind editor would shout. The students were mesmerized.

Feeling uplifted and reminded of all the good that takes place in a university, I returned to my office. The phone rang just as I resumed my seat and I was grateful to hear Joe's voice. "Larry Coleman is out on half a million in bail. His wife paid it."

"Larry's wife is a successful attorney. She can manage that. What's the charge?"

"At this point, assault with a deadly weapon. But that could change to attempted murder if the evidence shows that Larry premeditated the shooting."

"Did he account for how he got the gun?"

"Well, in a way. He said he has been carrying the gun every day since last year when George and the others were bullying him. It's small enough to fit in his jacket pocket, and he has a license to carry a concealed weapon and permission from the university."

Nevada law permits gun licenses to any adult without a criminal record, and since it was against the law to bring a gun to a school, Larry must have also persuaded authorities that he faced substantial danger to get permission to carry concealed on campus.

"Is he still claiming self-defense?"

"He is. He insists George dragged him outside to beat the shit out of him, and that after being knocked down a couple of times, he drew the gun and fired."

"But I saw George walking away."

"I know. And you'll probably be called to testify when this thing goes to trial."

Great. That undid the revitalization I felt during Edwin's class.

"Another thing, hon. Wynan wants to meet later. He has some news about those land maps you found."

We agreed Wynan would come for dinner.

Joe would make lasagna. Joe's lasagna cheers me up almost as much as Edwin's teaching.

I had no sooner ended my conversation with Joe than Dorothy Weinstein called to tell me she was transferring George to a hospital in San Francisco. "The bullet injured his spine and I want a special neurosurgeon in the Bay Area to deal with it."

With Larry free on bail and George still alive and well enough to be flown to San Francisco, I felt a bit lighter on my way to the library to what I hoped was the last meeting of the week for the assault policy committee.

Manny Lorenzo had left a voicemail while I was on the phone, expressing his condolences for our troubles and, like Sadie, assuring me that in a few weeks, this too would pass. He made no reference to our competition for the job. Manny's call was clearly his way of telling me we were still good friends and he still had my back even as we competed.

Another surprise waited for me when I ran into my second rival on the path leading from the library. Victor Watts was balancing books and a laptop, but stopped when he saw me.

I was startled to see him still on our campus, and my face must have shown it. "What brings you back to Nevada?" I asked hoping to sound casual.

"Oh, I never left. My wife and I have rented a place up at Lake Tahoe. We love September sailing and are hoping for some snow later on so we can ski." Victor smiled. "However the dean's job turns out, I plan to enjoy Nevada as much as possible."

"Oh, how nice." A lame rejoinder if ever there was one. I wondered if he knew about Larry and George. He did.

"Sorry to hear about the shooting last night."

"It was awful. I hope it doesn't make you think badly about our school." I meant that.

"It doesn't. I was a war correspondent for over a decade. I know violence can show up anytime and anywhere."

I nodded, uncertain of what else to say.

He hitched up the books in his arms and turned to go. "On the bright side, Red, last night's episode may have relieved the school of two of its worst personnel problems."

The callousness of his remark stunned me. But as I watched him leave, I had to admit Victor Watts was shockingly right.

Jamie

Jamie's bedroom door remained locked until early evening. No breakfast and no lunch, and certainly no wandering about the house. She was being punished for the hole in the closet wall. Hungry and scared, she sat on the edge of her bed, waiting to hear the sound of his car in the driveway and wondering what he planned to do next.

The deadbolt on her door snapped. He was still dressed in a suit and tie. "There's food on the kitchen counter. Go downstairs and start dinner." His voice matched the coldness in his eyes.

Pieces of frying chicken, some potatoes, and broccoli awaited her. She pulled a bag of flour from the cupboard and poured oil into the skillet. The very skillet that she had once thought would gain her freedom was now back on the stove, a dent in the rim the only reminder of her escape plan.

The two of them sat through another silent dinner. As she cleared the table, she said, "What's going to happen to me next?"

"Nothing's going to happen to you next," he said. Dressed again in boots and jeans, he looked large and powerful at his end of the table. "You go back to your normal routine tomorrow. Except, of course, for the closet in the front room. That's obviously off limits."

"Did you repair the hole?"

"Not yet, but the door is nailed shut, so don't try anything. Or something else *will* happen."

Not for the first time since she had been abducted from the garage, Jamie felt a painful sadness. Tears filled her eyes and made her voice choke. She grabbed the back of her chair for support. "Why, why, why?"

"Why what?"

"Why have you taken me?" She swallowed hard. "What is supposed to happen between us? What are you waiting for? What exactly do you expect of me?"

He stared at her for a moment. "As I've told you before, I am waiting for you to get used to living here. To taking care of this house and someday, I hope, to feeling more comfortable with me."

She knew it was reckless, but she persisted. Why not? Her escape plan was ruined. What else could she try? "Tell me about your stepmother."

His face paled. "Why do you want to know about her?"

"I look like her, don't I?"

"You could be her sister...or her daughter."

"What was her name? Tell me about her. How did she come here?" Jamie sat down in her chair and stared back at him. His facial nerves twitched and his eyes widened. He pushed back in his chair and placed his hands flat on the table. His hands were strong but his nails were manicured. Not the hands of a rancher, she thought. What does he do for a living?

As he talked, some light came into his dark eyes. "My stepmother's name was Alice. She was hired as a day nurse for my mother, who had suffered a major heart attack and was too weak to care for me or the house."

"How old were you when Alice first came?"

"Ten or eleven. I don't remember."

"And after she came what happened?"

"In spite of everything Alice and my father did to take care of her, my mother died. Alice left for a while, but then my father hired her back to cook and clean and keep an eye on me during the day while he worked."

"How long did that last?"

"My father fell in love with her, and they were married the next year."

"And you loved her too."

The man turned away and seemed to be staring at some object in the middle distance, but not at Jamie. "Yes. I loved her too."

Jamie took a deep breath. *Go for it*, she thought. "Did you love Alice as a stepmother, or was there more?"

The man's chest heaved. "This is hard for me to talk about. But, as you seem to have guessed, there was more. Alice was in her twenties and much younger than my father. When I turned sixteen, I was taller than her, big for my age, and...and yes, I fell in love with her." The man turned to Jamie, his face red with exertion and pain. "And, yes, damn it, I know what you want me to tell you. My father caught us together one afternoon in the front room, which had been my mother's last bedroom."

"What happened after he caught you?" Jamie felt frightened and not so certain she really wanted to know what happened to Alice.

"My father took me out back and whipped me with his belt until I fainted." The man looked down at the table, his breathing heavy and labored. He pushed against the edge of the table. "When I came to, it was midnight and I was lying in the grass out back. Alice was gone. Her clothes, her books, everything."

"Did you ever see her again?"

"No. And that's enough. I understand your curiosity, but I can't talk about this anymore." He left her sitting at the table, wondering how she was going to maneuver her way out of the incredible task of replacing Alice.

Chapter 26

In addition to her proposal that we adopt the California policy on sexual assault, Karen Milton suggested the university hire a special person to handle all aspects of the process for dealing with that kind of crime. "As director of all student affairs, I am already too busy to cope with this. Other universities and colleges have created a new position and I think we should too. The title would be Director of Assault Prevention and Response."

"Would this person handle the entire process?" asked Howard.

"I think so," said Karen. "I'm not sure the provost should be the one to determine the appropriate discipline for..." She paused, uncertain as what word to use to describe the accused. "...violating the policy."

"Why not?" asked the attorney.

"The provost is also very busy, too busy to spend time reviewing and evaluating all the facts in an individual case."

Bridget jumped in. "Besides, the provost is charged with protecting the university's reputation. That's been one of the problems in the past at other universities. It's just natural for a top administrator to want to soft pedal or minimize events that make us look bad."

It was my turn again. "I'm not sure I agree. If we hire a special person to handle this, she or he will have to first receive the victim's complaint. Then console the victim and offer counseling, maybe even medical help. Then, that same person has to investigate and gather evidence that an assault has occurred..."

"So?" said Bridget, glaring.

"So, that person is likely to become an advocate for the survivor somewhere along the way. Which is fine. But someone else should render judgment."

"The Dean of Journalism is exactly right," said Shelby Vane from the other side of the table. "Another person, a neutral party, should decide the punishment if the accused is found guilty."

Bridget swung her head toward him. "Granted, Shelby. But, as I said, I don't get the impression that our particular provost is exactly a neutral party when it comes to this subject."

"Not very flattering to the provost," said Bud Chekovski, who must have wished he had a chairman's gavel because he slapped his hand on the table to get our attention.

"Folks, we're getting close to the time when we have to vote on all this and write it up. I suggest you continue emailing your thoughts to me and I'll see if I can construct a motion or two for our meeting next week."

My turn. "Bud, since you receive all our email, can you tell us where we seem to stand as a committee?"

Bud winced. "All over the lot, I fear."

Great.

Another chance to be part of a failed effort.

Howard chimed in. "Maybe we should use Red's idea and bring some student leaders into this discussion."

"Too late," said Bud. "Too damned late."

Karen Milton caught up to me in the hallway. "Red, you may get a call from a rather difficult parent."

"I get those calls all the time. What's up?"

Karen paused. She looked acutely uncomfortable. "Well," she began, "one of your journalism students, a young man, has been accused of assaulting a woman in her dorm room."

Disasters come in threes. Or was this four?

"Oh, Karen. I'm so sorry. Who is the man?"

"Normally I keep all the names confidential and there would be no reason to tell you this, but it's Peter Delacroix."

"Senator Delacroix's son?"

"Afraid so. The senator called me this morning and said she planned to talk to you before she goes to see the provost and the president. She's on something of a rampage."

"But Virginia Delacroix is one of the co-sponsors of legislation to protect female students. She's been a champion of women's rights for years."

Karen looked miserable. "Exactly. It's so ironic. And now her darling baby boy is being accused and the female student is demanding a university hearing and says she will file suit if we don't handle this effectively."

I leaned against the wall in the hallway. "I don't know Peter Delacroix very well, but he was in one of my classes last year. He seemed very shy. Not what I think of as the predator type."

"I know," said Karen. "That's what struck me when I talked to him. But you never know."

"Do you think the young woman is telling the truth?"

Karen leaned against the wall beside me. "I always think the woman is telling the truth. That's why I think we should hire someone else to handle these situations more objectively than I can."

I patted Karen's hand. "I'm sure you do your job well."

Karen gave me a grateful smile. "The Senator is sure to call you."

I started to leave, but Karen wasn't finished. "Watch out for her, Red. She's cozy with the provost."

The evenings were starting to get cooler; the roses that climbed the front of my house were in full riot, displaying their one last bloom before the first frost. I put Joe's lasagna in the oven, opened some red wine, retrieved the bourbon from the cupboard, and checked to make sure there was cold beer in the refrigerator. I also put on a fresh pot of coffee. I never know what cops are going to want before dinner.

Wynan had been checking out the status of the Morgan-Lassiter properties and Joe and his people had been scouting from Landry to Reno.

Joe was with Wynan when they drove up to my house, took off their dirty shoes, and left them near the kitchen door.

We spread the maps out on my kitchen table.

"Here's what I've found out about the Morgan-Lassiter parcels," Wynan said, pausing to take a long draft on the beer I'd given him. He pointed to the two-acre parcel outside of Landry. "The records say this one was sold in 1977 to a developer who left it alone for three years and then filed plans to build housing. But never did."

"And then what?" Joe asked.

"Then the land was acquired as an addition to a larger ranch owned by Andrew Vane."

I perked up. "I think I may know his son, Shelby Vane. He's a professor in our College of Agriculture at the university."

Wynan patted my shoulder. "That's great, Red, because when I went to the ranch house, the woman who answered the door said she knew absolutely nothing about that piece of land. She also made it clear that she had no interest in helping me. Said something about the police not being among her favorite people."

"I'll talk to Shelby," I said. "His older brother was falsely convicted on a rape charge some years ago, so that's probably why the family is so unfriendly to police. But I think Shelby respects me, and he might be willing to tell us what he knows."

Or, I thought, maybe I could pick up more information about Shelby before I tell Joe and Wynan my suspicions.

Joe unrolled another map. "What about this large parcel further away?"

"I had no luck at all with that one," said Wynan. "I'm not sure I even covered much of it. It's about fifty acres of mostly hilly land, and swamp. You can't drive onto it, and the perimeter I covered on foot was fenced in with eight- foot high steel construction fencing. I couldn't see any buildings or animals."

"Do we know who owns it now?"

Wynan took another draw on his beer and pursed his lips. "The owner is listed as a bank in San Francisco that acts on behalf of a blind trust. They pay the Nevada property taxes, but couldn't tell me the identity of the true owners on the trust, and even with help from San Francisco PD, it will take a California judge a month to get us into it." Wynan sighed and sat in a chair. "And, damn it, we don't have a month." A large hand came up and covered his eyes as his head bent down.

"Do you want to reconsider calling the FBI?"

The pain in Wynan's face was unbearable. "We still have no evidence of kidnapping. But I'm at my wit's end. Maybe we could use the Feds' help on this."

Joe put his hand on the older man's shoulder. "Let me see what I can do. I have some buddies in the Reno office."

I put my hand on Wynan's other shoulder. "Let's drop the maps for now and I'll set this table so we can eat supper."

Nell arrived as we were having coffee and placed a stack of papers next to Wynan. "There are about two hundred here," she said, gently taking Wynan's hand. "The printer wished us well."

Over large type reading "Missing Student" was a color photograph of a beautiful girl with cropped black curly hair, large brown eyes, and a full smiling mouth. An orange cat nestled in her arms. "Jamie with her cat, Marmalade, taken a year ago," said Wynan, a catch in his voice. "I guess it's time to put up posters. Probably should have done this days ago."

"I've lined up some journalism student volunteers for tomorrow," said Nell. "We'll put these up all over campus and the neighborhood of Jamie's apartment."

After Nell and Wynan left, I joined Joe on the couch. A baseball game was on television but Joe had muted the sound.

"I know we can't take any time away from here now, at least not until Jamie is found." I tucked my head into his chest. He stroked my hair. "But after the search is over, I would love a weekend in Graeagle."

Joe had inherited his parents' cabin in Graeagle, a place important to both of us. Last year after a dreadful quarrel and a serious breakup, Joe and I reconciled and he had taken me to the cabin. In Graeagle, we discovered how much we cared for each other and how good we could be together. We took walks, talked about all our hopes and fears, our childhood troubles, our professional ambitions. We enjoyed three days of good wine and wonderful lovemaking, and returned to Landry promising to give our relationship a chance to thrive.

Since that weekend, our lives had gotten busy again. Joe was appointed chief of detectives, and while his individual caseload decreased, his responsibility for overseeing all the others increased. Landry's not as big a community as Reno, but it is a college town and we did have our share of incidents. I had become involved in long hours working on the school's reaccreditation and my application for the dean's job, requiring a brilliantly written letter and an impressive updating of all my publications. Members of my faculty continued to come to me with problems of their own, plus dreams and desires and hopes I would be the next dean. If I got the job, I would have to keep all my promises to them. If not, who knew what a new guy would decide?

Joe and I spent time together, but didn't live together. Many nights we ate at the same table and slept in the same bed, but too often we were too tired for the long talks and the shared family stories that had bound us closer in Graeagle.

I chalked it up to his new responsibilities at work, but Joe told fewer jokes, had stopped talking about his family and his deceased best friend. He'd even stopped talking about the boy in Chicago he shot by mistake, the case that still put him into moments of deep depression. I knew, however, that particular tragedy was never very far from his mind.

I'd stopped telling him about my mother, who had disappointed me, and my father, whom I adored even as he disappeared into dementia. I knew Joe and I should talk more about what was important to us. I missed the conversations that revealed our deeper emotions and secrets. Those talks made us closer. But somehow we'd gotten out of the habit.

As Sadie had said, "You and Joe are like an old married couple who never got married. You spend time together but you are not building a life together. You have allowed routine to substitute for intimacy. You take each other for granted. You fight over small and stupid stuff and don't take the time to make up. That's a recipe for a very poor endgame."

I listened to Sadie, but when I just stared at my wine glass and didn't react, she said, "Red, you're getting ahead at the university but you are not getting younger. Do you even want to have a future or a family with this man?"

That's when I stopped staring at my wine and looked at Sadie. "I do want a future with Joe. But I don't know what that future looks like and...I don't know how to make it happen."

Jamie

Jamie hunted through every room in the house. In the laundry room, she found one of the knives he had hidden. Not the strong eight-inch blade, but a smaller one. She'd decided to make one more try to create another escape hole. This time she would try the floorboards. She knew the house had no cellar, but maybe there was a crawl space and she could get to it and find a way out. Knife and dust cloth in hand, she explored all the floors in the kitchen, parlor, laundry room, hall, every place to which she had access.

The man had left early again but had left her bedroom door unlocked. He'd only denied the empty front room, along with her ground floor view of the lake.

She longed to get back to the lake. Maybe she would see the men, the trespassers, in the rowboat again. Next time, she would shout at them no matter what.

Meanwhile, she poked and pried and prodded and scratched and looked for another weak spot.

By late afternoon her fingers were bleeding and the knuckles of her hands were raw. The dust cloth had not provided the protection gloves would have given. Damn, he would notice her hands.

She took the knife back into the laundry room and turned on the clothes washer. Once the agitator blades had started, she poked at them with the knife to see if she could damage the blades and stall them out.

The water turned pink with the blood from her fingers, but ultimately she had stabbed at the blades long enough to cause a sharp grinding sound and a halt. She would tell him she had tried to fix the washer and hurt her hands. That would explain the condition of her knuckles and fingers.

She put the knife back in his hiding place and sat at the kitchen table, waiting for his return.

Chapter 27

The next morning I woke up alone and feeling blue. Joe had dodged my suggestion we go to Graeagle for a weekend. "We'll see," was all he had said. I spent some extra time patting Charlie's silky head, feeling sorry for myself, and then shook off the blues. I still had not found any serious clues to Jamie's whereabouts, and I knew I should get back to focusing on that.

But focusing on Jamie was not to be. Senator Virginia Delacroix was waiting in my office.

"She's been here since eight. I gave her coffee." A roll of Nell's eyes told me to expect a tough meeting.

"Good morning, Senator."

Virginia Delacroix was a handsome woman, strong features, elegant navy blue suit, carefully styled blonde hair swept into a wave on one side of her face. "Good morning, Dr. Solaris. I hope you don't mind my visiting unexpectedly, but I also assume Dr. Milton told you I would contact you."

"She did. I'm sorry to hear about Peter." I sat down at my conference table opposite her.

She placed her coffee mug delicately on the table as if afraid it would break. She smoothed her hair and unbuttoned her suit jacket. "I need your help."

"I'm not sure what I can do." The senator's face was so tragic I felt a surge of pity for her.

"You were Peter's teacher last year?" She played nervously with a diamond and gold bangle on her wrist.

"Yes, he was in one of my writing classes."

"He spoke highly of you."

"That's nice to hear. Peter was a good student."

"I'm glad you remember him, and I was wondering if you could appear at Peter's hearing and speak on his behalf. He did well in your class, I believe." She ran her hand over her hair again. Her hand trembled slightly.

"Senator, I'm sorry. I don't think I can do that. It would be highly inappropriate for me to seem to take sides in a university hearing on...sexual assault."

"I don't know how well you know my son..."

"Not well. He was rather shy with me."

Her back straightened and her voice grew stronger. "Peter's shy with everyone. You probably don't know, most people don't, but Peter doesn't relate to other people very well. He never has since he was a little boy. He was an adorable baby, but then he changed. He keeps to himself. He can be charming, but usually he's quiet, unobtrusive. But, as you may have observed, he's terribly bright. It's just that drinking and sex are not part of his life."

I nodded, unsure of what to say next. How often have I heard a parent swear their college student didn't drink or was still a virgin?

She pushed her hair roughly away from her face. "It's impossible for me to believe Peter would do what he's accused of doing. He's a kind, gentle boy who can barely make conversation with young women. He doesn't date."

"That must be lonely for him."

"Probably, but that's his life. When I asked him about the accusations, he shook his head. And when I asked him if he had done anything to...with that girl, he burst into tears."

She paused to catch her breath. "Crying is very unusual for Peter. Except for occasional impatience with a math problem, showing his emotions is rare. Clamming up is what Peter usually does, and that's what he's doing now. He won't tell his father or me anything."

"I understand. I am so sorry about all this."

She stood up. "Dr. Solaris, my son is a loving, wonderful young man. If you can't help, I don't know where to turn."

"Senator, I wish I could help, but I can't get involved. Please believe that. Perhaps you should go back to Karen Milton and tell her what you have just told me."

She looked at her watch. "I doubt Dr. Milton will care. I'm due to see the provost in fifteen minutes. Perhaps Ezra will have some ideas on how to help my son." Ezra? Yes, of course.

The dull stare in her eyes told me we were done. "Thank you for your time." She picked up her handbag and left.

Yes, Senator, do see the provost, I said to myself. McCready may not give a damn about your son or any other student, but he knows a powerful political ally when he sees one.

I busied myself for about half an hour with paperwork before Nell came in. "Mark Froman is here. Wants to see you."

Oh, wonderful. Another tough meeting. Just what I needed. No doubt Froman would want to talk about the shooting. And he did.

Froman stood in my office doorway looking even taller than usual. Instead of the thousand-dollar suit he had worn the previous time, he was wearing jeans and work boots and a denim shirt that made his shoulders look particularly broad.

"Thanks for seeing me, Red. Sorry I didn't have a chance to change into a suit and tie, but my best mare had a bit of trouble birthing a foal this morning and I had to stay with her."

"How's the mare doing now?"

"Oh, fine. She's a good breeder normally. Just taking her time this morning. Foal's a bit spindly, but I think he's healthy." He sat at the table this time, avoiding the slender chair in front of my desk. I moved from my desk to join him.

"What brings you here, Mark?" As if I didn't know.

"The shooting, of course. What's the latest?" I had to make an effort to conceal my impatience. Once again, Mark Froman acted as if he was entitled to first party information no matter what the subject.

"Well, as it stated in the paper this morning, George Weinstein is at a hospital in San Francisco pending spinal surgery, and Larry Colman has been released on bail pending a trial for assault with a deadly weapon."

Now it was his turn to be impatient. He waved his hand dismissively. "I know all that. What I don't know is what you are going to do about Coleman. I mean, when you're going to fire him."

"Larry's a tenured professor, Mark."

"Yes, but you can fire him for cause even if he is tenured. Considering the man shot a colleague and seriously wounded the fellow."

Nell entered with more coffee. Mark looked up at her. "Any raw sugar around here?"

Oh, for Christ's sake.

Nell cocked her head to one side. She was used to arrogance. "Just regular white," she said, and turned on her heel without waiting to hear what was sure to be another request.

"Hmm. Females around here are a little touchy this morning." Obviously Nell and I and his slow-laboring mare were all lumped together in his mind.

"Very few academic units carry gourmet condiments," I said. "And we've been very busy and very sad at this school today."

He sipped his coffee and eyed me over the rim of his mug. "About firing Coleman."

Again, I practiced patience. "If Larry Coleman is convicted of a felony, he will automatically be terminated by the university. That's our rule. But until then, he is presumed innocent, and he claims self-defense."

"You were there. Was it self-defense?" How the hell did Mark Froman know I was there? Oh yes, friends and informants in the Landry Police Department.

"I wasn't there the whole time, and that's all I can say about it now."

Froman pushed himself away from the table with a grunt I'm sure was meant to indicate his displeasure with me. Oh well. One more opponent to my getting the dean's job probably didn't matter, since I was sure the provost was opposed. "You're a stubborn woman, Red Solaris. Thanks for the coffee."

"You're welcome."

He stood once again in my doorway, one hand on the frame, his head almost touching the top of the frame. He smiled. "And you're one beautiful woman. We should have dinner sometime. I'll show you around my property."

"I understand you have quite a lot of property."

"My dad bought half the county, and then after old man Lassiter died, I bought half of the other half." Froman laughed. "I mean it, Red. I think you and I could have a good time."

Lassiter property. Jesus. I worked hard on a smile back. "Thank you, Mark. But I don't think I'm your type."

His smile dimmed. "You're right about that. You're *not* my type. I like a smart woman, but I like a woman smart enough to follow good advice."

"You mean follow instructions."

"Maybe so. See you around, Red."

Lassiter property in Froman's possession. I had to follow this up. But how? I called Sadie.

"I need to know more about Froman. How can I find out?"

"Well, I suppose you could try his ex-wife, although I don't know how much she might be willing to tell you. Why do you need to know more about him?"

"Oh, Sadie. He's so pretentious. But for some reason, he quizzes me all the time about everything. I have to figure him out. Particularly because he just said something that suggests he might know about my missing student and I need a way to follow up without his knowing."

"Hmm. Interesting. I'll give you Diane's number in Dallas. I haven't talked to her in years, so I don't know if it will still work, but you could try."

The former Diane Froman, now Diane Peterson, picked up on the third ring, and didn't seem the least bit reluctant to discuss her ex-husband.

"What's that idiot done now?" She had a lilt in her voice that suggested she enjoyed hearing bad news about Mark Froman.

"Ms. Peterson, I don't know for certain, but did you ever know him to become involved with a student?"

She expelled a breath so loud I could hear it. "Are you kidding? Listen, Dean Solaris, I found him with a cheerleader in a motel room six months after our wedding. And I doubt she was his first student, just the first one I found."

"Were there others?"

A pause. "Not that I knew of, at least not while we were married. Cocktail waitress, yes. Our attorney's wife. And, believe it or not, once our attorney's seventeen-year-old daughter. Needless to say, no longer our attorney after that. But the cheerleader was the only college student I discovered."

So Froman liked them young.

Diane Peterson must have read my mind. "Dean Solaris, he liked them young and old and in between. The man thinks of himself as a great seducer. He's sure he can talk any woman into anything."

"Do you think he would force himself on a woman?"

"Christ, no. Mark's no rapist. He prefers to persuade his conquests. Took him two years to lure me into his web, but he got me. Man's all patience and persistence. Then, of course, once he's gotten you into bed, gotten you to fall for him, he gets bored and looks elsewhere."

"That must have been very difficult for you."

"It was. But I'm over it now. And glad to be home and happy in Dallas. I never much cared for his ranch."

"Did you know anything about the land he purchased?"

Another pause, this one longer. "I thought you were interested in his sexual exploits. Not his business." Her voice was lower and the lilt was gone.

"Only in land he might have purchased while you were married."

"Sorry. I know he bought land, but I don't know anything about it."

Jamie

She failed to find another way to escape. She searched through every inch of the house that was available to her. She tried again to work on the door to his room, hoping she would find his satellite phone. Nothing. She was once again seriously considering setting the house on fire that night so he would have to let both of them out. Wouldn't he?

She thought about pretending grave illness. She would put soap in her mouth and writhe around on the floor, alternately screaming and foaming. Unless he wanted her to die, he would have to take her to the hospital. Wouldn't he?

She would attack him with the skillet. Try to bash him hard. Not knock him out, but just hurt him badly enough for him to know how desperate she was, even willing to risk his violent retaliation, major injury, even death. He would have to take that seriously. Wouldn't he?

Midafternoon found her sitting in the parlor staring at the biblical verse on the wall. *Let a woman learn in quietness with all subjection.*

Maybe that was her way out. Submitting to him. After all, she wasn't a virgin. She'd known lovers in college. She could pretend long enough for him to drop his guard. And then one night after he had satisfied himself and fallen asleep...

The thought made her nauseated.

No, shouted every bone in her body. That was what he wanted, what he had been hoping for all along. She was not going to let him wear her down, exhaust her into capitulating to him. She would rot in that house before she would ever let him put his hands on her.

But meanwhile, she would pretend. She would soften him up. Maybe to the point where he would let her outdoors, untethered. He would watch her but all she'd need would be a minute outside the house.

Chapter 28

Shelby Vane's office was on the top floor of the Mountain West College of Agriculture, a wide, sprawling building on the newer part of campus away from the quad. Instead of the classic brick of the journalism school and its sister buildings in the center of campus, the Ag college was modern steel and glass. Even the elevator I rode had an outside glass window so you could see the treetops and the mountains beyond as you rose to the top floor.

I had not telephoned ahead. I hoped Shelby would be in his office, but I wanted to surprise him. Maybe if I flustered him a bit, he would impart more information about his family's ranch lands than he would if he had time to prepare for my questions. The Ag school website listed his office hours as three to four p.m. I hoped I wouldn't have to compete with too many of his students for his time.

He was alone, leaning far back in his chair, his boots on his desk, muddy soles to the doorway, eyes closed.

"Hi Shelby. Sorry to disturb your nap."

He jolted awake, surprised at my sudden entry. "Afternoon, Dr. Solaris," he stuttered, awkwardly righting his large body and moving from behind his desk to shake my hand.

He indicated a chair in front of his desk. "I wasn't asleep. I just wasn't expecting you. What brings you to the Ag school?"

I sat forward on the edge of the chair, my back straight, my eyes level with his. "Well, I have an odd request. I hope you don't mind a few questions about your family."

"If it's about my brother, I don't answer those questions anymore." His big face took on a sour expression.

"No, Shelby, it's not about your brother, and it's not about any of the committee issues either. And my name is Red. The formality-hating journalist, remember."

His features relaxed. "Yeah, I've heard your nickname at the school is the Red Queen." He leaned on his desk. "Okay, Your Majesty. How can I help you?"

"I'm interested in a piece of ranchland your family acquired some years ago, land that used to belong to someone named Lassiter."

Shelby leaned back in his chair again and put his big hands behind his head. "Hmm. You must mean the five acres on the south side of our ranch. Not great property, but my Dad always wanted it for the water rights and the grazing. We ran more cows in those days."

"So your father bought the land. When?"

"Why do you want to know?"

"My question involves a problem I'm having with a student, and it would really help me to know some of the history of that particular piece of land."

A shrewd look crossed his face. "Would your inquiry have anything to do with a policeman who bothered my mother yesterday? Tall black guy."

No way to avoid answering that. "It would. The tall black police officer is from Las Vegas. He and I are investigating a student problem that is connected to the name Lassiter and some land that Lassiter owned."

"Did Lassiter do something wrong? He's dead, you know."

"That's what we want to find out."

"Well, I'm still not sure how your student problem connects to my ranchland, but I'll tell you what I know. My dad approached old man Lassiter years ago before I was born and asked to buy those five acres. At first Lassiter refused. Wouldn't say why. A few years later, he offered the land but at such an outrageous price, my dad refused. Then we heard Lassiter sold it to a developer who went belly up. After Lassiter died, Dad finally bought the land from the developer at a decent price. Not a very exciting story, but that's it."

"Are there any buildings on that land?"

"An old shed for hay storage, but nothing else."

"Would you mind if the police and I took a look at the shed?" Shelby's eyes narrowed and he shifted his bulk in his office chair. I knew immediately my blunt request was a mistake.

"Okay, you better tell me what's going on that you need to come on my property with police."

I cast about in my mind for the best way to gain Shelby's cooperation without alerting him to my real purpose. "As I said, we are concerned about someone named Lassiter and some property he once owned."

"Did something happen on that property?"

Now it was my body shifting in the chair. "We don't know." Oh, God, this was not going well. "We're just checking out whatever we can, and we found that name in the land records."

"I see." He sucked his lips into this mouth and his eyes narrowed again. "You're being very obtuse, Red."

"I have to be, Shelby. Student privacy is a big deal with me."

"I understand. I'll consider your request as a favor to you. But I'll need some time to think about this, and to talk to my mother. She's very suspicious of police investigations since my brother's ordeal and I don't want to upset her." He rose from his chair. "I'll let you know, Red."

At dinner that night, Joe had that look on his face that meant he disapproved of my taking risks talking to large men with muddy boots. "What makes you so sure this guy Shelby couldn't be involved with Jamie's disappearance?"

"I can't imagine it." But the truth was I could imagine it. Big guy. Work clothes. Boots. Shelby Vane fit the vague description of the suspect. "I mean, of course it's possible, but Shelby seems like a gentle guy and he did say he would think about it."

An hour later, the phone rang.

It was Shelby. "I've talked to my mother and she says you can look at the shed, but she wants me to be with you when you do. So that means early morning before my first class."

I held my hand over the receiver and told Joe.

Then, "Shelby, thank you. Early morning is fine. There will be three of us—the girl's grandfather, one other police officer, and me."

"Come to the house at six and I'll take you to the shed."

Jamie

The man came home later than usual and brought Chinese take-out with him. The food containers were white with no writing on them, but the bag listed a Chinese restaurant in Reno. He had bought her new clothes at Macy's and she knew that was in Reno. He must work in Reno during the day. So this place must be in northern Nevada, and that meant she was still in the same part of the state as Mountain West University and what she knew would be her grandfather's search area.

She dished up the fried rice, sweet and sour pork, and cashew chicken into separate dishes. The bag also contained chopsticks and soy sauce in packets. She laid it out on the table and waited for him to come downstairs to the table.

He walked into the kitchen, and as he passed her standing near the sink, briefly touched her shoulder. "Smells good," he said, seating himself.

He seemed in a good mood so she smiled at him and he nodded in response. *Take it slow*, she thought. Her conversion had to be credible. He had to believe she was coming round to his point of view. He had to believe she could care for him. Make friends, persuade him to trust her enough to let her go outdoors. That was the plan.

He handled the food well with chopsticks. That was interesting. Manicured nails. Business suits. Could use chopsticks skillfully. The more she observed of him, the more she wondered how he was a working rancher at night and a businessman by day. And if he was a real rancher, he was also a cosmopolitan rancher. She wondered what more she could learn if she could get him talking again.

"I know you said you didn't want to talk about Alice anymore, but I do want to know more about her. I think if I did, I would be better able to understand how to adjust to these surroundings."

He paused, chopsticks holding a bit of chicken in the air. "What more do you want to know?"

Jamie cautioned herself. Proceed smoothly. Ask him nothing that reminds him of the day he and Alice were caught in bed, the day Alice left. "If she was much younger than your father, why do you think she married him?"

The man put down his chopsticks and drank from his glass of beer. She noticed that when he drank beer at night, it was always expensive Japanese or German beer, and he always poured the beer from a bottle into a glass. Another clue, perhaps. "My father was what you might call house poor but land rich. I think Alice hoped she could persuade him to sell some of his land and build her a new and much grander home than this one. I think Alice always wanted more comfort, more luxury, than living here provided."

"And what did your father say to that?"

"He used to say that living simply was the right way to live, the Christian way to live."

"And how did Alice react to that?"

"She eventually gave up on the bigger house idea and began to campaign to sell the land so we could move away and live in a city like San Francisco."

Jamie smiled. She adored San Francisco. "And did your father think that would be living in Satan's playground?"

The man smiled a small bitter smile. "He didn't say that exactly, but you're close to the mark."

"So it wasn't always a happy marriage."

"They fought."

Often, Jamie suspected. She wondered if a father who had beaten his son into unconsciousness would be violent with a contentious wife. "Did he beat her?"

"Once or twice. Usually he just took away her car keys and locked up the house. His usual response was to force her to sit in the parlor and read the Bible out loud to him for hours."

"So Bible reading was used as punishment?"

The man sighed and went back to picking at the chicken pieces on his plate. "I'm sure my father thought of Bible reading not so much as punishment as corrective behavior."

Jamie decided to take a risk. "Is Alice still alive?"

A fierce expression came into his eyes. "No. Alice is dead. But my father had nothing to do with her death, if that's what you're suggesting." He smacked his chopsticks down so hard they clattered on the plate. "Alice just packed up and left."

One more try before he gets too angry and stamps out of here. "And your father?"

The man's shoulders heaved. She saw sweat stains under the arms of his shirt. "My father died a year after Alice left. His heart was broken."

"Did you see her again?"

He was breathing heavily and she was sure his eyes had begun to water. "After my father died, I left here and went away to school. I looked for Alice every weekend and every vacation. I spent years and money, hiring private detectives and traveling all over the country. Finally, one of the detectives I had hired found her death certificate in Louisiana."

Jamie felt an honest sympathy for his pain, but she couldn't forget her plan. She had to establish friendship, trust and, abhorrent though it was to her, imply the possibility of intimacy. She could see the sadness in his face and softened her tone. "You never saw Alice again."

"Not until the first time I saw you."

Chapter 29

Wynan Congers was at my front door at five the next morning. I settled him in the kitchen and gave him a cup of coffee and some scrambled eggs and bacon.

"Thanks. And thank you for talking to this guy Vane. Do you think we can trust him?"

"I think so. And honestly, we don't have much else to go on right now."

"Joe said you felt sure Vane is not our suspect, that we haven't forewarned him. You know how dangerous that could be for Jamie if he has her."

"I do know. And I do know it's risky going to him. But it may be the only lead we have right now, and my instincts tell me Shelby is not our guy."

Wynan looked gloomily at his eggs. "Nell and her student helpers put all those posters up yesterday afternoon. Maybe they'll help."

I had grown to like Wynan Congers. Not just because he was a loving grandfather but also because he was a strong and decent man—a good man for Nell, and a good friend for Joe and me. I also hoped what I told him about Shelby was right.

The road to the Vane ranch was two lanes that ran through the country outside of Landry past a series of other small ranches. Cattle, mostly Black Angus, stood in sharp relief to the green grass that nourished them. The wooden split rail fences had just a touch of frost on the top rails, reminding us that September was full of warm days that began with cool mornings and would soon turn to late fall and crisp cold. Just before the turnoff to Shelby's we came upon a sod farm, still operating with giant sprinklers keeping the sod green and ready.

The Vane ranch house was built low to the ground, a long one-story structure with a barn off to one side. Purple asters and orange chrysanthemums lined the driveway. A tall cottonwood, bright with brilliant yellow color, dominated the lawn.

The moment Joe and Wynan saw the owner on his front porch, dressed in boots, jeans and baseball cap, I could almost hear a simultaneous click in each of their well-trained police minds. Shelby did look very much like the description of the suspect. Joe gave me a sideways look that registered his renewed doubts about the wisdom of my visit alone to Shelby Vane.

"Morning," we all said at the same time. Behind Shelby, we could see an older woman's face in the window, her mouth drawn thin with disapproval. A Jeep appeared from behind the house, driven by a boy who looked like Shelby probably did when he was fourteen or so. The boy jumped out and handed his father the keys.

"Not much of a road going to the shed," said Shelby, indicating we should all pile into the Jeep. I sat in back with Wynan, Joe in front with Shelby. The boy stood on the bottom step of the porch, watching us in silence as his father started up the engine and we jolted down the drive. About a quarter mile on gravel and then we turned into a field bisected by a narrow dirt path. The Jeep jumped and bucked at every rock in the road. Past a stand of yellowing cottonwoods, we saw the shack, small and weathered gray.

Shelby stopped the Jeep and climbed down. Without saying anything to us he strode toward the shed and lifted a large two-by-four that was across the door.

The door swung open.

Inside were bales of dry hay and a rusted wheelbarrow with a shovel and scythe in it. The shed measured about ten by eight feet, hardly large enough for two people to enter, much less for a large man to keep a girl captive.

"If she was in here, she'd have escaped easily by now," Wynan said. "Unless she was tied up good."

Shelby looked startled. "You think someone was in my shed?"

"No," said Joe, who had entered the shed and was inspecting it with his flashlight. "There's no sign anyone has been in here recently." He emerged and brushed the dust off his pants and stamped his feet.

Shelby put one foot up on the running board of his Jeep and twirled the keys in his hand. "Anyone going to tell me what the hell is going on, and why we all had to get up at the crack of dawn to get over here?"

"We're investigating a problem with one of Red's students, Dr. Vane. That's about all I can tell you right now." Joe brushed off more dust and turned to get back in the Jeep.

Shelby's neck turned red and the color crept up to his cheeks. "Sorry, Detective, that's not good enough. You're talking to a man whose brother was railroaded by false accusation. Tim did time in state prison for a crime he never committed. So I need to know more. Why is my land, my shed, even of interest to you guys?"

Joe looked steadily at Shelby and made a decision. "Because we believe that a man who may be a member of the Lassiter family has had something to do with a student's disappearance. And this was once Lassiter land."

Shelby inhaled deeply. "Okay. But this is just one of the smaller parcels of Lassiter land. There's a much bigger one about twenty miles from here. Why don't you look there?"

"I tried," said Wynan. "But it's protected with high steel fencing and I couldn't see much when I walked a couple of miles of the perimeter."

"Yeah, that was old man Lassiter," said Shelby. "He never wanted anyone to get into there. His house was way back in the woods and he had no trespassing signs posted on all sides of the land around."

Wynan frowned. "I didn't see a house."

"You won't see it, either," said Shelby. "The house is only accessible by a dirt and gravel road that leads in from the north side of the property. And that road has an eight-foot gate and an electric fence and warning signs."

Joe, Wynan, and I must all have looked incredibly dispirited, because Shelby stopped twirling the keys and said something unexpected. "I know a way into that property on the south side."

"That's great, Dr. Vane. Can you show us?" asked Wynan.

Joe raised his hand. "Wynan, we don't have a warrant to enter that land."

Shelby shook his head. "Well, it's risky going in anyway. The only safe time to sneak in is late afternoon, when the watchman goes home."

"There's a watchman?" Wynan looked surprised. "Hell, the property must cover fifty acres. Who can watch over a spread that large?"

"He drives a Jeep full-speed over that land. I've also seen him on a dirt bike. Most of the property is scrub pine and sagebrush. The only trees and grass grow alongside a lake in the middle of the property. I think the watchman probably pays his closest attention to the south side. Some kids cut an opening in the south fence last year and got in. The lake is a little wider on that side, and when the wind's up, it's good for windsurfing."

Joe moved closer to Shelby. "Have you ever gotten into that property?'

Shelby looked sheepish. "If you promise not to arrest me for trespassing."

"I promise."

"I was on that lake last week, and it's a eutrophic lake, if you know what that means."

"Shallow, cloudy, full of plants."

"You remember your biology, Detective. Well, my friend, Skip Kramer from Biology, wanted to go up there and gather some specimen plants for his lab. We know how to get in and out of there, even with two of us portaging a small boat through a meadow and squeezing through a small opening in the fence. A good thing, since the other day we saw that watchman's Jeep barreling down on us like a bat out of hell. We barely made it back to our truck."

"Did you use the opening the kids made?"

"Nope. Skip and I made another opening earlier this summer and then concealed it with tree branches so the watchman couldn't spot it easily."

"Can you take us there?"

"I can, but not today. I take my mother into Reno for dialysis today and I can't skip that. There's no one else except my boy, who isn't old enough to drive on the roads. I can take you there tomorrow, but if we want to avoid that watchman, we should go late in the day. Sorry, that's the best I can do."

"A student's life may be at stake," I said.

"I understand, but you're not even sure your student is up there at Lassiter's place. It's pretty far away. And one thing I am sure of is my mother's poor health. Tomorrow's the best I can do."

"We've waited this long, we can wait until tomorrow," said Wynan. "Besides," he said, "I want to try for a warrant so that if we find the house, we can get into it for sure."

Joe turned to him. "You really okay with delaying, Wynan? Getting a warrant's a long shot with no compelling evidence."

"I know a judge who might help me out, and just might also accept my word for probable cause." Wynan dug his hands in his pockets and paced back and forth in front of the shack. "But I'll have to fly down to Vegas to see him and talk him into it, so I need the extra day to do that. I want to be absolutely sure we can get into any building on that property."

Shelby took his foot off the running board and put his keys into the ignition. "So we'll go tomorrow then. How about we meet at my house at four tomorrow afternoon? I think the watchman may leave the property about four thirty, so we can dodge him."

Shelby looked at Joe and Wynan, then made a sucking sound with his lips over his teeth. "I know you men are both cops, but that watchman is as tough and mean as a rattlesnake. Rumor has it he was in Special Forces. He caught Skip and me one day last summer. We managed to persuade him to let us get on our way and not to come back. But he carries a Bushmaster semi-automatic rifle and, if we see him again, I'd rather not be party to a gunfight."

"Did he spot your opening in the steel fence?"

Shelby's brow furrowed. "I don't think so. He seemed to be satisfied when we practically ran with the boat. We left him by the lake. And as of last week he doesn't seem to have inspected that section of the fence. But you never know. We may have to create another opening. Bring wire cutters."

Jamie

The house did not have a vacuum cleaner so Jamie used a stiff whiskbroom to clean the upholstered furniture in the parlor. She pulled the seat cushions off the sofa and carefully brushed the base of the sofa. The broom caught on the crevice that separated the base from the back. Freeing the whiskbroom required her to poke her fingers into the crevice. Something hard and sharp was in there. She poked again and flipped out a small plastic card. It was a Nevada driver's license.

She took the driver's license to the window to examine it. She stared at the image in disbelief. It had been issued to Alice Lassiter. The face in the photo on the license could have been Jamie's. So could the height and weight. The birth date was April 7, 1957. The date the license should have been renewed was April 7, 1987, when Alice was thirty years old. But according to the man, Alice had left the house when she was still in her late twenties. A chill ran through Jamie's body. Who packs up her clothes and books and leaves without her driver's license?

Jamie tucked the license into her pants pocket. She replaced the sofa cushions and went back into the kitchen. An hour later found her still standing by the sink, staring out the window at the meadow and the steel fence, still rehearsing the questions she wanted to ask without arousing his suspicions. She was certain she needed to find out much more about the time Alice had spent in the house.

But that evening was not to be her opportunity. The man came home late, slamming the car door and then the front door and calling out from the hallway. "I've eaten. Feed yourself and go to bed." His voice sounded angry, very angry. He did not appear in the kitchen but she heard his footsteps loud and hard on the wooden stairs as he went up to his room.

Chapter 30

It had not been a good day. Even though Joe and I were excited about the possibility of finding Jamie on the Lassiter property, we were still concerned by Wynan's willingness to wait for another day to hone in on his granddaughter's whereabouts.

"I think Wynan's scared," said Joe, after we dropped Wynan off at the Reno airport and were headed back to Landry.

"Of course he's scared. So am I. But why not insist on getting into that land? Why not go to Shelby's friend in Biology and ask him to help us get through that fence *today?*"

"All I can figure is Wynan wants to do this by the book," said Joe, turning onto the highway that led to Landry. "He told me last week when we were having a beer together that he'd once bungled a kidnapping case by rushing in without a warrant. The kidnapper's attorney cited all the illegal search and seizure stuff and the case never even went to trial."

"And the kidnap victim?"

"Her body was found years later buried in the basement of the house, but by that time the kidnapper had relocated to some Latin American country that doesn't extradite."

"So Wynan wants to be careful this time. But what will he use for probable cause to get this judge in Las Vegas to issue a warrant?"

"God knows. We'll just have to wait and see."

*   *   *

Nell was agitated when I arrived at the office. "Sorry I'm so late," I said to her. "We spent more time than I had expected at the Vane ranch." I told her about the plans for tomorrow.

"That's hopeful," she said, "but meanwhile the provost's office called and McCready wants to see you in the president's office at eleven and it's already five minutes to."

I hurried to the ladies room on the third floor, splashed some water on my face, combed my hair and pulled it back into a bun. I was still wearing the sweater and slacks I had worn to the Vane ranch. I preferred to wear a suit to President Lewis's office, especially if Ezra McCready would be there. But it was too late to change, so I decided to hope for the best and set off across campus.

The day had turned warm and I regretted the sweater as I walked quickly across the quad to the administration building. The bell tower tolled eleven just as I crossed the wide lawn, still green and punctuated with beds of white vinca and alyssum. A breeze had come up and the leaves stirred in tall oaks that lined the edges of the lawn. This was where the summer commencement had been held last June and I wished I could turn the calendar back to that day. I was happier then. The former provost had just told me my faculty wanted me to apply for the permanent dean's job. My best senior student had graduated magna cum laude and I had hugged her so hard when she came off the podium, I nearly lifted her out of her shoes.

But that was then, and now it was early fall. The oak leaves would soon turn dark red. The fabled Nevada winds would blow them to the ground and snow would follow. And I had been summoned to the president's office. I was half-convinced I was about to be fired, or told that one of my rivals was getting the job and I would go back into the faculty.

Even with assurances that the shooting of George Weinstein had not been an event I could have prevented, I felt sure it was going to block my career. Perhaps for a long time.

I climbed the steps to the administration building slowly. Even though it would make me late, I wanted to enjoy the warmth of the day and the beauty of the campus for a few more seconds.

The clock on the wall of the president's office read five minutes past eleven. His secretary, a cheerful brunette named Margie, stood up and smiled. Margie probably weighed two hundred pounds, but she moved swiftly from behind her desk to give me a hug. "So sorry about the shooting," she said into my ear.

"Thanks, Margie."

Margie gave me a rueful smile. "Go on in," she said. "They're waiting for you."

The president's office at Mountain West is impressive. Spacious and paneled in mahogany, furnished with heavy leather couches at the far end and a large round beautifully polished conference table in the middle of the room. Tall windows overlooked the quad, and Philip's desk was a small eighteenth-century table set to the side near the windows so the light fell on its surface.

Nearby was a small circle of four leather chairs, two of which were occupied by Philip Lewis and Ezra McCready. Both rose and indicated a third chair for me.

"I apologize for being late," I said, "but I've been occupied at a location we thought might lead us to our missing student."

"Ah yes," said Philip Lewis. "Ezra showed me your memo about her. Beautiful girl. I saw the posters as I walked onto campus this morning."

"Another problem for the school of journalism," said McCready. He was wearing a lightweight wool suit and shoes as highly polished as the conference table. His hands were folded in his lap and his long legs stretched casually out from the chair. Cool and calm, with a smugness in his expression that infuriated me.

Philip Lewis leaned forward in his chair and put his thin pale hand on the armrest of mine. "Red, we called you here this morning to discuss the plans for the rest of this fall semester in the school of journalism—plans for dealing with the Weinstein shooting and a missing student, as well as the governance of the school and the preparation for the last of the reaccrediting meetings in October."

I could hardly bear to look at either of them. We had slaved over the written requirements of the accrediting team all summer long, and now I hated the thought of going through the final meeting with the accrediting team when we were in crisis mode.

Ours was one of the select group of accredited journalism schools in the country and had been for decades. But to keep our status, every seven years we were examined by a team of distinguished academics from other schools. They looked at everything: graduation rates, faculty research, teaching evaluations, every dimension that could be seen to describe our success or failure. They would insist on interviewing the entire faculty and getting at all the dirt. How was I going to pull us together in time?

"The accrediting team is bound to be concerned about the leadership of the school," said McCready.

Oh shit, here it comes.

"And for that reason we are not going to name a new dean at this time," said Lewis. "In the interests of stability, it seems best for you to stay as interim dean until after the team has left. The faculty is very supportive of you and we want to present a cohesive unit to the accrediting team."

Except for Lewis' shallow breathing, the room was very quiet. McCready sat up in his chair and crossed his legs.

"I see." My head was starting to pound. The air felt much too warm.

Philip Lewis rose unsteadily from his chair and called for his secretary. "I am going back home now for a nap. You and the provost can continue this discussion here if you like. Margie can bring you some coffee or some lunch."

After Lewis had left, the provost sat back in his chair and stretched his legs out again. "I'm wondering, with all your responsibilities at the school, if it's wise for you to also continue serving on the sexual assault policy committee."

"I'm not sure how one thing has to do with the other."

The provost turned his head and looked at me, dark eyes flashing. "I'm thinking of your time. You will have a great deal on your plate in the next few weeks, what with the publicity the shooting will bring, not to mention preparing for the accrediting team."

"Much of the data preparation for the team has been done over the summer, Dr. McCready. And I think the publicity will die down for a while until we know more about George Weinstein's future health problems, and until Larry's trial date comes up." I was dying to know about his meeting with Virginia Delacroix. "May I ask a question?"

"Ask."

"Did Senator Delacroix see you?"

"She did." He gave me a stern glance. "I fear there again we have another example of your awkwardness at handling people."

"I couldn't do what she requested of me."

"No, you couldn't. But you could have handled her better."

"How?"

"She's a United States Senator. I think she felt she had been treated somewhat dismissively when she left your office." He got up and walked to the window. "Don't worry about her. I took care of her concerns and you can put the matter out of your mind."

What in hell did that mean?

McCready turned back to me. His hands were clasped behind his back and he looked very much the stern headmaster about to discipline an errant school child. "Now I have a question," he said. "How about the missing student?"

I swallowed hard. "The police think they have some good leads on where she might be. I'll know more tomorrow."

He turned his head and looked again toward the windows. "Anything you can share?"

"Nothing firm. But I'll let the administration know when I do."

"Well." He walked away from me, hands still clasped behind his back. "I still think your time should be spent on the issues of the school instead of university assault policy."

"I disagree," I said to his back. "I think I have an important contribution to make to any future policy that so seriously affects the life of our students, especially our female students. In fact, in light of the disappearance of..."

He turned suddenly and walked back toward me until he towered over my chair. "Do as you please, Dr. Solaris. You seem accustomed to getting your way."

I stood up and faced him. "I just believe I can handle this, Dr. McCready. Really, I do."

He cocked his head. "I'll be watching carefully. I will be very disappointed to read more bad press for this university or your school or your colleagues. Philip thinks highly of you. As for me," he said, with a thin smile, "the jury's still out."

"I am trying hard not to disappoint you, Dr. McCready."

On my way across the quad, I called Sadie on my cell phone. "Lunch? I could use a friend and a glass of wine."

"I'll see you there."

Gormley's Grill was crowded when I walked in, but Sadie had the table that Wilson, the owner, always kept for her in the corner of the room. She sat quietly, a dim overhead light shining on her beautiful hair.

I sank into the chair opposite her and Wilson brought me a glass of Pinot Noir.

I told her about the morning at the ranch and the meeting in the president's office.

I talked nonstop and Sadie listened patiently, her blue eyes fixed on me, a little smile of sympathy turning up the corners of her mouth.

"McCready's worried about you, you know," she said, when I paused in my narration and took a breath.

"I know. He's sure I am going to mismanage something."

"No, I don't think that's why he's worried. He worries about you succeeding, not failing."

"I don't get it."

Sadie smoothed her hair and reached out for my hand. "Listen. If you become the next dean of journalism, you'll be the youngest dean on campus. And if you keep building the journalism school and getting it through its difficulties and generally doing well, you'll develop a reputation for success on this campus. The Regents will notice you, and you just might be a candidate for McCready's job someday. Especially if Philip Lewis retires and we get a new president who doesn't like his second in command."

"Me. Provost? C'mon, Sadie. Not a chance."

"Not now, no. But someday. And that's what worries McCready and probably what tempts him to clip your wings now…if he can."

Sadie was always on my side. And probably wrong about the provost. Then again, I found myself smiling at her idea. Maybe I had more rivals than I realized.

After lunch, I stopped by Karen Milton's office in the Student Services Building. Her office was small but cozy, with a large window overlooking the quad. A couch and two armchairs were placed on either side of a coffee table. Watercolor paintings of Nevada scenes hung on pale blue walls. A coffee machine and china mugs sat on a corner table along with a box of tissues. A bouquet of fresh flowers centered on the coffee table. This was a room for quiet talk, a place where students could share their worries and unburden their troubled minds.

I sat in the armchair opposite hers. "I was with the provost this morning. He scolded me for failing to handle Senator Delacroix properly."

Karen nodded her head.

"He said he would manage the Peter Delacroix situation. Has he?"

Karen gave me her gentlest smile and spread her hands across her lap. "There is no Peter Delacroix situation anymore. The girl has withdrawn her accusations along with her request for a hearing."

"Oh, Karen. Why? Did the Delacroix parents buy her off? Is that what McCready advised them to do?"

"I don't know about the provost's advice. But I do know the girl comes from a small rural town. I doubt her family is rich. However, at no point in our conversation did she mention Peter's family."

"Did she seem intimidated?"

"No, and I have seen a number of victims who were intimidated. If not by the accused, by his friends, or by her friends. I've worked with a lot of girls—and a few boys—who'd been bullied into silence."

I rubbed the soft upholstered arms of my chair. "Did the Senator tell you anything about Peter?"

"Oh yes, I got a call about how he's much too nice and much too bright and much too shy to have ever done what he was accused of doing. I also got a strong indication that the parents were convinced the girl was running a scam to get them to give her money. The Senator seemed certain that, if anything happened in that dorm room, it was the girl seducing the boy."

"So, what do you think now?"

Karen leaned back so the sun coming in through her window warmed the side of her face. "I think I will never know what happened between those two students. I'll never know what was consensual and what was forced."

"And you don't know whether or not the provost encouraged the girl to withdraw?"

"Nope. I don't know that either."

But my stomach told me that Ezra McCready had a great deal to do with the dismissal of an accusation against Peter Delacroix. Bringing a United States senator's son into a university hearing would simply not have fit into the provost's agenda. I leaned toward Karen who looked gloomy and defeated. "I'm so sorry. What a discouraging outcome."

Karen smiled weakly. "But not an unusual one, I fear. Day after day, my mission in life is to create a safe and successful campus. Yet I know that often a reporting student or a responding student fails to believe me when my investigation and my findings don't support their views of what really happened."

"Do you think we should just turn all these cases over to the police?"

This did not improve the look on Karen's face. "The police don't always do any better than I do. A number of complaints that go to them never get to trial. The cases stack up in the department files. The prosecutors don't want to touch anything that doesn't seem like a sure win."

"But Karen, sexual assault is a crime. If a guy breaks into a girl's dorm room, slaps her around, steals her wallet, she calls the police, right?"

"Maybe. Maybe not."

"What if he beats the crap out of her, breaks her nose? Then doesn't she go to the cops?"

Karen leaned across the coffee table and took my hand in hers. "Red, your heart's in the right place, and of course you're making sense. But relationships between people, especially sexual relationships, can often lead them to stupid and cowardly decisions."

I sat back. "I should know this. When I was a newspaper reporter back in Ohio, I was amazed at the number of domestic violence cases that never went to court."

"Bullies often go unpunished. And if I rely solely on the police to get the campus bad guys, I may end up letting serial rapists get away with it and roam free around here. Did you read about that case back east last month?"

"Three Ivy Leaguers in a parking lot outside the dorm?"

"Do you think that was their first attack?"

I sat with Karen quietly. We drank some tea. The sun left the side of her face and highlighted the rug under the coffee table. Enough talk of Delacroix and serial criminals.

I liked Karen and my instinct was to cheer her up. "Sadie Hawkins thinks that McCready is worried about my becoming dean of journalism because it would put me in a position to compete for his job someday in the future."

I was rewarded with a grin. "Sadie Hawkins is one of the smartest women I have ever known. Next to you, Red Solaris."

Jamie

As Jamie washed the dishes from her own supper, she heard his footsteps on the stair and then in the hallway. He was still dressed in his suit pants with an old sweater over his shirt. He walked to the refrigerator and extracted a handful of ice cubes that he plunked into a glass. Then he produced a bottle from the top shelf of one of the cupboards and poured a drink. He turned to her. "Want one?"

She nodded. A drink might steady her nerves.

He poured a second glass and handed it to her. They sat at the table. "Sorry about dinner tonight," he said.

"That's all right," she said, trying to sound sympathetic. After all, he was being polite, and she wanted to take advantage of any sign he might change his mind about keeping her locked up.

"Bad day?" she asked.

"Frustrating day."

"You said when you came in you had already eaten. Sure you're not hungry? I could fix something."

His head lowered and his hands circled his glass. "I stopped at a bar on the way home. I had a mediocre cheeseburger and a few beers." He took a long swig. Oh, God, she thought. He's drunk.

"Maybe I should go upstairs and leave you alone."

"No, Jamie. Stay here. Talk to me. It will distract me."

She sipped on her drink. It was risky talking to him, staying in the same room with him if he was as drunk as she suspected. But if he were drunk, maybe she would have a chance to overpower him. Maybe. The muscles in her arms tensed. She waited, thinking. She leaned in. "What would you like to talk about?"

His head came up. His eyes were a little bloodshot and his speech slurred slightly. "You always want to talk about Alice, so what else do you want to know?"

"How old was she when she left?"

His head cocked from one side to the other. "Twenty-six."

"So she was ten years older than you."

"Yep."

"And twenty-three when she married your father."

The man swayed in his chair, nodding his head.

"Did she drive a car?"

He looked puzzled. "Of course she drove a car. How else would she get here to take care of my mother and me? Why do you care about that?"

"I just wondered if her car was gone when you regained consciousness and discovered she had left?"

The man slouched forward, elbows on the table. He reached for the bottle and poured himself another drink. "Alice was gone. Her clothes, her books, her car, every goddamned thing that was hers was gone. Gone for good." His fists clenched and the gesture reminded her of his strength.

Jamie stood up quietly and left the kitchen. She'd never heard him swear. But for all his claim to strict religious beliefs, he had taken the Lord's name in vain. And that alarmed her. There were too many things about this man that didn't add up. What profession allowed him to live so far from civilization? The house, its furniture and his work clothes suggested he was poor, at least working poor. His well-tailored business clothes said he had money. His decision to kidnap her, imprison her, and conduct his twisted idea of a courtship said he was mentally unbalanced. And yet there were times when he seemed rational, even shrewd.

As she sat on her bed, she decided he was a complete enigma. She also began to wonder if she couldn't overpower him, might she still outwit him? He'd just revealed some vulnerability. The thought made her more determined, but not less afraid.

Chapter 31

A long memo from Bud Chekovski sat on my desk when I returned from Karen Milton's office. It started with his summary of all the conflicting points of view that had been emailed to him from the committee members. He had managed to squeeze what he called "some consensus" out of all our writings and his memo ended with suggested motions for us to consider at the next meeting.

His first motion was to adopt the California policy, "yes means yes," with consent required throughout any sexual encounter.

The second motion was to create a new position of Director of Sexual Assault and Response. This was Karen's idea and addressed her hope to be freed of the responsibility for receiving and investigating complaints.

The third described a committee of selected faculty who would preside over any university hearings and stipulated that attorneys or other representatives could be present for both the accuser and the accused, although the lawyers would have to remain silent during the hearing. No doubt, this reflected Shelby's desire for due process.

The final motion called for a three-person committee of the university lawyer, one faculty member, and one student who would determine the punishment should the accuser be deemed guilty by a "preponderance of the evidence."

I had hardly finished reading when Bridget Thomas called in a state of what my father used to call "high dudgeon." Her intense indignation roared through the phone. "Lawyers in the room? To do what? Intimidate the girl? Scare her into thinking she had some lawsuit to face if she didn't present an unlikely eyewitness or irrefutable forensic evidence? Holy shit, Red, this is awful."

Bridget went on and on. While I was listening patiently, an email popped up on the computer. The provost had obviously read Bud's memo even though it was supposedly only sent to committee members. It was clear the provost had little use for university committees when it came to conducting hearings.

Perhaps that's what he told Virginia Delacroix. Had the provost promised the senator he would put an end to special hearings on assault? Had he promised her he would handle matters himself?

Poor Bud Chekovski. He was in for a drubbing.

The provost's email went on, "As for a triumvirate debating an appropriate punishment, I regard that as a recipe for injustice. That decision is mine alone."

I had a nagging suspicion young Peter Delacroix had been dealt with gently, very gently.

I put Bud's memo back in its envelope, said goodbye to Bridget, and closed my computer.

Home and Joe were all I could think about. Finding Jamie Congers was the only plan my mind could follow.

Wynan called from Las Vegas while Joe and I were cooking supper. He was in a hurry to catch a plane back, but told Joe that he had met with his old friend in Vegas who'd persuaded a fellow judge in Reno to grant a search warrant for the Lassiter house.

But the warrant was just for the house and outbuildings, and just for Jamie. No exploring the entire fifty acres or the lake until we had further proof a crime had been committed.

The Reno judge was firm about wild goose chases that violated a person's right to privacy.

"If we have a warrant tomorrow, do we have to use Shelby's cut in the fence? Can't we just drive to the gate on the north side?"

"No. That would alert the owner and give him too much time to either move Jamie...or Jamie's body. Wynan and I still need Shelby to show us how to get in and we still have to sneak up on the house."

"I want that 'we' to include me."

"Sweetheart, it's much too dangerous for you."

I sat down hard on the kitchen chair. "C'mon. I found the Morgan-Lassiter property on the maps. I persuaded Shelby Vane to help us. I deserve to see this through."

Joe put down his chef's knife and came over to me. He pulled me up out of my chair and into his arms. He kissed me and held me and kissed me again, a long deep kiss that usually meant we were about to abandon whatever we had been doing and go upstairs to bed.

"Whoever is on that property kidnapped a woman and may have killed her. I can't risk something violent happening to you. I can't even let Shelby come with us past the fence opening. No civilians, just police. Honestly, I can't, and Wynan won't let you come in either."

"May I at least go partway with you and stay behind if you find the house?"

Joe sighed and kissed me again. I pushed away from him. "I'm not accepting sex, even great sex, as a substitute for accompanying you and Wynan tomorrow."

"Okay. You can come to the property. But you have to stay in the car with Shelby, and if we spot anyone or anything, you and Shelby beat it out of there. Now, how about great sex just to seal the deal?" He grinned.

I gave in. I always gave in to Joe. The man had the greenest eyes and a smile that made my knees go weak.

"Dinner can wait," he said. "I'll turn off the burner under the soup while you go upstairs and take off your clothes."

"Gee whiz, I have to take off my own clothes. How romantic."

"Okay, wait for me. But remember the last time I undressed you, I got complaints about buttons ending up on the floor."

"Those were your buttons, sir." I headed for the stairs.

Once in my room, I said, "I really appreciate you letting me go along tomorrow."

"Just remember you're staying in the car. Sweetheart, my responsibility is to keep you safe. You're a civilian."

"Rubbish. I'm your favorite amateur detective. As a reward for being good at it, I should be in on the finale."

"I'm serious. Even if I let you go along, Wynan would never stand for you getting anywhere near that house."

"You have to get used to letting me make decisions about my own actions. You don't get to just overrule me because of some stupid protocol. If I was a cop, you'd let me join you all the way."

Joe was very quiet and did not make a move.

I went on. "I know. I'm not trained. But you can't take an army of police into that property tomorrow without risking the owner will see what's coming, and move or kill Jamie, if he has her."

Joe nodded.

I pressed my advantage. "And we have to cover a lot of ground in a short time. You need all the help you can get to check out that property."

Joe rubbed his chin. "You make a good point. But I still can't risk putting you and Shelby in any position to be injured. The man we are looking for is dangerous. You have to promise me you'll let Wynan and me find the house. He and I know how to use guns. You don't."

"Maybe someday you can teach me how to shoot."

Joe smiled, a wicked tempting smile. "Okay, Sherlock, but not tonight."

I took off my right shoe. Joe followed and took off his right shoe. Then my left shoe. Then his left shoe. Right socks were next, removed slowly with much grinning. I took off my shirt. He took off his. It was our game, mirroring every removal. Finally, we were both naked except each of us had kept one sock on one foot. We faced each other, standing straight. The first one to touch the other would lose the game. I was as still as a statue. Joe was…well, for the most part, absolutely still. Joe's smile turned into a wide grin. I knew how to win. I slowly raised my arms up and clasped my hands behind my head.

Joe lost.

And then we were in bed and his soft mouth found its way down my neck to my collarbone and he pulled off my remaining sock, and his fingertips made a slow crawl from my toes to the inside of my knee. Even if I sometimes questioned the wisdom of dating a moody cop, I never had doubts about dating a former basketball player. Those guys really know what to do with their hands.

I woke two hours later to the beeping of my cell phone on the bedside table. Wynan was back in Reno and would pick up the warrant tomorrow. He was at Nell's apartment. Wynan was often at Nell's apartment. I hoped they stayed together no matter what we discovered had happened to Jamie.

A full moon shone through the maple trees on the front lawn. Soon the leaves would turn a brilliant orange. I lay in bed, one hand stroking Joe's bare body, hoping he'd wake up and make love to me again. Perhaps it was the threat of serious danger awaiting us the next day, but whatever the reason, it aroused passions neither of us had felt for some time.

Jamie

Jamie couldn't sleep. She worried about the not yet empty bottle of tequila in front of the man downstairs. She listened intently for the sound of his chair scraping back from the table, for his steps coming up the stairs toward her bedroom, toward her.

She could not lock her door from inside.

Outside the window, the moon shone through the branches of a huge willow that grew on the lawn. She thought water from the lake must find its way through the ground to nourish the enormous tree. She got up and tried for the hundredth time to open the window and gain access to the bars. There was a slight give, but the window held firm. Maybe if she broke through the glass, he would be too drunk to hear. Maybe if she got to the bars and worked at them the way she had worked on the hole in the closet, she could push them out. And then what? The willow was ten feet away from the house and no other tree was near the window. She would have to pry the bars open enough so she could squeeze through with enormous effort and fall or jump to the ground. She looked down. It would be a long fall. Enough to break a bone or sprain an ankle.

And, of course, punishment if he caught her.

She returned to her bed and found herself sobbing into her pillow. She fought her tears. He was drunk and it was important she hear him if he came upstairs. She had to listen. Listen hard.

Chapter 32

My desk was tidy but covered with piles of memos, messages, spreadsheets, and reports Nell had carefully tended. This was the usual paperwork that normally faced me on a bright early fall morning. But I was not feeling at all usual. I was edgy and nervous about the afternoon that lay ahead. I flicked some of the papers off the top, caught sight of the envelope containing Bud's memo, and put it on the bottom of a pile. It would just have to wait for my response. I was in no mood to deal with the petty politics of a university committee when I faced the prospect of hunting for a young woman in more danger than any of them.

I turned my back on the papers, and looked out the window that faced the quad. A group of students had set up a platform and a microphone.

One of them unfurled a banner and strung it across the back of the platform, tying it up on two upright poles. The banner displayed in large black and red letters "Rally for a Culture of Consent." I opened the window enough to feel the cool autumn breeze and hear the voices of the students.

As I watched, the group grew larger. Three young women and a young man stepped up on the platform. The tallest of the women stood in front of the microphone, her long blond hair moving in the breeze. "Thank you. Thank you for showing up," she called to the crowd, which numbered perhaps a hundred students, males and females.

A few faculty members stood with them. I recognized Howard Evans. Karen Milton was standing on the side of the crowd.

"Tonight at 6:30 we will rally to replace a culture of assault with a culture of consent on this campus," the blonde shouted. The crowd applauded and whistled. "And we are happy to see so many of you are here to support us, and happy to see that so many of you are men, and that so many of the men are fraternity men." Another roar of approval.

Another woman with cropped, unnaturally bright orange hair took her place at the microphone. "Listen, everyone. Get all your friends to come to the rally tonight outside of the Student Union. We're ready to insist that Mountain West University have a new policy on sexual assault, but we need a whole lot of student support."

I felt vindicated for suggesting students participate on our committee. Clearly they saw this as their time and their issue.

"What if we don't get a new policy?" came a shout from someone in the crowd.

The blonde was back at the microphone. "The students at Syracuse protested when they closed a student center designed to help assault victims. Some of the students even occupied the building with the chancellor's office."

"Colgate had a student protest too," added the girl with orange hair.

"Why don't we just march over and occupy the provost's office?" shouted a burly kid near the platform, flexing his muscles. Football player, most likely.

"Come to the rally instead," shouted the blonde. "We can occupy the provost's office later, if no one listens to us."

I laughed to myself.

Wouldn't Ezra McCready just love that move?

The wind came up and blew some of the leaves off the oaks, showering the speakers and sprinkling the lawn.

The crowd began to disperse and the banner was taken down. I noticed Howard helping the students remove the microphone. Karen seemed to have left early. I closed my window, almost sorry I'd miss the rally. But I planned to be busy that evening, backing up the hunt for the Lassiter house even if I couldn't join Joe and Wynan.

It was noon when I started to clean up my desk and prepare to go home. I sensed rather than saw the woman in the doorway. Dorothy Weinstein, George's wife, was dressed in a tweed suit and a silk blouse that gathered around her thin neck.

Her face was lined and sallow, but still finely featured. I had thought her quite beautiful when we first met, beautiful but unhappy.

"Oh, Dorothy, please come in and sit down. I thought you were in San Francisco."

She moved slowly, like a woman walking through waist-deep water. She put her hand on the back of one of the chairs by my table and stopped. Dark shadows were under her eyes. I suspected she had not slept for a long time.

"Please sit," I repeated. "Can I get you some coffee? My assistant is on her lunch break, but I know how to find the pot in the break room."

She coughed a small raspy sound. "Thank you, no," she said. "But I will sit for a bit."

"Dorothy, you look at the end of your rope. How is George doing?"

"He's coming along," she said, easing into the chair, every move still in slow motion.

"I feel badly. If I had known you were back in town, I would have come to your house if you needed to see me."

She removed her gloves, finger by finger. Her breath was shallow and uneven. "I just flew into Reno this morning. I haven't been to the house yet."

I sat next to her and put my hand over her pale freckled one. Her hand was unbelievably cold. "What can I do to help?"

Sharp inhale. "I just came from the District Attorney's office. He told me about Larry Coleman's arraignment."

She made another effort at a deep breath. I gripped her icy hand. "I'm so sorry you have to go through this."

"I told the District Attorney that I wanted him to drop the charges against Larry Coleman."

I must have looked astonished.

"I know that will seem odd to you, but I also told the district attorney I was going to come here and ask you not to testify to what you saw that evening."

"Good God, Dorothy. Why? What did the DA say?"

"He's thinking about it, particularly since I told him if he pursued the case to court, I would testify on behalf of the defendant."

"Please help me understand this."

The woman was trembling, her hands freezing, but her eyes were clear and her voice grew stronger with every sentence. "George deserved what happened to him. He's been a fearful bully all of his adult life. Not just to his peers here, but to his family. He was especially cruel to my parents, who were invited to come and live with us when my father's investments failed."

"I remember hearing that your father once went to the hospital with severe bruises. Was that George's work?"

Her chin went down to her chest. "It was. Although I have to say, most of George's bullying was verbal rather than physical. That must have been true for you, Red."

It was. I had some vivid memories of encounters with George when he tried to bully me into agreeing with him.

She sighed. "Surely you must have wondered if George was responsible for your predecessor's fall down the stairs."

"I did. But it turned out to be someone else instead. However, I know Larry Coleman shot George, because I saw it with my own two eyes. I grant you, it was after George had struck Larry so hard he fell to the ground, but shooting a man is an extreme reaction to a fistfight."

Dorothy's chin came up and the look on her face was closer to rage than despair. "Normally, I would agree. But George has made life hell for too many people. Including me. Larry Coleman was a victim of George's tyranny all last year and he just did what someone was bound to do someday." Her expression changed to fierceness. "You remember the party Larry gave to celebrate his tenure?"

I did. The entire faculty plus Nell and her assistants were invited. Larry's wife, a corporate attorney with a handsome salary, had bought a large house in the same part of town that housed Philip Lewis. The bar was lavish and the food was excellent. By ten almost everyone was slightly if not seriously drunk, including the host.

Larry had raised several toasts. To his wife. To me. To the faculty of the school and at the end, his face flushed with drink, he raised his glass once more, "To the assholes who tried to sabotage my tenure."

George had laughed out loud and raised his glass in return. "Atta boy, Larry. You tell it like it is. You're tenured now and you don't have to take shit from anyone."

Larry had looked at George the way a rattlesnake looks at a rabbit.

"I remember that party vividly, Dorothy. What does it have to do with the shooting?"

"George and I stayed late. After most of you had left, I went to find George. He'd cornered Larry in the kitchen. Just the two of them. I heard Larry say 'go to hell.'" She paused and searched in her handbag for a tissue. "Then George pushed Larry up against the refrigerator and banged his head on the door and called him a little shit. That's what he said. And he told Larry someday he was going to make sure he left Nevada forever." She paused again. "In a box, if necessary."

So that was why Larry had been carrying a gun all this time. I sat back in my chair and let my mind roll around this for a few minutes. Dorothy seemed to welcome my silence. At length, I said, "I will give this considerable thought and I'll talk it over with the DA."

'Thank you. I assure you, if I testify at his trial, Dr. Coleman will very likely be acquitted."

"What's the prognosis for George at this point?"

"He'll live, but his spinal cord was severed just below his neck."

"Oh, dear. That sounds as if you'll have a great deal to do taking care of him." Poor Dorothy. The hell would never end for her, I feared.

Dorothy rose from her chair and turned toward the door. Her movements had quickened. "Well, someone will have a great deal to do taking care of George." A thin smile appeared. "But I don't think it will be me."

"Dorothy, before you go, do you feel safe still being married to George?"

She cocked her head to one side and put her gloves back on. "I do now. George is paralyzed and no longer has use of his arms and legs, or of the hands he used to make into fists." She stopped by the door and looked at me, her eyes steady and still fierce. "My husband will depend on the good will of his caretakers for the rest of his life. Bullying will no longer work for him. Not if he wants to be fed and bathed. I doubt George Weinstein will ever be able to hurt anyone again." She closed my door behind her.

After she left, I called the district attorney's office. I told him what Dorothy had said and he repeated what he had said to Dorothy. At the end of our conversation his voice lowered as if telling me a confidence. "I have no idea what I'm going to do next, Dr. Solaris. This is a really weird case."

Indeed.

Jamie

The man slept late, all that morning. At noon, he walked into the kitchen and sat at the table. He hadn't shaved and his eyes were red at the rims. Jamie made him some eggs and toast that he ate silently. Then, without a word to her, he had gotten up and gone back upstairs. Hungover, she thought. But he had left her alone.

When she came downstairs, she had found the bottle empty on its side in the middle of the kitchen table and had thrown it away. She hoped it was the only liquor in the house besides the beer in the refrigerator.

He did not come back downstairs until late afternoon. She was in the parlor, watching the sun set on the lake. She had thought all day about what to do next and decided on a new approach.

"I'm sorry about last night," he said. "I rarely drink hard liquor and I'm not used to it."

"I'm glad you're feeling better," she said. "We need to talk."

He sat heavily in one of the upholstered chairs. "No more about Alice. Please." He waved his hand in the air as if to dismiss the thought. His eyes were dark and his voice was weary. "I'm hungry. I need something to eat before we talk about anything."

She walked into the kitchen and pulled out a chicken she had roasted the night before. She sliced some pieces and put it on a plate with some bread and cheese. She was not going to cook him a full meal. She had other plans for that night.

He sat at the table and began to eat. After a few minutes he got up, got himself a glass of water, and sat down again. "What's on your mind?"

"What really happened to Alice?"

Chapter 33

Joe, Wynan, and I had agreed we would meet at my house at three o'clock. I drove home an hour ahead of time. I was hoping there would be time to tell Joe about my conversation with Dorothy Weinstein before we headed out to Shelby's ranch.

I changed into jeans and put on mountain climbing boots and an extra heavy sweater. I knew Joe would still refuse to let me join the search, but I figured I should be prepared to hike into the property in the event of some unforeseen emergency. No matter what, I was going to be ready and waiting if Jamie Congers was found and there was some way I could help her.

I pulled a large wicker picnic basket out of the front closet. I folded a blanket and put it into the basket followed by a first aid kit along with my big flashlight. No telling what shape Jamie would be in when we found her, and I wanted to be equipped. In fact, as I put bandages and medical tape into the basket I realized why I was so determined to be close to the search. No matter what, if the girl was still alive, she might be in shock and seriously hurt. She would need care and comfort, and I was the woman prepared to supply that.

Joe and Wynan showed up at exactly three. Both were dressed in heavy pants and jackets and what looked like army boots and gear. And both carried handguns that neither made any attempt to conceal. I knew there would be a rifle and a shotgun in the trunk of Joe's car.

"No Bushmaster semi-automatics, guys? What if you run into the watchman?"

Joe grimaced. "The Landry police department doesn't issue that kind of weapon. Wynan and I will just have to be faster and smarter."

The drive to the Vane ranch seemed to take longer even though we had driven the route before. The day was still warm, the pastures held fewer of the black cattle, and the sprinklers must have just finished watering the sod that glistened green and lush in the afternoon sun.

Shelby Vane's mother was sitting in a rocking chair on the front porch when we drove up. She watched as Joe and I mounted the stairs to the porch.

"Afternoon, Mrs. Vane," I said in a tone as friendly as possible. The woman turned her face away.

Shelby opened the door. He was wearing boots, jeans and a heavy sweater and carrying a shotgun. "We may need this," he said, gesturing with the gun.

"We have our own weapons, Shelby. You can leave that here. I don't want you going any further than you need to point out the right direction to the house. Just get us to the fence opening and then you and Red will both stay in the car."

"Be careful, son," said the old woman without looking at any of us.

Shelby kissed his mother and he and I got in the front seat of his Jeep, while Joe and Wynan got into Joe's car. Shelby led the way and we went back out onto the two-lane road and drove faster than before. We passed sod farms and ranches, one with sheep. The trees grew in clusters next to streams.

The meadows stretched endlessly; some seemed to go all the way to the mountains in the distance.

After a few miles, the terrain became hilly, and we saw more of the sagebrush and tall pines that cover much of the northern Nevada high desert.

Shelby pulled over to the side of a grassy rise. We could not see much from the road, but birds circling above and a flight of geese suggested a body of water nearby. Shelby and I got out of the car. I waited by the side of the road. I had put the picnic basket of medical supplies in the backseat. Shelby walked up the hill and gestured to Joe and Wynan to follow. I followed a few minutes later and found the three men at the top of the rise in front of a tall steel fence.

The men removed a pile of tree branches from in front of the fence and Shelby tugged at the fence section until it opened wide enough for all of us to pass. Shelby kept looking around but no one else was near. "This is it. But I think I should lead the way. I know this land better than you, and it's a long way to the top of the lake where the house is...or used to be. It's a lot of land for just the three of us to cover before dark."

"You and Red are going to go back down to the road and stay in the car," said Joe. "Neither Wynan nor I are willing to risk the lives of two civilians going in after this bastard. Red's brought along medical supplies in that picnic basket, so if the watchman comes by and challenges you, just say you are hikers looking for a way into the lake."

Joe and Wynan looked at each other. Shelby protested. "But you guys don't know where the house might be, and I know this land better than either of you."

Joe sighed and shook his head.

Wynan cut in, "Listen, Shelby, I'm deeply grateful for the help you have given us so far. And, yes, you do know the land, but you don't know this guy or what we'll run into."

It was then that I saw the rifle propped up against the fence. Wynan picked it up. "Shelby, give us the best directions you can based on your memory."

Shelby grunted. "Go in this way until you reach the lower edge of the lake, then your best bet will be to turn left and go up the west side until you reach the top, the north shore side of the lake," said Shelby. He pulled a pair of leather gloves and a pair of long clippers out of his pocket and handed them to Wynan. "There's high grass and shrubs on the way and thicket when you get there, so these will be good if you need to cut through some of the dense stuff."

Wynan accepted the clippers. "How long do you figure it will take us to get to where you think the house is?"

Shelby looked at his watch. "Two hours or so, unless you run into problems." He scanned the landscape again. "You should get to the top of the lake by six-thirty. It will still be light, but you won't have much time to search for the house. It would be a lot faster if we could widen that fence opening and drive my Jeep in."

"We don't want to alert anyone to our presence," said Joe. "Your Jeep would make too much noise. If the watchman is still on the property, he'll hear it. Worse, the kidnapper would hear it and try to make a run for it. No, we can't take that chance. We have to move on foot, find that house, and get in before whoever may be inside knows we're there."

"Then let's get moving," said Wynan, patting his chest pocket where he had put the search warrant. The exhaustion in the older man's face had been replaced by fierce excitement. We knew we were all were out of options, but Wynan was invigorated by the idea that he was on the verge of finding his granddaughter. Alive.

Joe checked his cell phone. "I haven't seen a tower for miles, and there's no reception up here." He put down his backpack and opened it up. Inside were four satellite phones, thicker and slightly larger than conventional smartphones. He gave one to each of us. "I rented these this morning. Don't drop them. They're expensive."

"How does it work?" I said, turning the unfamiliar phone in my hand.

"Just like a cell. I've programmed the number of my sat phone into the others so all you do is push this button here at the base and you'll get to me. But don't call unless you absolutely have to."

"And if you call us?"

"That means Wynan and I need reinforcements. Call the station if you get a text on the screen. They know to be on alert if we need them. There should be a patrol car and two officers stationed about a mile down the road."

I pulled Joe away from the group. "Please take good care of yourself," I whispered.

"Red, honey, I do this for a living."

Wynan came over to us. "Let's go. We're losing light." And then the two of them were up the ridge and through the fence and gone.

Shelby fidgeted. He kept rubbing his thumb across the top of the sat phone. His other hand ran back and forth across the steering wheel. Joe and Wynan had been gone for ten minutes. He opened the driver's door.

"I can't stand this," he said. "Those guys don't know this part of the country that well." He shifted out of the car and leaned in to grab his backpack from the back seat. "Stay here, Red. I'm going to catch up to them."

I watched Shelby climb the rise to the fence opening, his big body lumbering up the incline. As he grasped the edge of the fence opening, I could see his hand was trembling. Something bothered me.

After a minute, I got out of the car. Shelby's nervousness preyed on my mind. I decided to check it out and climbed up the rise to call him back. But he had moved fast and was several yards ahead of me. He reached the lake and turned, not left as he had instructed Joe and Wynan, but right, going to the east side. Something was wrong. I decided not to call after him. I pocketed the phone and put on my gloves. Now I worried that Joe and Wynan had a problem at their backs as well as ahead of them.

Keeping well behind him and as much out of sight as possible, I followed Shelby. I was soon pushing my way through tall grass as high as my shoulders. The leaves of the grass were narrow and sharp-edged, and swayed and cut back and forth, denying me progress as well as offering me concealment. Sometimes I could only see the top of Shelby's head. Finally he broke into a clearing where the grass was shorter and sparser. I stayed behind for a moment, using the tall grass as cover. The day was still warm enough to make me sweat in my heavy sweater, but I knew that as the sun went down I would be grateful for the wool that made me sticky.

The clearing led to a stand of cottonwoods. Tall and graceful, the leaves glowed. It had been cold enough at night to turn the sturdy trees to huge globes of yellow. I waited a moment and then followed Shelby's path into the stand of trees. Birds flew over my head from the direction of the lake, and a late afternoon wind came up as it often does in this part of the world. My legs were starting to ache just as I saw Shelby cross another small clearing and go into another grove of trees. He stopped and looked around and then looked at his watch. I looked at mine. Almost five o'clock. He picked up his pace, moving with surprising speed for a man of his weight.

I also turned east and speeded up to keep Shelby in my sights. The sun was behind us, but as it hit the lake, it sent blinding glints into my eyes.

The land turned hilly, and I had to climb slopes to get from one grassy meadow to another. In the valleys between the slopes, more thick groves of trees kept me from seeing very far ahead. As I cleared each ridge top, I looked for some suggestion of a building, but saw nothing but miles of meadow, and further away from the lake, more sage and short pines. The water had taken on a murky look and seemed more swamp than lake.

Shelby had slowed some and the light was dimming but I could still see him ahead. He seemed to know where he was going. And the longer I followed him, the surer I became that my trust in him had been misplaced. He had sent Joe and Wynan off in a different direction, probably the wrong direction. But Shelby moved as if he knew exactly where he was going and was determined to get there.

As I came through yet another stand of trees, the lake widened and turned watery again. "It's really two lakes, connected by a swamp," Shelby had said in the car as we drove from his ranch. "The bigger lake is called Morgan's Lake. I don't know if the other one has a name. Morgan's Lake once belonged to the family of

Emily Morgan, who married old man Lassiter's father. She inherited the land, and I think they put their joint property under the name Morgan-Lassiter on the map that you found." Shelby had seemed to know a great deal about the history of the property.

I stopped to catch my breath and wished I had thought to bring a canteen of water. I looked around. If Jamie Congers were being held captive somewhere near here, she would have had one hell of a time escaping without sturdy shoes and heavy clothes to protect her from the grass and thickets.

It was still light but the sun was low in the sky when Shelby pushed into a thicket. I followed as closely as I could. The brambles tugged at my sweater and scratched my face. Then I saw the top of the lake up ahead and a clearing that stretched for what I guessed was a mile or more. Shelby turned inland away from the lake.

I waited in the thicket until I was sure he could not see me, then ran across the clearing and into another shallow valley with trees on either side. I was sure I could still see Shelby ahead, but a tree branch brushed across my face. I pushed it away and rubbed my face with my gloved hand. When I looked up again, Shelby had disappeared.

Where had he gone? That bastard. He had deliberately misled Joe and Wynan. What was his plan? To get to the house before us and make sure no sign of Jamie remained?

I still found it hard to believe Shelby was a kidnapper or a seducer. Froman might be. Maybe he and Froman were in this together somehow. Shelby knew Froman had bought the land. Maybe he knew Froman had brought her here. He had maneuvered Joe and Wynan to the other side of the lake so he could get to the house and warn Froman?

That's stupid. He could have just telephoned.

Maybe there was no house. This was just a diversion.

Damn. I had to call Joe, but first I had to figure out where I was, so Joe and Wynan could join me.

I scanned the scene, turning a full three hundred and sixty degrees. No sign of Shelby. Then I noticed what seemed like a reflection through the trees. The sun was setting and the last light had illuminated something. Possibly a glass window. Still keeping a lookout for Shelby, I kept my head down and walked cautiously a few yards toward where I had seen the reflection. I saw the glint again and went up to the crest of a small ridge and looked down the other side.

A road appeared below me. A dirt and gravel road that looked like it could be the driveway to the house. I looked around. No house. I walked down to the road and followed it a few feet as it curved around. This must be the way to the house. I pulled my satellite phone from my pocket and punched the button Joe had shown me.

"What is it?" Joe's voice sounded distant but clear.

"Joe, Shelby left the car and went in another direction, I followed him to..."

"God damn it, I told you to stay in the car. Where the hell are you?" His voice was a low hiss.

"I told you," I tried to whisper, unsure of where Shelby might be.

"I can't hear you. Speak up."

"Shelby was acting strangely and he went to the east of the lake, not the west. I'm on the east side, a little ways in from the top of the lake and Joe, I found a road that might go to a house."

Jamie

The man sipped on his water. "I said no more talking about Alice."

Jamie put her hands on the back of a kitchen chair and braced herself for his anger. "You scare the hell out of me. How do you expect me to ever get used to being in this house when I'm terrified, when I break into a cold sweat every time you come near me?"

The man looked weary. "I know you're afraid, but I am not going to hurt you. I am not going to force myself on you. Please understand that."

Her hands gripped the chair back. "And yet you make me feel as helpless and trapped as if you had already raped me and might again."

"Nonsense."

"No. Don't you realize, that's exactly the way a woman feels when a man tries to overpower her, to control her. That's what rape is about."

The man rose from his chair and stuffed his hands into the pockets of his jeans. He rocked back and forth on his heels. "Perhaps we should go into the parlor and read some scripture. Maybe that will calm you down and make you feel better."

She ignored the familiar pinpricks in her neck and pressed on. "No more Bible reading. I was raised knowing the Bible, and much of it is about compassion and kindness, not oppression and obedience. You've perverted the Bible to suit your own ends. You don't use it for worship, you use it for mind control."

He frowned. "That's absurd. You're a deeply religious woman, Jamie. I know that about you. You go to church every Sunday."

Something clicked in Jamie's mind. "How do you know that about me? How do you know about my religion, or the size of my clothes, or the brand of shampoo that I use?"

"Let's just say I have done research on you. Now, please, let's go to the parlor."

"No. No Bible reading. It won't work. Not on me any more than it did on Alice."

Spittle appeared at the corners of his mouth. He slammed his fist down on the table. "No more about Alice. I told you that," he shouted.

Jamie took a deep breath and pulled the driver's license out of her pocket.

She put it on the table face up so the man could not avoid seeing Alice's face. "I found this in the parlor sofa. It's been there a long time."

He reached for the license.

His face flushed and his eyes watered.

Jamie stepped back from the table and crossed her arms in front of her. Her shirt felt sticky across her back. But something told her this was her chance to prevail. "What really happened to Alice? She did not drive away from here without her license."

The man swallowed hard and shook his head. A tear ran down his cheek.

"And you never found a death certificate for her in Louisiana, did you?"

He made a choking sound. "No." The license trembled in his hand as he stared at it.

Jamie licked her lips. Her mouth was as dry as cotton. "Would I be right if I said your father killed Alice after he had nearly beaten you to death?"

More tears streamed down his face. He bent over the back of a chair, nearly choking. Foam appeared on the corners of his mouth. "She wasn't as strong as I was. She couldn't take the whipping."

"Where's her body?"

His chest heaved, his voice choked to a rasp. "I don't know."

Jamie slammed her fist on the table. "Where is Alice's body?"

His tall body was trembling from head to foot. "She's buried on a hill overlooking the lake. About a half-mile from here."

"You must know now why I can never stay here, never be with you." She tried to steady her voice. "I know what you want, but it's not going to happen. I am never going to be able to bear living in this house. I hate it here."

His eyes returned to her, his hand clutching his chest.

"I care for you, Jamie. I really do."

"No, you cared for Alice. You loved her. But you can't transform me into Alice. I'll never be her, and I'll never be yours."

"You keep saying never. You don't know what more time with me might..."

Jamie leaned toward the man and slammed her hands on the table. "Never. Never. Never!" she shouted.

He shuddered. A loud moan parted his lips. He raised his head and opened his mouth wide.

The sounds of a large wounded animal reverberated around the room. "Please, Jamie. You have to stay."

"No. I can't stay. You have to let me go."

His shoulders fell and his head hung over and nearly touched the plate of unfinished food. Then, he pushed the chair away and moved toward her. "I know. I want you to be free. I do."

She walked backwards toward the kitchen door. He staggered and broke his fall by putting his hand on the wall. He leaned against the wall, then turned toward her, but his legs no longer supported him, and slowly he slid down until he was sitting on the floor. He stopped with his back against the wall, his shoulders shaking and his head buried in his arms.

Jamie strode to the kitchen door and reached for the padlock. "What's the combination?" Her voice was hard and firm. She knew he was defeated.

"I'll tell you in the morning," he murmured to his knees. "It's going to be dark soon. You can't leave in the dark. We are miles away from anywhere. You'll get lost and hurt yourself. In the morning, Jamie, in the morning."

Jamie strode to where he sat against the wall and squatted down until she was no more than a few inches away from his bowed head. "What made you think you could force me to love you?"

He looked up with bloodshot eyes. "You're so young, so lovely, and I'm so much older now. I thought this would be the only way. I thought that after you got to know me better..."

"Not going to happen."

"I can take care of you, Jamie." His voice became firmer. "I have money. I can give you anything you want."

She stood up. "I want the combination." She walked over to the back door.

No response, just a shaking of his shoulders. Jamie raised her voice. "The combination. Now."

His head rose and the look on his face told her all she needed to know. Jamie reached for the padlock, and punched in the first digit of Alice Lassiter's birthdate.

Chapter 34

"Drop the phone, lady." The voice came from the right and I looked over. Through the gloom of dusk I saw a Jeep parked under one of the trees. A short, stocky man was standing in front of the Jeep. There was still enough light to see he had no hair, small eyes set far apart, and a flat nose—the face of a pit bull.

He wore a thin sweater that displayed forearms the size of hams. His chest was broad and striated with thick muscles that seemed like plates barely attached to his body. His hands held what I took to be the Bushmaster semi-automatic Shelby had described. The gun was enormous. The barrel was at least sixteen inches and it was pointed at my chest.

"Drop the phone. Now." He gestured with the gun, waving it ever so slightly back and forth. "I'd hate to see this baby cut a good-looking woman in half."

I dropped the phone.

Still using the gun as an indicator, he waved me over to the other side of the gravel road. He pulled a sat phone from his pocket and punched in a number. His voice was low and menacing. He spoke in a sharp voice like a bark without taking his eyes off me. "I've got a female trespasser here." He paused, listening. "She's about thirty or thirty-five, roughly my height, red hair." He paused again. "Right. I'll walk her in. Unless you want me to bring her in the Jeep." Another pause.

I stared at him. No way was he the man who had entered Jamie's apartment. Too short, too heavyset. How many men were involved? If this guy was any indicator of the sort who had kidnapped Jamie, I'd be astonished if she was still alive. Or if she was...poor Jamie. I wondered what these animals had done to her. I could almost hear my heartbeat. Where was Shelby? Was he the man on the other end of the phone? Where was Joe? Oh, God. Probably a mile away on the other side of the lake.

The man leaned down and picked up my sat phone, still pointing the gun at me. He dumped the phone into the backseat of the Jeep and gestured with the gun again. "Walk," he said, indicating the road ahead.

It was getting darker, but I could just make out the gravel and the curve ahead. I looked at the trees that lined the road, hoping for a glimpse of a man following us, a man with a gun strapped to his body, a man who would know what to do and how to disarm my captor. But no shadow moved and no sound occurred.

After a minute or so, the road curved around and I saw it. A two-story house with bars on all the windows visible from the road. A tall brick cube of a house, imitation Federal style, with a low-pitched roof and windows arranged symmetrically around a center front door. I wondered how someone had trucked all that brick this far into this wilderness. It looked like a jail.

The gravel drive ran past the side of the house to a wooden barn with a door closed with a heavy six-by-six bar. A black sedan was parked on the gravel on the side of the house. Off to my left, the last rays of the sun hit the lake. How was Joe ever to find this place, or me?

Jamie

Jamie punched the next digits of the code into the padlock. She tugged on the lock to free it from the hasp. It didn't move. She started the code again.

His phone rang. Still sitting on the floor, he tugged the phone from his pocket. "What? What does she look like?" The man staggered to his feet, still holding the phone. "Bring her to the house."

Jamie paused, confused. Her? A woman. Here? Oh my God, had someone found her? Was the woman alone?

"No, leave the Jeep where it is. Just walk her here."

Jamie punched in the code again. This time the lock snapped open. Too late. The man was next to her. He grabbed her arm and pushed her back toward the table in the kitchen.

"No," she shouted. "You said I could be free." She lunged for him.

But he had gained his balance, and avoiding her swinging fists, grabbed both her hands. She leaned forward and bit his wrist. He howled and dropped her hands. She stepped back and prepared for a knee kick to his groin, but he was too fast and grabbed her again. He wrenched her arms behind her back.

"Jamie, I don't want to hurt you. I can't let you go now. Someday, maybe. But not now. Relax." With one hand, he grasped her wrists behind her back, locked his other hand in a firm grip around the back of her neck, and pushed her down the hall into the parlor. He shoved her down onto the sofa. "Stay here. Don't move and don't make any noise. If you make any noise, I swear I'll knock you out cold and tie you up again."

"Go to hell," Jamie sobbed as he locked the door to the hallway.

Jamie sat, huddled into the sofa, trying not to weep or scream. She had been a few seconds away from walking out the back door, but for that damn phone call. What woman?

She tried to calm herself. She had unlocked the padlock and knew the combination.

The man was vulnerable. She could figure out a way to manage him after he had dealt with this woman who showed up. She took deep breaths.

She felt into her pants pockets. The paper clip was still there. She walked over to the hall door. Then stopped. Better to wait until he let her out again. Better to make another try at the back door. He had understood that she'd never give in to him. He knew his cause was lost. Be quiet, she thought, be patient.

Her blood turned cold. Letting her punch in the combination had just been his way to calm her down. He would change the combination tomorrow. He would never let her go, because now she knew about what had happened to Alice.

Chapter 35

I felt the tip of the gun barrel press against my spine. "Keep going," the voice behind me said. My knees almost buckled but I steadied myself.

A small porch fronted the house and offered slight covering to the massive and windowless front door. A light came on over the door, then went off again.

"We're here," shouted the voice behind me. The door opened. A tall figure stood in the doorway. "Bring her in," said the figure, retreating back into a dark hallway. The tall figure turned and moved down the hall. The gun pressed me in through the door and down the hall to a lighted room. As I passed through the hall, I noticed two closed doors, one on the right, one on the left, and a stairway to the left.

We entered a kitchen. The tall man had his back to me and did not turn, but there was something familiar about his stance. He was taller than Shelby. But he was not Froman. The shoulders were wide but not wide enough. He put his hand up. He must have covered his mouth because the words came out muffled and exaggerated. "Sit her down and face her toward the stove, away from the table."

I knew that voice. With his attempt to disguise it, I couldn't quite place it. But I knew this man, and sooner or later he'd figure that out and then I would pay for that knowledge.

The gun directed me to the chair and I sat. I felt the tall man come up behind me and pull my arms back and tape my hands together. Cloth that felt like a dishtowel came over my head and across my eyes and ears. Hands tied the towel tight and the knot caught my hair.

"Ouch."

"Shut up," said the watchman with the gun.

Hands lifted the edge of the towel and stuffed what felt like wads of paper toweling into my ears. But I could still hear him say, "Tell her to be quiet and not make a move. I'm going outside to check for others." It was harder to hear but I was beginning to figure out his voice.

"She was calling someone on her sat cell when I caught her. She called him Joe."

God, where was Joe? He must be trying to find me. He must have found the road and the Jeep by now. He must have called Wynan and Shelby to help him find the house. Where was Shelby? The voice behind me was not Shelby's, so that meant he was somewhere else.

I heard a door open and close.

Minutes passed with no sound but the faint breathing of the man with the gun. I heard the scrape of a chair being pulled across a hard floor. The door opened and closed again.

"No one out there. And it's pitch dark now." How did I know that voice? I struggled to identify it. Another chair scraping on the floor. Then I felt tape going around my ankles. "Okay, lady," said the voice of the watchman. "Now tell us what the hell you are doing here."

He was letting his watchman talk for him. He knew me, too. Was he pretending not to know me? "My boyfriend and I were camping out here," I said, trying to keep my own voice from trembling.

"Bullshit," said the watchman. "No one camps out here. It's private land." I head another scraping of something like metal on wood. The gun on the table?

"We wanted to camp near the lake and go fishing in the morning." My breathing was labored.

"More bullshit," said the watchman. "You were a quarter mile away from the lake when I found you on the road. And you had no equipment."

I struggled to maintain the fiction I'd started. "I was looking for wood for a campfire."

I waited for a response.

Finally, the voice of the tall man. "Go get the Jeep and bring it around to the back of the house. I don't know where her boyfriend is, but we need to get her off the property now." Definitely not Froman's voice. Oh my God. I knew who he was.

A chair scraped. The heavy tread of a man wearing boots. The door opened and closed. I sensed the tall man near me. I needed to calm down. My mind wasn't working because I was too damned scared. What would they do to me? What had they done to Jamie? What about Joe out in the dark woods, not knowing about where I was, and worse, not knowing about the watchman with the semi-automatic?

I wanted to ask them if Jamie was here, but I was terrified that they would kill me right away if I betrayed my reason for being there.

I waited for him to speak again. I wanted to be certain. Silence.

I waited to hear the sound of the Jeep. Again, silence.

Ten minutes and still no sound of the Jeep. The chair scraped the floor, and again, the heavy tread of a man in boots. A door opened.

"Shit, what the hell..." A loud groan and I heard a fall. A loud bang against the stove. I felt a body fall against my legs and then move off again. Then I heard two voices. One was Wynan's. "Where's my granddaughter, you son of a bitch?"

Another was Joe's near me. "Steady yourself, Red. Hold on. I'm going to rip off this tape on your wrists." The towel came away from my eyes.

I saw Wynan with his hands around the throat of a man taller than he was.

They moved back and forth like two great animals.

Wynan raised a fist and smashed it into the man's face, knocking the man to the floor and sending one of the chairs sailing across the room.

Joe freed the tape from my hands and lifted me to my feet. He held my arms tightly in his hands and stared at me. "Jesus, Red. Damn it, this was close. Too close." He was furious. But I didn't care. We were all still in danger.

"Joe, where's the watchman? He has a gun."

"We captured him by his Jeep. Shelby's got him trussed up like a Christmas turkey. He's guarding him with the gun he was carrying."

Behind me, a fist cracked against bone. Wynan shouted. "Where is she? I swear I'll rip your head off." Another punch. I turned in time to see the tall man fall to the floor holding his hand across his face. Blood poured from behind his hand and down his chin. Now I was sure. "Joe, I know him. I know who..."

A woman's voice screamed from another room. "Grandpa, I'm in here! Grandpa, it's Jamie."

Jamie, my God.

Joe released me and we all ran into the hall. Wynan beat on the door. "Jamie, stand away from the door," shouted Wynan.

Joe stood back and gave the door a kick. The door held. Wynan turned around, kicked backwards like a mule, striking the door just below the doorknob. He kicked so hard he almost lost his footing. The door gave in. Behind it stood a girl with black curly hair and large eyes flooded with tears. She was in her grandfather's arms before Joe and I could turn back to the kitchen.

The tall man was sitting on the floor, holding his jaw. He lifted his head and I held my breath looking at the tear-stained and bloodied face of Ezra McCready.

Chapter 36

It was a long night.

Joe searched the rest of the house while Wynan stood guard over McCready. Jamie and I sat on the parlor sofa, my arms around her shoulders, while she described her ordeal.

It took the Landry police a while to get to the house and another several minutes to staunch the bleeding in McCready's nose, handcuff him, and get him into a police car.

It was another hour getting Jamie to the hospital in Landry and then waiting to learn enough about her condition.

Wynan couldn't take his arms from around Jamie, even in the hospital.

He had insisted she spend most of the night and be thoroughly examined in spite of her repeated protests. "I'm not hurt, Grandpa. He didn't hurt me. He just kept me."

And then it was another half hour quizzing Shelby over coffee in the hospital cafeteria.

"Sorry," said Shelby, slurping coffee from a mug. "I meant to catch up to you, but when I got to the south shore of the lake, I figured since you and Wynan were going up the west side, I'd check out the east side. If I found something, I'd call on the sat phone. If not, I'd join up with you at the top of the lake."

"I see," said Joe evenly.

I was still annoyed. "Did you know I followed you?" I tried to imitate Joe's professional tone of voice, but I was sure Shelby sensed my irritation.

"No, Red. I never saw you." He put down his mug. "Again, sorry to have caused you worry, but I've always been able to take care of myself, and I thought I could help."

"Shelby, I have to tell you, I was sure you were up to something when you veered off in another direction. Why didn't you follow Joe and Wynan so you could be together when you got to the house?"

Shelby looked sheepish. "When I reached the lake, I remembered the last time I had seen the house and realized I should have told them to go east of the lake instead of west. I felt like an idiot and thought I could make up for it by finding the girl myself." His eyes widened. "Prove that we Vanes are good guys. My brother would really like it if I did that." He paused, looking first at Joe and then at me. "I planned to call Joe when I saw the house, Red. Honestly."

There was something in Shelby's big, rumpled face that softened me. I began to believe he was telling the truth.

"At least we found her," I said.

"You found her, Red. You discovered the driveway to the house."

Joe turned his face away. He was probably still mad as hell about my decision to leave the car. I turned back to Shelby. "So how did you catch up to Joe and Wynan after all?"

Shelby laughed. "Oh, I heard them coming through the woods like a herd of wild boar. They were moving fast and making no effort to keep their movements quiet. Joe was honed in on the GPS on your cell phone and I don't think he gave a shit who heard him."

After the sun came up, we gathered in Joe's office at Landry Police headquarters. Wynan, Jamie, and Shelby sat in chairs facing Joe's desk.

I perched on the windowsill. We were waiting for a report from Joe's team, who'd been working feverishly during the night until early in the morning.

A stocky gray-haired detective named Norman O'Hare came in with a sheaf of papers in his hand.

"Where's McCready?" asked Wynan.

"In a cell downstairs," said Norman.

"How's his nose?" said Joe.

"Busted. The doc looked at it. Put some ice on it and said he could patch him up until we got him to a jail with a psych ward where they can treat him."

Norman turned to Joe who was looking through the papers. "Can I bring you up to speed on anything, Joe?"

Joe looked up from the papers, his face drawn and pallid. I had gotten an hour or two of sleep on the couch in his office, but Joe had been working all night since the arrest of Ezra McCready. "Has the team found Alice Lassiter's body yet?"

"Not yet. McCready's directions to the site were a little on the vague side. I'll let you know as soon as we have anything."

'Thanks. Please stay here for a few minutes while I fill in the rest of these people about what we've learned. And please speak up if I forget anything."

Norm settled on the couch against the wall as Joe began.

"Here's the short version of what we know so far: Daniel Lassiter married Alice McCready a year after his first wife died. He beat her to death four years later when he found her in bed with his sixteen-year-old son," Joe said.

A collective sharp inhale from almost everyone in the room as we absorbed the weight of his words.

Joe continued. "According to Ezra's statement last night, just before Daniel died, he showed his son where he buried Alice."

Jamie shuddered. Wynan put his arm around her shoulders. "Do you want to stay for this?" he asked. She nodded.

Joe's voice softened a bit. "Lassiter's will left Ezra the house and a large inheritance. Ezra collected some of the money, took off, and assumed Alice's name—in honor of his love for her, he says. He enrolled in an Oregon high school and went to college and then on to graduate school. The summer between high school and college, he petitioned to have his name changed legally to Ezra McCready. He also had all his Nevada property put in a trust in the bank in San Francisco that Wynan discovered."

"Joe, breathe," I said.

Joe flashed me a frown. "McCready's statement says he didn't want to be associated with the Lassiter name, so he had the bank sell the other properties but kept the original family home by the lake because Alice's grave was there."

"When did he move back to the house?" asked Wynan.

"Apparently a couple of months ago." Joe scanned the next page of notes.

"How'd he have time to install all those bars on the window?" asked Jamie.

Joe shook his head. "Actually, he tells us the house always had bars on the windows even when he was a kid growing up there. Apparently his grandfather, Pastor Edward Lassiter, had security issues."

"When did he put in the padlocks?" asked Jamie. She looked wan but generally healthy. She held her grandfather's hand and her voice trembled slightly.

"He didn't tell me that, Jamie," said Joe, with a gentleness I was pleased he could still muster. "But he did admit he had been watching you for several weeks and planning your kidnapping for some time."

"How did he find out so much about me?" Jamie's lip trembled.

"He's the provost," I said. "He had access to all your records, and once he got the key from your handbag, he gained access to your apartment."

I turned to Joe. "Does he deny or contradict anything Jamie has told us about him?" I couldn't believe a man as smart as Ezra McCready would just spill out the entire story without demanding a lawyer. I could still see him in the president's office lecturing me.

"McCready doesn't deny a damn thing," said Norm from the couch. "The watchman has asked for his attorney. He's ex-military and tough as nails, says he was just doing his job as a security guard. But McCready's a different story. He looks broken to me. He just sits on the floor of his cell with his head in his hands. Won't eat. Weeps a lot."

I tried to imagine feeling sorry for McCready, but my mind couldn't make that leap.

Jamie sighed and squeezed Wynan's hand. "He never hurt me. He really wanted me to fall for him, but I couldn't."

"Of course you couldn't," I said.

"Filthy son of a bitch," said Wynan.

Jamie seemed lost in her thoughts. "It wasn't that he was cruel or ugly or anything..." Her voice went down an octave. "It's just that he was so creepy."

I got down from the windowsill and went to the girl and put my arms around her. She put her hand over mine. "Oh, Dean Solaris, I was so scared of him. I still can't believe how scared I was."

I continued to hold her.

"Did they find the gray van?" asked Wynan.

Joe shuffled the papers again. "In the shed behind the house, along with Jamie's car. McCready's been doing a lot of driving."

"Why did McCready move back here to Nevada?" asked Shelby.

Joe looked at another one of the papers. "Apparently he came back here because President Lewis offered him the provost's job last spring." Joe picked up another paper. "Over the summer he rented an apartment here in Landry for a while until the semester began and..."

"And he saw me on campus," said Jamie.

By noon I knew I had to go home, take a shower, change my clothes, and get to campus.

The school, hell, the whole university, would be in an uproar over the news about the provost and Jamie's return.

Joe motioned to one of the patrolmen in the hallway. "Please take Dr. Solaris to her home," he said.

"You coming?" I asked.

"I still have paperwork to do to get McCready transferred to a jail with a psych ward where he can be examined."

"Later?"

"I don't know."

"Are you still angry with me?"

Joe pulled me into an alcove while the young patrolmen waited patiently by the door. Joe's face was inches from mine and his eyes were dark and held no affection. "You should have waited in the car instead of pursuing Shelby. You could have called on the sat phone if you were worried about what he was up to. I asked you to wait."

"I called you when I found the driveway."

Joe's chest heaved with exasperation. "You had no business being anywhere near that driveway." He gripped my arms. "Don't you realize the watchman might have shot you? McCready might have taken you hostage. Any number of really dangerous things could have happened to you because of that stupid move." Joe's breath was hot and sour.

"But I found..."

"I know what you found. I also know that your impulse to take risks drives me crazy. For all your insights, for all the help your big brain can be, you still don't know how to protect yourself or accept intelligent advice. You always think you know better."

I put my hand on the side of his face, but he shook his head. His breathing became heavier. "Honestly, I don't know how much longer I can live with this."

Pain started in my chest and went down to my stomach. "You mean live with me, don't you?"

"I'm too tired to answer that question now." He pulled me back out into the hallway. "Please take her home," he said to the patrolman, and turned on his heel.

Chapter 37

Back home, I stood in the shower for a full twenty minutes letting the hot water pour over my aching body. I was out of my mind going over and over what Joe had said. I'd only seen him that angry once before when he thought I was secretly in love with someone else. But he knew how to admit he was wrong, and maybe he would this time.

Then again, I had been lured by a glint from a gun. I'd been a fool again, and there was every chance in the world that this time, I would not be forgiven.

When I got to the journalism school, Nell was the first person I saw. "What a time we've had," she said, giving me a big hug. "Let me get you some coffee, and how about a sandwich?"

Edwin appeared in the hall. "Red, my dear, from this morning's TV reports, I gather that you have been moonlighting as a police detective."

"Just my old habits as a news reporter, Edwin. I have to be on the scene whenever something exciting happens."

"Well, I want to hear all about it at tomorrow's faculty meeting. At least, all that you are free to tell us."

Nell handed me a stack of telephone messages. "Philip Lewis has called twice. Says he wants to see you the minute you get to campus."

*   *   *

I was still in a somber mood and very tired as I walked across campus toward Philip Lewis's office.

"Red, are you okay?" It was Howard Evans rushing across the lawn to meet me.

"I'm fine, Howard. Thank you. But I'm heading to an urgent meeting with the president, so I can't stop right now."

"Isn't it astonishing about McCready?" Howard was flushed with excitement. I nodded and turned again toward the administration building. Howard kept pace with me. "I mean, frankly, I for one am glad McCready's gone. But it's not very good for our university's reputation to have our provost charged with...what was the charge the television reporter said...'abduction with intent to defile.' That's pretty heavy, isn't it?"

"There are still some questions about the provost's intent."

"McCready must be mentally ill, don't you think?" Howard called after me.

I did.

As it turned out, so did Philip Lewis. The university president, sitting at his desk absorbed in thought when I was shown in, struggled to his feet. "Oh, my dear," he said.

I took his hands in both of mine and told him to sit again, while I took the chair opposite his. Philip Lewis looked ghastly. His face was gray and his hands shook, but his tone was reassuring and strong. "You've had to go through so many trials, Red. I hope they've made you strong, even as they must have made you sick to your stomach."

"I'm still here, Dr. Lewis. Although I admit there have been times recently when I felt like giving up."

"It's time you called me Philip."

I started to object but he raised his hand. "I'm not very well these days. Give an old man his way." He brought his hand up to rub his chin. "Did you know McCready was mentally ill?"

"Not until last night. I just thought he was cruel and difficult."

Philip pressed his jaw with his fingers and shook his head.

"Would you like me to pour you some water?"

"Thank you."

I left my chair and walked over to the carafe on the conference table. Two glasses were beside it and I poured into both. A folder titled "Dean of Journalism" sat next to the glasses.

The president drank eagerly from the glass of water, then paused to catch his breath. "I didn't know McCready was cruel, or difficult, much less sick enough to kidnap a woman. My God, how I admired that man. He had a wonderful reputation as a dean at his previous university. Great leader, they said. They thought the world of him. His research had made him famous." Philip drank again. "The search committee raved about him. I knew him slightly and thought he was brilliant, would make a great university president someday. I must have been much foggier than I realized when I interviewed him."

"We all misjudge sometimes. Myself included."

Philip smiled. "But you redeemed yourself and changed course when you had to. And, the ability to change, my dear Red, is a characteristic of great leaders."

My heart rate increased. Maybe I still had a chance for the job described in that folder on the table.

"Which leads me to a much happier subject," Philip said. "Even though I admired Ezra McCready, I was never going to let him give the dean's job to anyone but you." He rose from his desk and made his way over to the table. He picked up the folder.

"Even Manny Lorenzo?"

"Manny's a great guy and a splendid scholar. I just spoke to him an hour ago. I urged him to come here as interim provost and then to apply for the permanent job."

"Fantastic. Did he say he would?"

"He said he would. He really wants to come here. If I could avoid the protocols around here, I would just outright hire him now. But you know the faculty will insist on a new search."

"Manny will make a sensational provost."

Philip turned toward me with the folder but lost his balance and started to fall. I caught him in my arms. We held each other in a tight hug for several seconds. When he recovered his balance, he made his way back to his desk but remained standing. He handed me the folder. "Dr. Solaris, I hope you will accept the position of permanent Dean of Journalism. Nothing would make me happier."

I hugged him again. "Nothing would make me happier either."

He sat down in his desk chair with a loud sigh. "I have more news. News I think you will like. Fred Stoddard has agreed to come out of retirement and take over my job. He'll serve as interim president."

Fred and Manny. I was elated. At last, a university management team I could respect and admire.

"I wish you didn't have to leave."

"So do I. But I'm on my last legs. And with your promotion and Fred's return, I leave knowing my university is in excellent hands. That's a good way for an old man to feel. That's what I call a good final act."

"Before you go, may I ask one favor?"

"You may."

"I'm on the sexual assault policy committee. We've been really struggling with trying to come up with a policy we can all agree upon."

"I'll talk to Stoddard and Lorenzo tomorrow when they arrive for our first joint meeting. My view of the sexual assault policy is that I want it soon, but I also want it right."

Nell was jubilant. "Can we plan a party? At least cake and coffee here at the school?"

"Maybe tomorrow afternoon."

"Oh, I'm not going to be here tomorrow afternoon."

"Why not?"

"Well, Wynan wants to sell his place in Las Vegas and move up here and I agreed to help him tomorrow afternoon. He's looking for a house that would be large enough that Jamie and Marilyn could stay with him until they graduate."

Marvelous how some things work out.

I picked up my cell phone and saw a text from Bill Verden. "Never doubt my ability to predict the future. Long live the Queen."

Finally I dialed Joe's number, but got his voicemail. I left him a message about my new job and tried to sound conciliatory about his anger with me. But, damn it, I didn't feel apologetic for discovering that road, that house, and leading him to Jamie's rescue. More and more—even if sometimes I was a wretched fool—I'd begun to trust my instincts, and I wished Joe Morgan could too.

The thing was, my instincts also told me to trust my deepening feelings for Joe Morgan, and I was scared he didn't reciprocate.

Karen Milton's was the last phone call of a tiring and exhilarating day. "Congratulations," she said. "It's all over campus, you know."

"Thank you. How goes it in your part of the universe?"

"Badly, I'm afraid to say. A second girl has filed a complaint against Peter Delacroix. She went to the police and to me. It happened the other night. Same routine—Delacroix borrows a book from a girl, then waits for the opportune moment to return it to her when she's alone in her room. He brings the book along with a flask of drugged alcohol."

"Unbelievable. Shy, sweet Peter Delacroix. What's going to happen to him this time?"

"The DA has agreed to prosecute him. He's about to get his politically well-connected ass fried."

"Senator Mom notwithstanding?"

"You got it."

I drove home through the main street of Landry, then past the police station, hoping to spot Joe's car. I hoped we could talk. But his car was nowhere in sight.

Sadie Hawkins was out of town visiting her son, and I faced the prospect of celebrating my new job alone. The sun was setting and the sky looked as if it was on fire. The buildings and houses of Landry were bathed in peach-colored light. Our wide open sky in late summer and early fall provided amazing sunsets that guaranteed I would never leave, even if I ended up living in Nevada as a solitary single woman.

By the time I pulled into my driveway, the sun had gone down, leaving behind a scrim of blue and purple. Charlie greeted me at the door. I was standing by the sink, opening a can of dog food and looking out at my backyard when I heard a familiar sound. Joe's car in the driveway.

I gave Charlie his food and waited. Then I couldn't stand it a moment longer. We had to make up from our quarrel.

I pushed open the kitchen door and almost hit Joe, who was coming in with a large carton in his arms. He put the carton down on the butcher-block island in the center of the kitchen. He took me in his arms. "Congratulations, sweetheart. I knew you were going to get that job."

"How'd you find out?"

"Your message. Besides, it's all over town. Nell told Wynan who told Norm, who..." I stopped him with my mouth and we lingered there.

There were no apologies. That was Joe. And no, we were not going to talk about his earlier angry remarks. Not yet.

I looked in the carton. Joe's enormous soup pot was nestled next to his favorite cast iron skillet, items he sometimes brought over to cook at my house, but items he always took back to his apartment. Precious possessions. Upright and next to the pot was a leather case that I knew was filled with his extra sharp chef's knives.

Joe removed the skillet from the carton and began to wander around the kitchen. "I'm wondering where to hang this," he said, his eyes roaming the walls.

"And I'll need part of that lower cupboard for the soup pot."

I had a steel rack with hooks over the sink. Joe removed an old fry pan of mine and put up his cast-iron treasure. He went back to the carton and pulled out a special knife rack. He held it against the wall near the sink where I assumed he wanted to install it.

I stifled the temptation to applaud. "If you leave this stuff here, how are you going to cook at your place?"

Joe shrugged. "I'm not. I figure with the demands of your new job, I'll be doing all my cooking here from now on." Charlie let out a low groan of delight. Never doubt that dogs understand English.

Joe headed back to the open kitchen door.

"Now what?" I asked.

"My clothes."

I knelt down and pretended to shift pots in the lower cupboard. Then I stopped, closed my eyes and put my hands over my mouth, trying hard to conceal a triumphant grin.

Bourne Morris

Bourne Morris began writing at Bennington College where she studied under the late poet laureate, Howard Nemerov. After college, she worked at *McCall's* Magazine and then went to Ogilvy&Mather, New York during the "Mad Men" era. David Ogilvy and his colleagues treated her wonderfully, promoted her several times and then sent her west to become head of their agency in Los Angeles. She had a splendid run in advertising.

In 1983, she joined the University of Nevada Reno as a full professor in Journalism where she taught until 2009. She learned about campus politics when she served as chair of the faculty senate. She retired to write mysteries in 2009 after an equally wonderful teaching career.

Henery Press Mystery Books

And finally, before you go...
Here are a few other mysteries
you might enjoy:

SHADOW OF DOUBT

Nancy Cole Silverman

A Carol Childs Mystery (#1)

When a top Hollywood Agent is found poisoned in the bathtub of her home suspicion quickly turns to one of her two nieces. But Carol Childs, a reporter for a local talk radio station doesn't believe it. The suspect is her neighbor and friend, and also her primary source for insider industry news. When a media frenzy pits one niece against the other—and the body count starts to rise—Carol knows she must save her friend from being tried in courts of public opinion.

But even the most seasoned reporter can be surprised, and when a Hollywood psychic shows up in Carol's studio one night and warns her there will be more deaths, things take an unexpected turn. Suddenly nobody is above suspicion. Carol must challenge both her friendship and the facts, and the only thing she knows for certain is the killer is still out there and the closer she gets to the truth, the more danger she's in.

Available at booksellers nationwide and online

Visit www.henerypress.com for details

CIRCLE OF INFLUENCE
Annette Dashofy

A Zoe Chambers Mystery (#1)

Zoe Chambers, paramedic and deputy coroner in rural Pennsylvania's tight-knit Vance Township, has been privy to a number of local secrets over the years, some of them her own. But secrets become explosive when a dead body is found in the Township Board President's abandoned car.

As a January blizzard rages, Zoe and Police Chief Pete Adams launch a desperate search for the killer, even if it means uncovering secrets that could not only destroy Zoe and Pete, but also those closest to them.

Available at booksellers nationwide and online

Visit www.henerypress.com for details

KILLER IMAGE

Wendy Tyson

An Allison Campbell Mystery (#1)

As Philadelphia's premier image consultant, Allison Campbell helps others reinvent themselves, but her most successful transformation was her own after a scandal nearly ruined her. Now she moves in a world of powerful executives, wealthy, eccentric ex-wives and twisted ethics.

When Allison's latest Main Line client, the fifteen-year-old Goth daughter of a White House hopeful, is accused of the ritualistic murder of a local divorce attorney, Allison fights to prove her client's innocence when no one else will. But unraveling the truth brings specters from her own past. And in a place where image is everything, the ability to distinguish what's real from the facade may be the only thing that keeps Allison alive.

Available at booksellers nationwide and online

Visit www.henerypress.com for details

WHEN LIES CRUMBLE

Alan Cupp

A Carter Mays Mystery (#1)

Chicago PI Carter Mays is thrust into a house of lies when local rich girl Cindy Bedford hires him. Turns out her fiancé failed to show up on their wedding day, the same day millions of dollars are stolen from her father's company. While Carter takes the case, Cindy's father tries to find him his own way. With nasty secrets, hidden finances, and a trail of revenge, it's soon apparent no one is who they say they are.

Carter searches for the truth, but the situation grows more volatile as panic collides with vulnerability. Broken relationships and blurred loyalties turn deadly, fueled by past offenses and present vendettas in a quest to reveal the truth behind the lies before no one, including Carter, gets out alive.

Available at booksellers nationwide and online

Visit www.henerypress.com for details

DEATH BY BLUE WATER

Kait Carson

A Hayden Kent Mystery (#1)

Paralegal Hayden Kent knows first-hand that life in the Florida Keys can change from perfect to perilous in a heartbeat. When she discovers a man's body at 120' beneath the sea, she thinks she is witness to a tragic accident. She becomes the prime suspect when the victim is revealed to be the brother of the man who recently jilted her, and she has no alibi. A migraine stole Hayden's memory of the night of the death.

As the evidence mounts, she joins forces with an Officer Janice Kirby. Together the two women follow the clues that uncover criminal activities at the highest levels and put Hayden's life in jeopardy while she fights to stay free.

Available at booksellers nationwide and online

Visit www.henerypress.com for details